PRINTHOUSE BOOKS PRESENTS

Welcome to My Hood
The Life of A Don Diva.
Fiction

T.E. COOPER

©T.E. Cooper; 2013

PrintHouse Books, Atlanta, GA.

Published   10-30-2013

www.PrintHouseBooks.com

VIP INK Publishing Group; Incorporated

2

Welcome to My Hood

Cover art, designed by SK7.

ISBN: 978-0-9911719-2-7

Library of Congress Cataloging-in-Publication Data

T.E. COOPER

Welcome to my Hood;

The Life of A Don Diva.

1. Drama 2.Mystery 3.Erotica 4.Urban Literature

5. Women's Fiction 6. T.E COOPER

T.E Cooper

Raised on the streets of Charlotte; North Khak aka The Queen City; Meme and her best friend Kyra are what you call "Don Diva's". After a tortured family life, Meme and Kyra set out on their own with Meme's two little sister's in tow. Meme's Street Certified boyfriend; Eric, is about to show them the finer things in life.

From The QC's; infamous Beatties Ford Hood to The Glamorous Ballyntyne, will Meme be able to keep her friends close and her enemies closer? Can she overcome the hurdles she's about to face? Even with Kyra keeping a big secret?

Will Meme come out on top, a Don Diva?

Welcome to My Hood

This book is dedicated first and foremost to my children.

Deondra, Kyre, Mishak.

Then I'd like to throw in there:

Monwazee Watts,Sr. (you know I love you!)

Lil' Monwazee & Monjharii (love you guys!!)

T.E Cooper

T.E. COOPER

Welcome to My Hood
The Life of A Don Diva.
Fiction

VIP INK Publishing Group, Incorporated

Atlanta, GA

Table of contents.

T.E Cooper

Welcome to My Hood

1. The Beginning.

Where do I start? Well, first off let me say, this isn't what I expected. I thought I was destined to a life with just me and my 4 children. Why, you ask, well let's start from the beginning.

I was born to a gold digger who only married my father cause he had a little doe. As far as mom dukes was concerned, she could do without kids. Just nasty little brats that took your looks away! Well my dad wanted a kid so, here I am. Born on; Halloween '76. My mom said I gave her hell coming out, so I guess that's why she gave me hell in life.

My mom wasn't the stay at home and be a mom type you see, so I wasn't the happy bundle of joy some people associate with their first child. She tried to skip home once and leave me with my dad. I was only 3 months! Can you believe that? Well anyway, she eventually came back, ran out of money I hear. But she didn't stay long, this time she took me. Getting a divorce and collecting child support seemed like a plan to her. At the time I was 2 years old.

9

T.E Cooper

Mom and dad never got that divorce. My dad was so stressed out over the fact that ma dukes wouldn't let him see me until the money started rolling in he had a heart attack. Crazy but true. We were living in Philly. Well as you would guess my mom didn't care that he died just that she would get a check for as long as I was in school. Well that was the beginning of my life of hell.

For starters, she met this guy. The perfect man looks to die for, talk game from hell and of course a sex game that would make your mother cry. Slick was a man of many disguises and many secrets. At first life was good. We lived in the projects, and I loved it. I starting calling Slick "daddy" and making friends galore! My mom had a best friend that lived downstairs in the flats. She had 3 boys and 1 girl. All of them were older than me but that didn't stop me from following them around everywhere. Especially, Sandra, her and her best friend couldn't keep me and best friend's little sister away.

I remember when we caught Sandra and Tara with these guys. Boy was that something! "Where they go?" I asked Ce Ce. "Don't know, looked like in the stairwell of # 2." "Yuck! Thought they knew better than that." "Well you know Tara fuck anything

10

with a dick. She probably got his balls in her mouth going up the stairs!" "Girl you stupid. That's yo sista. How you gonna front on her like that." "Chile, please! That girl been fuckin and suckin since I was a little girl. This won't be the first time she took someone to those stairs." "Yeah, but I didn't know that Sandra was like that. Everybody knows bout Tara.""Girl you know the saying that birds of a feather flock together. If she hangin with my sista then she is a Freak!" "Ssh, they might hear us!" "Chile, Tara likes it when somebody watching. She a freak like that. She said it make her really wanna perform!"And there she was, Cece's sista goin down on dude like her life depended on it. And Sandra, I couldn't believe my eyes! She was takin it up the butt! The two of them was moanin and groanin like I never heard. When they came out they were all smiles; and the niggas! Boy was they peelin out! I mean I don't know how much money they got for their little freak show but that was when I saw how the game was done. Or so I thought.

When I went home that night I had a lot on my 7 year old mind. But you won't believe what I had to deal with next. That son of a bitch, Slick, decided that it was time to make me a woman. At least that's what he said. "What's up baby girl? Can daddy talk to you for a moment?" "Sure daddy.

11

T.E Cooper

What's up?" "Well you growin up to be a real cute little girl and daddy wants to know if any little boys been pushin up on you. You know you fillin out real nice and I know these little knuckle heads been noticing." "Not really. Just some kids at school notice that I wear a training bra. They tease me, but it's no big deal, I can handle me. Don't worry, I remember everything you told me bout these niggas, young and old." "That's my girl. You talk like a big girl; you look like a big girl, what else you got like a big girl?" "What cha' mean daddy?" "Let daddy see what these little niggas tryin to get at." "Huh?" "Take your clothes off and let daddy look at you. You don't have to be scared. It's just me and you no one else will see."

By this time I'm like you gotta be kiddin me. I'm not stupid by a long shot; go to a school for smart kids and all. So I know what this nigga askin. "You sure you can't see with my clothes on?" "Naw baby girl. I'll tell you what, we can both take off our clothes, that way you won't feel nervous." Nervous? No, nervous was what I felt when he brushed up against me when I was doing dishes. Nervous, was when I saw him feelin' on his dick when I was in the tub. This was total hysteria! "Come over here now and take off those fuckin clothes! You run your mouth like a grown woman now it's time I put that pretty mothafucka to use!

12

Time to make you a woman baby girl. Better me than the next nigga. At least you know me. Now come to daddy and suck this dick!" and there it was. At 7 I lost my virginity, I lost my soul and no one ever knew.

That started during the first weeks of school and didn't stop until that summer. "Your mom knows you fuck me better than her. That dumb bitch jealous of you! Can you believe that shit? Well anyway, she's sending your ass off so she can suck this dick. So we gonna fuck like never before and you gonna suck this dick like you ain't never gonna see it again." "Ooh, yeah, like that. Damn I'ma miss this shit when you gone."

Well to say the least my mom did ship my ass off. Just like the bastard said. She didn't even take me to the airport she sent me in a cab with called in instructions to the airline. Ain't that a bitch! Well life's a bitch and then you die. Just gotta roll with the punches.

North Cacalac here I come!

13

T.E Cooper

2. Rollin' Wit' the Punches.

I was shipped to stay with my grandmother, who was a strict Jehovah Witness. This also happens to be my mom's mom. Now to tell you a little about granny, she has 8 kids and only 2 have the same dad. My mom was the oldest and she only had one sister, everyone else was guys. They all were half Spanish and half black, so they all had that exotic look. When I moved in with my grandma my three youngest uncles were still living at home. They were all still in high school and sometimes they loved that I was there, but most of the time I caught hell. My mom was sending my check to my grandma to help take care of me, but I never saw a dime. My uncles on the other hand were fresh to death! They had all the latest clothes and shoes. Me, I had to wear the same pair of cowboy boots for 2 years! No joke. Anyway that wasn't the only thing going on; on the home front.

My aunt stayed a couple doors down and she had 3 kids. Me and my cousin, Chris, became inseparable. We did everything together. We stayed by the

Welcome to My Hood

woods and that was our playground. We ran around all the time in those woods. Messin' wit' possum traps my granddad had set and swimming in the creek. Well one day my cousin from cross town came over. My mom's middle brother; Michael's daughter. Now to say the least, she had to stay CLEAN! Okay. Well as I said before me and Chris loved the woods, and swimming in the creek and we had Miracle for the day.

So, we went swimming in the creek. We had it all planned out, we could take extra clothes for Miracle, and made sure she didn't get her hair wet. We had a ball, and didn't get her hair wet. But on the way out of our little hide-a-way, Miracle fell in the creek. Good clothes and all. She almost drowned and I had to jump in to save her. "Well, what are we gonna do?" Chris asked, concern all in his voice. "Okay, let's calm down. It's not dark yet and we still have time to get home. We gonna walk real slow like and take the long way. Now when we get to the house, Miracle, you gotta stay outside, k? Cause we gotta let you dry. We can kinda get around the hair thing." "K." Miracle replied.

When I say we went the long way, boy did I mean it. By the time we got home, Miracle was almost dry. If she just ran around outside a little while longer we were in the clear. So, we get to the house

15

and I go to check in. "Look, I'ma let grandma know we home and see what's cookin'. I'ma be right out. Now Miracle, you gotta stay outside and play race with Chris until you get dry." "K" was all I heard. I crept into the kitchen and said, "We back. What'cha cookin?" "Shake n bake chicken and stuff. Where Chris and Miracle?" Grandma asked. "Outside playin race." I replied. "Hmmp can't believe that girl outside. When she start to like outdoors?" "Dunno. Well I'm......" "Memorie, come outside, I'm almost dry now." Miracle said, out of nowhere. "WHAT!? What do you mean, "almost dry"?" my grandma replied. "Oh, didn't Meme tell you? I fell in the creek?"

That was my cue to jet. I mean, I didn't even warn my cuz, I just ran to the closet and started puttin' on winter clothes. My grandma got the extension cord and started to beat the shit out of me! My cousin walked right into an ass beatin'! She got that ass bare legged! That's how shit went down, down here in the south. My grandma beat my ass wet, in the tub, with a leather belt; I have been hit in the head with pots and pans! Not to mention the high heel shoes and boots. Getting snatched up by my hair (which made me hate long hair), and dragged across a room. You name it, my grandma did it. All the while; taking me to the Kingdom Hall of Jehovah's Witness; at least 4 times

16

a week. Including, knocking on peoples' doors early on a Saturday morning.

That was my life until I was about 9. Then my grandma sent me back to Philly. Well, I was back in Philly for about 2 weeks. I was kinda happy to be home with my mom and my 2 little sisters. (Yup, she had the niggas kids.) Before shit got really crazy. One night me and some of Slick's nieces were chillin' upstairs, all of a sudden I hear my mom scream out. Then I hear Slick callin' my mom all kinds of bitches and hoes. Then you hear what sounded like someone punching a brick. I ran to see what was goin' on and this nigga was whuppin up on my mom's ass! I mean she looked like shit! My sisters were cryin' and his sorry ass brother was just standin there lookin dumber than dumb. "Why ain't you doin something?" "Mind ya business. This here grown folk business." He responded. "Fuck You!" I screamed and ran downstairs to the kitchen. I grabbed the biggest knife I could find.

I ran back upstairs just when this son-of-a-bitch was about to hit my mom in the head with a pole. "If you hit her, I will kill you." I said with so much hatred in my voice the devil would have jumped back. "Baby girl what cha' doin'? I'm just talking to ya mom, I ain't gonna hurt her." Slick said, looking like the devil himself. "Put the knife down, Meme.

17

T.E Cooper

It's okay. I'm okay." My mom said "Not until he puts down the pipe and leaves the house." I stated, feeling far older than my nine years. "A'wight baby girl, I'ma let cha' ma go. Calm down sweetheart. I'm sorry I just lost my temper a little bit. But I'ma go and chill out wit' my bro and we'll talk tomorrow. Goodnight baby, see ya tomorrow. "Slick said, leaving the house." No Slick don't go! I'm sorry I won't question you again! Just don't go!" This shit coming from my dumb ass mom. Can you believe this shit!? What the fuck was wrong with her? Her face looks like someone had used it as a personal punching bag, and she beggin' this nigga to stay. What the fuck is that about? This nigga look at her, smile and leave. Good riddens if you ask me, but my mom stayed up all night cryin askin God to send this pathetic nigga back. What part of the game is this?

Well naturally the nigga came back 'bout a week or so later. He still actin' like he ain't did nothing wrong. Then he lookin' at me funny and shit. I already know where that is gonna lead. Damn! This nigga done snuck in my fuckin' room and standin' over me wit' his dick in his hand! Ain't this some shit! "Damn baby girl. You got some heart on ya young ass. More heart than that pathetic bitch you call momma. That shit turned me on. My dick got hard just lookin' at yo face. You sexy as hell when

18

you mad. Come here, I wanna fuck the shit out of you!" And he did.

Well stayin wit' my mom wasn't workin out, so off I go to NC. This is some bullshit if I ever heard of. I done seen more and done more than your average 11 year old, so naturally I developed a really foul mouth. I used my new found skills whenever I got a chance. At school, around the hood, wit' friends; you know whenever. Not to mention I started to feel like fuck the world.

I hung around my cousin Chris a lot which allotted me a host of male acquaintances. To say the least, girls didn't like me. Fine wit' me. I became a stone, cold tom-boy. Whatever a guy could do, I could do better. And since I got along better wit' guys, they taught me a lot. My crew when I was 11 to 12 was strictly boys. That proved to be valuable when I got older.

When I turned 12 I got sent back to Philly, "For good." My grandma said. Well not exactly for good, but this time I wouldn't be returning by myself. My mom and Slick decided to buy this grand old house while I was gone. When I returned to them, I had the most beautiful room attached to my sisters. We had a third floor that my mom turned into a play space for us. This was my mom's dream house that

19

turned into a nightmare. Almost every night now, Slick felt the need to beat my mom. I no longer tried to help, I learned my lesson, so I would sit helpless in my room, wait for him to finish with her and start with me. This became a ritual for about a year. Then one day, 4 out of my 6 uncles appeared in our driveway in a U-Haul, and off we went. Back to old North Carolina, and all the wonders it beholds.

Now to say we didn't have shit when we got here is an understatement. Sure, my mom took all the furniture, but we had nowhere to put it. My mom didn't have a job, and we had to stay with our cousin in a two bedroom apartment in one of the most-grimiest parts of town; The Ford. Now this was a totally different atmosphere than what I was used to. My mom was out partying every weekend and we could do whatever. The girls were into sex with boys our age and I wasn't. I tried to avoid that type of relationship as much as possible. I got too much attention as it was. With my Spanish roots you couldn't help but to notice me, even at 13. I mean, I was already in a C cup, okaaay! Not to mention, all men love long hair, and I had that down packed. I mean half way down my back and only needed a perm to thin it out twice a year. I wasn't light skinned but kinda in between a mocha and caramel. But the killa has always been my eyes.

20

My grandma on my dad's side had grey eyes, so guess who got those. With a slight slant and eyebrows that never needed arching. Attention was my middle name. Now don't get me wrong, I have never been vain, but the truth is the truth. As a matter- of- fact, I didn't want the attention, at first. I was like, "All you want is ass." This for the most part was true. That was with all boys at that age, then and now. So like always, I got in with a boy cousin of mine and hung tight with him. That was the start of the end.

T.E Cooper

3. Hangin' In the Hood.

When I started hanging-out wit' Bam, I knew I was headed down the wrong path. This nigga was like two years younger than me and slangin' that boy. I didn't care though; he was my cousin after all, so I loved him regardless. I hated school, whereas before I loved it. I felt out of place, like I didn't belong. And the only time I felt like I did belong, was with my cousin and his friends. He was real tight with these big timers from around our way and we used to hang out with them a lot. So much so, that they began to call me their little sister.

With them I felt loved, and protected at the same time. I started walkin' 'round the hood like I was the shit, ya know. I got the biggest dope dealers from the hood on my team, you couldn't tell me nothing. I remember once we all went to the movies, and this dude tried to push up on me. And I ain't gon lie, the nigga was dope. He was fine as hell! I'm getting ready to talk to the guy right, and

22

guess what these niggas do!? They start walkin' up on the dude telling him to back up and he couldn't holla; cause I was a virgin! Can you believe that? Me a virgin! Ha! If they only knew. Well to make a long story short, the guy backed down and quick. Not cause of what the niggas said, but how many of them it was. I was touched; to say the least.

I had to be about 14 or 15 by then and things at my house had really gotten crazy. Ever since we've been back my mom has treated me like an adopted child. Like, she never gave birth to me. It's like, only niggas and my sistas mean anything to her. Like the nigga she wit now. This nigga takin' stuff from the house and pawnin' it to the niggas I hang wit. They won't even take the stuff, cause they know it came from my house. And when the nigga get caught, he blames the shit on me! That ain't the fucked up part, the fucked up part is that she would believe him! I remember she put me out of the house at 3 in the morning and told me to go find the shit I stole cause her man told her I took it. Yeah for real. That's the type of shit I was putting up wit' now.

Well one thing I can say about my mom, she goes through men like most women go through drawers. When one leaves, you can believe she's got another one lined up. That's how it's been since

23

T.E Cooper

we've been back. Now this next nigga, well let's just say, wrong move. Sammy Johnson was a short nigga with a big head. The first day I met him, he was in my mom's bed wakin' up. I had just returned from the beauty parlor with a fresh new do and wanted to show my mom. Little did I know that I had a new problem. This new nigga wasn't as slick as Slick, but by then I knew scum when I saw it. "Sammy, this is my daughter, Memorie, we call her Meme for short. And speaking of short, what happened to your hair?" "Hello," I said." Well you know how I hate long hair. So I finally decided to do something about it. Do you like it? It's the latest style." "You look like a boy; that don't fit you. Why did you get it cut so short on one side and not the other? Looks like you couldn't make up your mind." My mom said. "Why you talking to her like that? It look fine to me. All the girls getting their hair cut like that." Said Sammy. Okay, I still wasn't too sure 'bout this nigga. Just cause he talking like that don't mean shit. I wonder what this nigga afta. "Thank you. Well see ya later." And I was out. I didn't want to hear my mom's shit talking anymore.

I went right to the store where everybody hung out to see what was poppin'. My cuz, Bam, and his crew was there chillin'. Then I looked and saw this nigga I ain't never seen before. "Yo cuz who that

24

nigga?" "Who?" Bam asked "That nigga wit' tha' jersey on." "Oh, that there is Manny's cousin from cross town. He getting down wit' the crew. Why you ask 'bout that nigga?" "Cause that nigga fine! Don't tell Manny I said that. I ain't got time for no repeats like at the movies. I'ma holla at him on my own." "How you gonna do that when Manny keeping that nigga close. He don't want him to fuck up, ya know. Teachin' that nigga the game and shit. So he probably ain't gonna let that nigga out his sight. Ya know what I mean." That was Bam's way of telling me to stay out the nigga's face. But that was like telling a kid they couldn't have candy. That just ain't gonna work.

So as I was checkin' the nigga out; all of a sudden Manny hollered at me to come here. "Yo Meme! Come here a sec." "Yo what up?" I asked. "This here my cuz, Waz, from over in the Valley. I wanted yall to meet cause I want you to show this nigga the hood. Cause don't nobody know this mutha fucka like you. I want you to show him every nook and cranny, every dope spot, every place to duck from 5 0. I want him to know the junkies and their families. He need to know what house is safe and where the snitches at. You know all that shit and I want this nigga to know too. After you do that then you bring him back to me. But before you come back this nigga gotta be able to

25

take me to every spot and know that shit wit his eyes closed. Ya heard me?" This was Manny's way of asking me for my help. "Well Manny, now that's a lot of shit. How much time I got to teach this square this shit?" "The nigga ain't a square, and you got as long as the shit take. Ain't no hurry, shit the nigga need to know his shit." "K. Well one other thing...." I was saying, and Manny interupted me. "I know, the payment. You a trip to be such a little girl." "Well you know what they say 'bout us small people, we got something to prove. So what's up?"

"Girl what you talking? You know I already take care of you." "Just time." "What cha mean, "time"?" He questioned. "Time to get to know your cousin, by myself. After all this is over." "What? Hell no! You trippin'. You ain't ready for no grown nigga lil sis." Manny said, shaking his head in disapproval. "How you know?" I asked, defiantly. "Look the nigga ain't no square. He's just new to this dope game. So be careful, cause I can't fuck this nigga up for fuckin' you over." Manny said, with a frown on his face. "Gotcha. Don't tell him what I really want. Ok. Cause I wanna just kinda rub off on him, you know." Laughing at me he said,"A'wight. Just watch yourself. Cuz ain't no square. Don't let the innocent look fool ya, just look at yourself." "Yeah, I gotcha." This was me, thinking I'm grown, not

26

listening to someone who knew.

Well to say the least, I got under Waz's skin. Pretty soon the nigga was lookin' for a sista even when there wasn't any business. Me, I was lovin' every minute of it, you know cause the new nigga in the hood seemed to be lost in me. Bitches was hatin' like hell and I hadn't even given the nigga any ass yet. Yup, I got him hooked. That's just what I wanted. Wait until I tell him I want to fuck. This nigga gon' go wild. He think I'm a virgin too! Well, technically I wasn't, but this would be the first time I would give it to someone freely, and willingly, ya know.

"What's up wit you, my princess, my Memorie." Waz was sayin' to me, "Well, I have something I wanna talk about." "What's up beautiful?" "Waz I think I'm ready." "Ready for what? Ooooh, you sure bout that baby girl?" "Yeah. I been thinking 'bout it real hard, and I think, no, I know I want you to be the first." "Be my pleasure beautiful, but I'ma make it right for you, and make it something you gonna remember." "A'wight. This time, I'm in your hands." We set a date. Can you believe that shit? We set a date.

Anyway this nigga was really goin' all out. It was gonna be on Sat. Oct. 31, my birthday. He got a

27

junkie to get us one of those penthouse suites, and man you would not believe what he had waitin' on me. He had to have come here before he brought me, cause the nigga had mad shit everywhere! I mean there was Gucci shit, Louis shit, Coogie shit, man all kinds of shit. "Wow, what's this all about?" "Well if you gonna go all the way wit' me, then I'ma go all the way for you." That was some romantic shit; he had me wonderin' who worked who. By the time morning came, I was way beyond ecstasy. I knew I was in love. Man the first time we did it, it was alright, but the next time! Boy, that was some shit out of the movies! The shit he did to me and the shit I did to him had me like, Damn! Oh well, I'm in it now all the way.

Now as much as I wanted Waz, and the shit I did to get him, you would think everything would be straight. Not! This nigga turned into a maniac! He wanted to dress me and tell me where to go and who not to hang with. I was like, "Man, I should have never gave him some pussy!" Like the time I went to the beauty parlor. I cut my hair some more, and what the hell I do that for. This nigga got a room and acted like everything was a'wight. Man was I wrong for thinking that shit. This nigga beat me like I stole something! I mean he beat me like his name was Slick and I was my mom. "What the fuck you doin?!" I screamed, "Who the fuck told

28

you to cut your fuckin' hair!?" Waz screamed at me. "Nobody! I just felt like it. You son- of- a- bitch, you gonna pay for this shit! I swear to God your ass gonna pay!" "Bitch I'll kill yo ass. You fuckin' hear me? I will kill you! Don't make threats you can't go through on. And from the looks of it you better shut the fuck up before I do that shit!" No comment from me, I was in total shock. I couldn't believe this nigga did this shit. I acted like I was cool and layed down and went to sleep. When I woke up this nigga had a bunch of flowers and shit, like that made it better. Fuck this nigga; he just fucked the wrong bitch.

Waz had been givin' my mom money and shit, so while I was at the room he told her a bunch of bull so she wouldn't be lookin' for me. I was like, a'wight I'ma stay here until I get straight then this nigga gonna get it. Well, I didn't have to do a damn thing. The whole crew got popped bout 2 days after shit went down. All these nigga's were on a Federal Hold, in the county. I mean shit was crazy, the cops was roundin everybody up. They tried to take my cuz, Bam, but that nigga underage, so what could they do? They had who they wanted and they had a lot of shit on them nigga's too. All kinds of people snitched on my folks. They were getting tired of being held prisoners in their homes, so they said. But most of them were junkies, just tryin' to get some payback. Like this one dude. He was mad cause these niggas blew up his car and apartment. Shit! That was his fault. He owed money and was talking shit, so you know they did what they had to do to set an example. Nobody else fucked up like that.

Then you had one of those pussy ass niggas, that know what they doin' when they doin' it, but don't want to do the time. This nigga been workin for Manny, for like, 3yrs! You would think loyalty would mean something to these niggas, but shit loyalty runs as far as the money goes and then you got shit. Well my niggas got a hell of a lot of time. I'm talking, life plus 140 yrs, and life + 90, and so on. These niggas didn't even have any murders either. They got that shit from guns and explosives and shit. I mean, when they pulled out that evidence, I knew my folk were fucked. I was like damn! But you know, shit happens and ain't nothing you can do about it.

Welcome to My Hood

4. Learning How to Game.

Well, by now my life was pretty wild. My cousin Bam got hooked up with this real pretty girl, who was pretty cool. She was a little younger than me, but shit, we had fun. She was my first, real best friend. Her name was, Kyra. That girl knew everybody, ya heard! Kyra knew how the game worked for real. This chick was gamin' niggas and getting paid. If my cousin only knew. He tried to get her to stop hangin' wit' me, cause he thought I was a bad influence. But that shit was dead. Once me and Kyra got together there was no stopping us.

Let me tell you how we used to get down before all the bullshit. I remember when she first came to the crib, she was wit' my little cuz Miracle. They was supposed to be spending the weekend, but just so happened that Kyra stayed a little longer. 'Bout 4yrs longer. She and her-moms wasn't really feelin' each other, so it was no big deal when her-moms never showed up. So my-moms said if she stayed she had to go to school. That was cool wit' Kyra except one little note she didn't tell us, she was

31

pregnant. Now when we finally found out, she was about 4 or 5 months. That's pretty far along. But, Kyra didn't care how far along she was, she wasn't having no baby. She made a call and left for about a week and came back ready to bop. Well that's when I found out what she was really doin'.

Now don't get me wrong, I was no angel, no angel at all. As a matter-of-fact, I was dealin' wit at least 3 niggas myself. One from school, one that worked at the pizza shop and one from the hood. They were all kickin' out too. You know gold chains, money, and shit like that. Now, I thought I was pretty good at what I was doing, but I wasn't anything like Kyra. She had niggas eatin' outta her hand! So I figured, I could learn something from her and maybe vice versa.

One night, Kyra was like, "Yo what up, wanna go to a party?" "Where?" "Over in Tanglewood." "Who you tryin to see? You know them niggas is crazy over there." "Just this nigga wit' a big dick and an even bigger bank. So what up, you know you wanna see that cute ass Eric. Lookin' like Genuine, and shit. I bet that nigga be fuckin' the shit outta ya, don't he?" she said as if it was a joke. "First off, Eric ain't to stable to be seein' me all up in some joint and not wit him. At least not in that neighborhood. And second, it ain't ya business

32

what me and him do." I said, trying to be coy. "Chile paalessse! Like you innocent and shit. Do Eric know how you be slobbin' all over Ashton at Ce's Ce's? Oh and what about Kimire? How them late night studies at the library? What type of head you got on you?" Kyra reminded me. "Look, I do a'wight wit my little hustle wit who I'm wit. Ain't no shame in my game and my game tight. But, ain't nobody got time for Eric commin' in there seeing me get my holla on and cutting a fool. Cause ya know that's what his ass will do. And was raised in the church and shit." I responded a little annoyed. "Well first of all girl, if that nigga want you to be all his then he need to start doin' more than a few fuckin' chains! Shit, just to eat my pussy a nigga betta come wit' a stack! And not no fuckin 100 either. I'm talking big stacks! I don't play that shit.

Oh and to suck a big black or white or Asian or whatever, you better have enough in ya bank to give me access to your damn bank account!" That's what she said anyway, I've known her to suck a dick for a ride, so whatever. "Okay, I'll go to the party, should I call Eric and tell him I'ma be in the hood?" "Hell no girl! We getting ready to go shoppin' on me and wait 'til that nigga see you tonight, cause if he ain't there when we get there, he gonna get a call and he will be there! Baby girl I'm bout to show you how to work the shit outta

33

that Spanish, Black shit you got goin' on! Ha, ha girl do you know how many real nigga's would pay good dollars to get in that ass. You better work what u got while you got it cause life is too short not to be paid!" With that we were out.

We went to Northlake and Southpark. I found this helluva dress in Southpark Mall. It was really a shirt, but I'm short so it'll pass. Anyway it was shear material on the outside and yellow silk for the lining. On the shear fabric were different shades of green and yellow and reds. Man, this dress looked good as hell on me. It was a Vera Wang original! And it was 5 stacks! "Girl are you sure you can spend like that on one dress?!" "Shirt. And hell yea! I told you I don't play that nickel and dime shit. That shit look good as hell on you too. Wait til this nigga see you tonight girl! He gon' wanna eat you out right there. And you can't tell me he don't eat pussy, cause that nigga got lips that look like they supposed to stay between a bitches thighs!" "You know you nasty as hell, but funny. Now where we gonna get my shoes, and when you gonna get you something?" "Oh girl you know I don't do this white shit. I gotta go to a hood sto' or something. Get me some fat ass Roc-A-Wear or maybe some Applebottoms. Cause you know with this ass I make Applebottoms look like the Shit!" She said smiling and showing me her big ass. "You

34

are so dumb." I said, laughing. "Dumb, but payed."
"I hear that sista! Let's shop on!" and shop on we
did. I mean I can go shoppin' wit' Kyra anytime!
She bought everything and no bullshit either, all
name brand, top designer shit.

I mean this bitch went to Jared's and got herself
this platinum Channel set with 4 carat earrings,
with matching necklace, ring and watch! That had
to set somebody back a grip! But she just pulled out
that little black card and Bam! They put her shit in
the box. We sat down and had champagne while
we waited on our jewelry. She bought me this
white gold and sapphire, diamond set. It might not
be platinum but it looked damn good on me. After
that we went to Northlake, and I went to Bakers
and I found some real fly ass heels! They were
yellow snake and leather stiletto, strap sandals! I
was in love. But when I looked at the price I said
they were outta they minds! 4 g's for some damn
sandals! I was like hell no, but Kyra was like, "Chile
please, you getting them shoes. 'Cause that's the
icin on the cake. Girl when I finish schoolin' you
wit' the shit you already know you gone be one
ruthless bitch! That was the understatement of the
year.

We finished up our shopping at Saks on 5th. We
both got some real fly ass lingerie that made us

35

T.E Cooper

look like some playboy models. We hit the perfume spot over at the Mills and hooked up some real shit. It had that sweet exotic type smell. That shit was sexy as hell! Even as we left the mall people were turning round lookin' for the source of the smell. Boy was I gonna knock 'em dead tonight! Wait til Eric sees me! You see, those others niggas ain't my type; I was just using them for a little extra experience, (crazy as it sounds). You see after Waz got life plus; I ain't fucked nobody else. Then I met Eric, and was like, I gotta be able to fuck this nigga stupid! I knew all about him, but he didn't know a thing about me, except what I told him and Kyra wasn't sayin' shit. I been plottin' to put the thang on this nigga from day one and tonight was gonna be my night. Kyra had just given me the gear I needed and the game I obsessed over. Ain't no stopping me now.

Welcome to My Hood

5. Some Next Level Shit.

This night I took special care of how I looked and took my time getting ready. Kyra was like, "Girl you gone kill 'em tonight!" "You don't look bad ya self mami." I replied "I knew you had some pretty eyes girl, but damn those mutha fuckas killin' 'em! They like, grey and green, I wish I had those puppies! And that hair! Shit, my weave don't look bad cause this shit cost me bookoo, but yo shit real and long than a mug!" "Thank you, thank you. Ha ha. What's all the complements for?" "I want yo ass to get ready, cause girl you gonna hear all kinds of shit tonight! Shit, you look like a damn supermodel, so be prepared. I get that shit all the time, but if they ain't rockin some real fly shit and I know it's real, they can keep lookin. Cause this big ass only bend over FO that cheddar. Ya heard!" she said laughing. We headed out and you wouldn't believe it! Kyra had one of those knuckle heads she fuck wit' rent us a fuckin' Porshe jeep! I couldn't believe this shit! We was rollin' in style and I liked the feelin'.

37

We rolled up in dat party like whoa! The nigga's was on us too. And of course the bitches was hatin'. Who gave a fuck. Ugly bitches, wit' all that fake ass shit on! Shit me and Kyra looked like the dubs we was, plus ten! Between the two of us, there wasn't a bitch in there that could touch us. They knew it and so did we. We strolled up in the joint and it was mad niggas everywhere! I mean, not only nigga's from T-Woods but niggas from the Valley, over on B-Ford, and Nation's Ford. It was like all the ballers was out this night and if it wasn't for the fact that I knew E hung out in this spot, I would be all over this chocolate nigga across the room. "Yo, I'ma go get us some dranks." Said Kyra walkin' off. She musta spotted something she wanted and it wasn't no drink. When I looked over she was all over ya boy I was just watchin! Well, I can't hate cause I got something commin'.

And commin' he was, when Eric and his crew walked up in the joint, bitches was all over 'em! I mean, it was like they was supa' stars or something. It was Eric, his boy Biggs, his two cousins (who were brothers), Ramel, and Romel. Then a coupla of their boys. They was rollin' deep and I noticed they had that little crazy nigga, Shakeem, wit' 'em too. Me and that nigga don't get along. "Hey, who drivin' that fly ass Porshe outside? 'Cause if it's a woman please tell me she lookin' for a man!" This

38

commin' outta Romel's mouth. "Tell E to check his girl." Somebody screamed. "My girl? Who the....? Shit, is that you Meme? Damn baby, you look good enough to eat! Who you rollin' wit', that Kyra girl?" Eric said. "Hey to you too boo. And yes, I'm wit' KY, and thanks, you lookin' damn good ya self. Take a good look, cause all this plus some is for you later on this evening. So go enjoy the party, I'll be in the Porsche jeep at the end of the night. Come holla." I said and walked off real slow like, so Eric could get a real appreciation of just how short my dress really was, my fine ass legs and of course my fine, round, perfectly shaped onion ass. And I know he was lookin', and so was a few of his boys. A few bitches was clockin too, but cool, the more hattas the betta, cause, I know I'm doin' something right.

By the end of the night at least a million guys tried to holla, but E wasn't havin' it he was on my ass like white on rice! "Yo, let's dip. I'm getting tired of this shit, 'sides I'ma havta' kill a nigga 'bout yo ass." E said. "Cool, let me holla at Ky and we out." I told him, scanning the room for Kyra. When I found her she was pussy poppin for a group of niggas in the corner, a real live freak show, just for them. "Hey Ky!" I yelled over the music. She heard me and ended her little show and came over, "What's up girl? I seen E all on yo ass tonight! That

39

shit was funny as hell when dude tried to get you to dance! I thought E was gonna kill that nigga, FO real. Where that crazy nigga at anyway?" she said all at once lookin' around. "Oh, you can believe he somewhere close. Anyway, we 'bout ta bounce, and I just wanted you to know. You leavin' or what. I don't want you callin' me cause some shit went down afta I leave." I said "Naw, I'm cool. I'ma leave in a minute with that fine ass brotha right there." She said pointing at dude from earlier. "What's his name?" I asked out of curiosity. "Oh that's Corey. And of course that nigga paid. Member that Lexus; l's 430 we seen outside? Well that's his, and that's not all. He ain't got all those ghetto chains around his neck, but he got on a custom made Rolex! Gots ta get him on my payroll." "Well do yo thang. Just call me if you need me." "Girl the shit you got planned for Eric, ain't no way I'ma call you, you gonna be occupied!" "Fo sho!" I said and was out.

Now when my girl said I had some shit planned for Eric, she was right. I was planning on makin' this nigga numero uno. I had whipped cream, chocolate syrup, strawberries, and this helluva black leather lingerie outfit with the pussy part out. Oh yeah, I had some shit planned for this nigga alright, and he won't even know what hit him.

When we got to the room I told Eric to go to the bedroom and relax. When he walked in that room his mind was blown. Kyra had already gotten the room in advance and we set it up before we went to the party. In the bedroom I had candles everywhere, and rose petals on the bed. There was a Jacuzzi that I had put some bubble bath in, and it was red and scented. The entire thing looked like something out of a movie. He turned around and looked at me and said, "What you tryin' ta do, lock me down? What else you got commin'?" he said lookin' at me with the most beautiful smile. "Oh sweetie, this is only the beginning. You have no idea what I got in store for you. Just get relaxed and watch momma work." I said with a wicked grin. "A'wight ma. What you got?" "First I want you to take off ya clothes and get in the Jacuzzi, pour some of that champagne, roll a blunt and wait for me." "You got a lotta demands, but you know I'm down." Eric said.

I left the bedroom and went into the bathroom to change. Now I had a variety of little outfits for this evening, for each little act I planned to pull. This was gonna be one for the record books, I promise ya that. I changed into this barely a bikini, thong bikini, that blended in with my skin so well you had to look twice to see I had something on. Just what I wanted. I pulled my hair up in a loose

41

ponytail, with tiny tendrils around my face. I looked to see if I needed some make-up, but as usual my face was flawless. I sprayed some of the perfume I made on and some gloss on my lips. I took one last look and was on my way. When I walked in that room, I knew I had something special. The look that nigga gave me said it all. I turned around slowly so he could get a good look at all I had to offer. He sat there dumbfounded, mouth open. "Damn, boy. Close yo mouth." I said laughing. "Shit, I can't help it. Girl I wasn't lyin' when I said you look good enough to eat." I just smiled and eased my way slowly into the Jacuzzi.

"Hey, I got something for you." Eric said reaching for his pants and pullin' out a sandwich bag. "Boy you know I don't fuck wit' that powder! You crazy!" "Hold on mami, this ain't yayo, these X." he said showing me the little blue pills. "So you poppin now?" I asked with a little annoyance in my voice. "When I feel like it. Ain't no harm. You trust me don't you? I won't never do anything to hurt you. Just roll wit' me and you straight. Ya feel me?" He said, kissing me on my neck. "So what you sayin', Eric, you want me to be yo main girl?" I asked "Naw, my only girl." He replied. "Yeah right. I know niggas, E, and they ain't got just one girl." I said, as serious as I could. "You know those niggas, not THIS nigga." He said with the most

42

serious face I'd ever seen. This nigga was serious and I could see it all in his eyes. Damn! That's all I needed to know. "Yup, I trust you with my life E, so don't lose it. Ya feel me?" I said, a little nervous at the prospect of being his, "only woman". "Yeah I feel ya, and I won't never lose it, I'ma keep it in my heart all the time." He said, kissing me again.

"Aww, you sayin you love me?" I asked him playin' cause it was way too early for that. That nigga'll be lyin if he say yeah. "Now, I'm not sayin' all that, but a nigga fealin' you and wanna see where it go. You fine as hell mami, with that Spanish look and those fuckin' eyes, I can stare in those pretty mutha fuckas all day. I need you on my arm. You fit for a king, and I'm that nigga yo. So all's I'm sayin is, let's see where it go." He said, as if it was the hardest thing in the world for him to keep it real wit' a woman. He already passed the first test. I asked him if he loved me and he kept it real. That's all I ask. "Yeah, I'm feelin' you too E. That's why I did all this, so I could tell you. So since we on the same page give me one of those pills and let's see what this shit do." And with that I popped 2 blue dolphins, double stack.

When those pills kicked in, in addition to the weed and champagne, I was fucked up! I was french kissin' E like his mouth was the best thing I had

43

tasted in years. I then took my roaming lips and tongue slowly down his neck to his chest. As I sucked on his nipples I played with his dick. It was the perfect size with a hook. It was smooth to the touch, with the perfect head. As I kissed his neck and sucked on his nipples and played with his dick under those bubbles that nigga whimpered! I continued my way down his stomach to my destination. When I got to his beautifully shaped, sized and colored dick, I took him in my mouth slowly. Inch by inch I swallowed him whole. The whole time playin' with his balls. I sucked and slurped like this was what I was destined to do on this earth. I took him out of my mouth slowly playin' with the head with the tip of my tongue while jackin' his shaft with the spit I just put there. I looked up to see what type of reaction I was getting and that was what I wanted. This nigga was past heaven. He had his mouth open and head hangin, lookin at me with bulging eyes. Like he couldn't believe I was doing all this. Little did he know, I was taught how to suck a good dick long ago and I knew what to do with it.

I continued suckin and jackin', lickin' and suckin' on his balls and the nigga let out another whimper. Uh oh, gotcha! I knew what it was when that warm, salty, juice flowed in my mouth. I sucked, slurped and swallowed everything his beautiful dick had to

44

offer like it was my last meal. This nigga was amazed. But boy was I not finished. After I sucked him dry, I sucked him back on bone and told him to get in the bed. I told him to wait 2 secs and I would be back. "No problem, I need a blunt after that shit! I don't think I could handle it if it wasn't for those dolphins." "Oh, we'll see what you can handle sweetie, I am far from through with you." "Good, cause I haven't even begun with you." He said with a seductive smile.

I got in the bed next to E and we just cuddled for a minute. "You know I could get used to this." Eric said. "What?" I asked, as if I didn't know. "Holdin' you in my arms. I like how you feel next to me." He said and hugged me close. "Yeah me too. You make me feel safe. Like no matter what, you got me." I replied. "And you know this, mami!" he said while kissing me on the neck. He was really makin' me wet with the way he was movin' his tongue up and down my neck. He moved slowly down to my ripe tits and started suckin' and swirlin' his tongue around my perfectly shaped nipple, sending chills down my spine. He slowly made his way down my stomach and when he reached his destination, boy was I in for some pleasure! He spread my legs open and just stared at my pussy for a minute. Then he slowly started to French kiss my pussy lips, real slow like. He licked and sucked on my click until I

45

was moanin like crazy. Then he took his whole tongue and started to slow stroke my pussy from front to back, savoring all my juices. He put his tongue in it, and started to fuck my pussy with his tongue! I mean he was in and out, suck my clit, and lick my pussy. Before I knew it I was holdin his head and fuckin the shit outta his mouth.

I came about two times in his mouth before he came up for air, smiling. "You like that? Well this pussy tastes so good I don't think I'ma stop just yet. It's so pretty and callin my name, mmmm look at that shit." He said as he was holdin my lips apart and slowly finger fuckin me. He played with my clit, fucked me with his hand, and kept lickin' me like I was a tootsie roll pop. How many licks does it take to get to the middle? Hell, I don't know but we can keep tryin! After fuckin me with his mouth for bout an hour he slowly pulled his dick out. And that mutha fucka is just beautiful. He placed the head on my clit and just kept rubbin back and forth, with some juices commin out his head and my pussy being so wet that shit felt like heaven. He was teasin' me now. He would rub the head of his dick up and down, then slip it in for a second and take it out, then do it again. That shit was drivin me crazy! "Please put it in and fuck me, please!" I begged out of shear lust. "You want this dick, then I'ma give you this dick." He said as he slowly

46

slipped all of his large shaft up in my pussy as far as it would go. Then he started to work a sista like I was a slave! He was fuckin' me so good I had to remember who was tryin' to lock who down. I flipped him over and prepared to give him the best ride of his life.

After we finished fuckin' and suckin' each other 'til the sun came up, we both went to sleep tired as hell. I fell asleep in his arms like that was the place God meant for me to be. When we woke up the next night, I was famished. "What's up wit getting something to eat?" I said. "Cool, we can order room service. I ain't ready for you to put no clothes on. I wanna keep lookin' at that fine ass body. Open yo legs and let me see my treasure." He said with a smile that told me if I did as told we would never eat. "Oh, I'ma let you look at this pussy again and lick it, but first, I need some nourishment." I said pickin' up the phone to call room service. "That's fine wit' me, just know I'm not through wit' that pussy yet." He said. I was in heaven, pure heaven. I couldn't believe that this nigga was straight up mine now. I don't care what nobody say, after all the freaky shit we did, he mine.

When I finally got home Kyra had called like a million times, so I called her back to tell her 'bout the amazing time I had with E. "Girl you won't

47

T.E Cooper

believe the shit that went down in that hotel room this weekend!" I told her all excited. "Well. Did you lock that nigga down or what?" she asked, "Man, did I?! I'll tell you this, I never knew he was a freak like that. Man the shit he did, ain't nobody ever did!" I said, "Uh oh, who locked who?" she asked with a laugh in her voice. "Shit, that nigga got me, but you can damn sure believe I got him too. Shit he ain't never had his dick sucked the way I tore that puppy up!" I said with confidence. "That's my girl! Well, what the nigga say when yall left? Was he feelin' the room and all that shit you did? Come on, tell me something good." She was sayin. "A'iight, girl, I think I'm in love! I mean that nigga got a sex game to rock the ages, ya heard! But you know he couldn't keep up wit cha girl. But all in all I think I got that nigga locked. I mean he talking bout me being his only and shit. You know the usual, but I'ma play it cool and see what goes down. But I swear I think I'm in love." I said, while Ky was listening intently. "Listen I'm on my way over. Mom's trippin', so I'll see ya in a sec." she said rushin' off the phone. I wasn't wonderin what that was about cause Ky's mom was bout like my own.

Speakin' of, she got her a new man, and boy is this guy a character. He walks around all the time with these dark shades on scratchin his arms and shit. I told my-moms he was a junkie, but she think she can save this nigga. Whatever. Then I heard it, sounded like somebody was fightin' in the living room. I jumped up and ran in there to see what was going on. That nigga was in there putting the beat down on my-moms like never before. "Bitch, where the money at?" with a punch and a kick. "Where the fuck is the money. I know you got it cause it ain't where ya put it last night. Now give it up or I'm kill ya ass!" My-moms was rolled up on the floor not moving, so I rushed over to see if she was still breathing. "Leave my mom alone, you fuckin' junkie faggot!" I screamed, trying to get my-moms up off the floor. "What you say, you little bitch! I'll beat ya ass too, you fuckin' hoe! Yeah, I know all 'bout yo slutty ass. Probably would have been straight if I fucked you, instead of this good for nothing bitch!"

At that moment, E showed up. This nigga was heated. He walked in, and punched ol' dude in the face so hard, that nigga hit the ground. And what he do that for, 'cause E was all over that ass! I mean he beat that nigga like that nigga beat my moms. I thought he was gonna kill the man. I started beggin' him to stop. "Please baby, it's okay, I'm okay. Please E stop!" But it was like, he didn't hear me or my-moms screamin' and hollerin'. "What's going on?" my little sisters had come outta they

49

room. That was when E stopped beatin' the shit outta dude. "Get the fuck outta my house!" the nigga screamed "Now, before I call the police!' Tell em they gotta go!" he said to my moms. And can you believe she told me to leave! I couldn't believe this shit. I'm tryin' to keep her from getting the shit beat outta her and she tell me to get the fuck out! "Fine, I'll leave, but don't call me when this nigga done beat you 'til he can't beat you no mo." I said going to my room to get some stuff so I could leave. "No, Meme! What about us! Who's gonna look out for us?" both of my little sisters screamed. "Go back to your room before I beat yalls asses too!" that nigga screamed at my sisters. I had to stop E from jumpin' on that nigga again, so I just grabbed both my sisters and walked out the door, with E close behind.

As we was leavin', Ky pulled up. "Yo what's goin on?" "Just follow us Ky, I'll tell you when we get where we goin." E said. "And where is that?" Kyra asked. "To my crib." E replied, still mad about what just took place. "You sure E? This a lot of responsibility and I can't ask you to take care of my sisters. They're my sisters so I gotta take care of them." I said. "Didn't I tell you to trust me? Don't worry 'bout shit. I got you and them. Yall 'bout to live like you was meant to. That's my word. That shit that just happened, ain't gon' happen no mo'.

50

Yall got me now and I got yall. That's all that matters." He said in a way that let me know, that was that. And now we are on our way to E's house, our house.

6. Well I'll Be Damned.

Now everytime me and E got together, we always went to a room, and I naturally assumed that he stayed in Tanglewood. But boy was I wrong. "Baby, where we goin'?" I asked. "Questions, questions. Why you can't just chill and let me handle things?" he said with a smile. "No it's not that. I thought you stayed in Tanglewood?" "Naw, that's where my fam stays. I got a crib by myself." He said, grinning like he just stole something. "And just where is this crib?" I asked again. "You'll see. Girls, yall hungry? Wanna stop and get something to eat?" He asked my sister's.

"Yeah!" was all you heard from the back seat. "A'iight, let's see, there's a McDonalds on this exit. That sound good?" he asked my sisters like he'd known them all their little lives. " Yea!" they said in unison. We pulled off the exit, and I noticed it was the Ballantyne exit, but didn't say a word. When we got to McDonalds E took the girls inside so I could holla at Kyra for a sec, before we got to his crib. "Girl, what the hell is goin on? And where the hell are we going?" She was still driving the

52

Porsche jeep and was lookin fly to be runnin from her moms. "You won't believe what type of day today it has been. I guess I'll have to fill you in when we get to E's house." I said. "E's house? I thought that nigga lived in Tanglewood." Kyra said confused. "Yeah, me too, but we was wrong. He won't even tell me where we goin'." I said. "Well girl, you off to a good start. Didn't we just get off on the Ballantyne exit?" "Yup. That's why I'm like, damn. This nigga got secrets. And I guess we 'bout to find out one." I told Kyra seeing E and my sisters come out of McDonalds.

"Well, alright, I'm right behind ya." I got out the jeep and walked over to E's CLS 550 Mercedes Benz. It was equipped with black tint, and black and white 22 inch rims. The paint was a pearl white just like on his rims. It was a fly ride, and E was a fly nigga. I couldn't wait to see what he was livin' like. I got in the car; E had already buckled up the girls, and had them eatin' their food in his car. "Girls, let's wait til we get to where we goin' before yall eat. I don't want yall to spill anything." I said, with concern on my face. "Girl, please. Leave them babies alone, they fine. I was gonna get it detailed and give it to you anyway." He stated, like it was only natural. "Say what?" was all I could muster. "Yeah, I'ma give you a ride, cause livin' out here you're gonna need one." "But this?" I said

53

awestruck. "What's wrong wit' it? You want something else? Something new?" he said, like I wasn't pleased. "NO! I mean, yes, I mean, it's perfect! Are you sure?" I said overexcited. "Baby girl, nothing is too good for you and when I stack some more paper I'ma get you and the girls something a little bigger to ride in. Ya girl Kyra ain't the only one that's gonna be ridin' in style from now on. And a little birdie told me Kyra sponsored our little weekend and all. Tell her I owe her one, cause we needed that. And tell her she won't have to sponsor anymore shopping trips either, I got you from now on." " Oh E!"
Was all I could say.

That is until I saw the house we was pullin' up at. OH MY GOD! I couldn't breathe. I could not believe that this nigga was livin' like THIS! House, no this wasn't no house, it was a MANSION! I mean, I ain't never in my life seen a house so big. "And you live here by yourself?" I asked. "Well, not anymore. I live here with 3 of the most beautiful women in the world." He said giving me a kiss. "Eww!" both girls said from the back. "And keep thinking that way too." Eric said back to the girls with a laugh. We all got out of the car and went up the stairs to the double doors. "Girl, I hope he got room for me. Cause I just can't leave, I think I'm in love too!" Kyra was just as excited as me and

Welcome to My Hood

the girls. "Okay, first let me show the little ones to their rooms, then I wanna talk to you Meme, cause I gotta leave for a while." Eric said as he took my sisters upstairs somewhere in the massive house. "Girl we gotta talk as soon as this nigga leaves. He damn sho got some secrets." Stated Ky.

Eric came back downstairs laughing like crazy. "Yo, those little girls a mess. They had me pinned down, smashing me wit pillows, yo, that was to fun. A'iiwt let's talk. Oh what I have to say you can hear too, Kyra." He said as he noticed Ky easin' out. "Look, to put it simple, this how I'm livin, and it's how I want you and now the girls too, to live. I'm feelin' the hell outta you Memorie, and I just wanna see where this gonna lead. This a big ass house, so Kyra you welcome anytime, to stay or just to visit. Whatever. Just do me one favor and don't bring them knucklehead niggas you be pimpin' where we at and we cool. Keep my baby company, and help me make her smile. That's wifey. So, let me show you how I do." E said, and then kissed me, handed me the keys to the CLS 550, gave me a grip for real, and said he would be back later. "Girl, yo ass must have put the thang on that nigga! This what I been talking bout. Gotta use what you got to get what you want and need. That nigga even willin' to play daddy to yo little sista's. If he ain't a keeper show me one." Kyra was just going on and on. Me I just

55

couldn't believe my luck. This just couldn't be happening "Pinch me Ky." I said out of the blue. "For what? This shit real. Ain't no doubt 'bout that. Hey, let's look around this big muthafucka, shit you gonna have to find yo way around." She said takin' off down the long hall. We walked around for what seemed like hours before we finally got tired and sat in what I think was one of the dens.

I had checked on my sisters, and to say they were fine was an understatement. It was like, he had this planned all along. My sisters' rooms were already ready, they had everything too. I mean, I didn't understand. They had clothes the right size and toys galore! They were in heaven to say the least. Then in the master bedroom. Man, that was some shit outta movie. The bed was huge! Then there was the fireplace, the 4 walk-in closets, and the bathroom. Boy, the tub looked like a pool and it was gold and marble everywhere! When I stepped in there I had to catch my breath. "It's beautiful." Was all I could say. Sittin' in the den at the bar I couldn't help but to think out loud. "Wonder how long he been planning this?" I said to no one in particular.

"Girl, I wouldn't even worry 'bout that. He got it all right. How did he know what was your dream bedroom? Did you tell him? I mean he got that shit

56

Welcome to My Hood

down to the last detail. Girl you lucky as shit."
Kyra was sayin'. "I don't remember telling him
nothing about my dream house, but here it is. And
I'm not lucky, I gotta be blessed. God, done finally
took pity on me and my sisters and decided to send
us an angel. That's how I'm lookin at it." I said, still
in a daze. "He said you could stay too. Please, stay.
I can't get around this big ass house alone." I
begged Kyra. "Girl you ain't gotta worry 'bout me
going anywhere. I told you, my-moms was trippin'
and I don't feel like stayin wit' no nigga. So best
friend, here we go on what I believe is gonna be
one helluva ride!"

T.E Cooper

7. Living Large.

I tell you, Kyra wasn't lyin. E was wonderful! I mean, he treated my sisters like they were his, he treated Kyra like she was his sista for real, and me, well he treated me like a queen. I mean, I have never been so spoiled in my life! I mean this nigga was livin' way larger than I could have ever imagined. He wanted me to stay in school, so I did that with pleasure. I drove my CLS 550, and wore the fliest clothes. I sent my sisters to a private school near the house and they were quite happy with the way things were going. I treated them like they were my own, and in all reality they were. I did everything for them, and loved doing it. It was like, I was meant to be a mom.

One day I woke up real sick. I mean, I was through. E looked at me and said he wasn't going anywhere that day cause of how bad I looked. "Hey, I'ma tell Kyra to do the girls today. I'm takin' you to the doctor." He said, sounding worried. "I don't need a doctor, just a little cold or something. I'll be a'iight." I said while heavin' in the trash. "Naw, you goin to the doc's. You been throwin' up all night. And you look pale and shit. Man, you goin' to the doctors. I don't want you getting Jewels, and Sapphire sick." He said worrying about my sisters. Oh how I loved this man.

"What's up Meme? You sick?" This coming from my youngest sister, Sapphire. "Just a little, you don't have to worry. I'll be alright in a little, I just need some rest." I told her trying to smile. "Jewel says you havin' a baby." She said matter-of- factly. "Oh no, sweetie, I just got a bug or something." I said getting a little worried. I hadn't seen my period in about 2 months, and I was gaining a little weight. I thought it was cause I was so happy. Could I be pregnant? Naw, couldn't be.

"Ms. Dupre'", the nurse called my last name. "The doctor would like to see you now." I looked at E, as he helped me up and over to the door. We went in and waited a little for the doctor to come in. "What do you think is wrong with me?" I asked E, still feeling horrible. "Probably just a bug or something going round. Don't worry. He probably gonna tell you to rest, get sleep and drink plenty of fluids." E said, not looking very convincing. "Wow sounds like you should be a doctor." I said with a half grin. "Naw, just been there before. I think I felt worse than you." He said "I doubt that. I feel like death." I

59

said and layed my head down on the pillow on the little medical bed. Just then the doctor walked in. "Hi, I'm Dr. Forrester." "Hello." We said in unison. "Well Ms. Dupre. It seems like we've found out why you've been so sick." "It's a bug ain't it?" Said E like he just won the lottery. "Not quite. Ms. Dupri, you're pregnant."
The doctor told me. And just like that my life changed forever.

Pregnant. Damn! What the fuck I'ma do now? What the fuck is this nigga gonna think, I'm tryna trap him or something? These are the thoughts that are going through my head the whole drive home. E was quiet as fuck, and I couldn't tell if he was pissed or what. He just drove home in silence. Should I say something? "E, um, can we talk?" I asked real nervous. "When we get home." Was all he said. Damn. This nigga pissed. Now I gotta find somewhere to go. I got me, my sisters and now a baby. This is too damn much. I can't have this damn baby! What the fuck I'ma do wit' a damn baby? I really fucked up a good thing this time. And wait 'til Kyra finds out! She gonna say "I told ya ass to protect yo self." And she should know. She has been in this situation more than once. Damn, that's who I need to talk to. She'll know what to do and where to go.

60

I was desperate to get home and talk to Ky. When we pulled up at his house, I jumped out the jeep and started towards the house in search of Kyra. "Meme, where you goin'? We gotta talk." E said, still no expression. "Look, I already know what you gonna say. And no, I didn't do this on purpose. And I understand if you don't want the baby. I'm going to find Kyra and me and her can handle this. And I know you probably want me to leave, but if you could give me some time, me and the girls will find somewhere else to go." I said, rambling on and crying at the same time. E looked at me stunned at first, then angry. "What you mean, "yall will take care of it"? You ain't doing shit 'wit my seed 'scept spittin it out! And I don't want you to go nowhere. Meme just chill." He was saying. "Baby look, yes I am surprised, but shit, I love the hell outta you girl. I'm damn happy you havin' my baby! I want you to have a girl, so she can look just like her beautiful mami." He said, coming towards me with a smile. I was speechless. Just then Kyra walked up.

"WE HAVIN A BABY!!" he yelled finally showing some real emotion. "Say what?" she said, "You heard me! Meme, is pregnant and havin' my baby! That makes me the happiest man in the whole world!" Then out of nowhere this nigga got down on one knee, right there on the steps of the house. "I kinda already knew you was pregnant. You had

61

all the signs. Plus, I been wantin' you to have my last name. I love you baby, will you marry me and make me an honest man?" Then he pulled out this little box, with a big surprise. "Oh, my God." Was all I could say for a moment. "Girl, you betta say yeah fo' I take off runnin' wit' that damn ring!" Kyra said all smiles. "You knew! You told her didn't you? And yes! Yes!" I said jumpin' up into his arms. Now how we were getting married and I was under aged, I couldn't tell you. But I was down!

Welcome to My Hood

8. And here we Go.

'Bout a week later I decided to go see my moms. I hadn't been to see her since that day she put me out and I took my sisters, but I had to get her to sign the papers for me to be able to marry E. I decided against takin' my sisters, Jewel told me that nigga would fuck with her when I was gone. The bastard. I just want her to sign these papers so I could go on with my life. When I pulled up my cousin Bam was coming out of his grandma's who stayed beside my mom. "What up cuz. Long time, no see." He said coming to give me a hug. "Look at you, you look good cuz. I see that nigga treatin you good." Bam said, lookin at the CLS. "Yeah, we doin alright.

I'm happy, and the girls are happy too. And you know Kyra stays with us too." I told him rambling, not really wantin' to go to my moms. "Yeah, that bitch!" he said, wit' no love at all. "What happened 'tween yall anyway. She never would get into it." I said. "Man, that girl foul. You better watch her trifflin' ass 'round ya man. That bitch is nasty, and if E knew what she was, she would be outta ya

63

house. Watch ya back wit that chick cuz." He said, then walked off like his day just got worse. I shrugged my shoulders, wondering what that was about and walked towards my moms.

As I walked towards the house, my neighbor from the apartment in front of ours told me to come here. "You goin' ta' check on ya' moms? She need it. You been gone a long time. How the girls?" she rambled on. "Fine." I replied. "Have you seen my mom around? Don't look like nobody stay there anymore." I said looking at the apartment in which I used to stay. "Oh, she probably up in there. You know that nigga don't let her leave the crib. You should come by more often to see ya moms. And she really misses your sisters, you should bring 'em by. Maybe that'll give her the strength to leave his sorry ass." My ex-neighbor said matter-of-factly. "Well, I'ma get on over here and see what's good. You take care of yourself and it was good seeing you." I said while walking away. I was still thinking about what she said 'bout my mom. Is she really letting this nigga keep her hostage? I gotta see what's going on. Even though we had our problems, she still my mom.

I walk up the little porch and knocked on the door. At first I thought no one heard me, so I started to

64

knock again when the door cracked open. "Who that?" I heard my mom ask. "Mom it's me." I said, all of a sudden real nervous. The door swung open and my mom came rushing out. "Where my babies? You didn't bring my babies?" she said like her heart was broke. "No mami. I came to see how you were doing, and how things were before I brought the girls. Can we go inside to talk?" She gave me an evil look, and proceeded into the apartment. When I got in I couldn't believe my eyes or my nose. The smell was foul, no rancid is more like it. The place was filthy and that's being nice. I was NOT bringing my sisters to this hell hole. "How you been mami? Are you okay? Talk to me." I said showing real concern. "Why you wanna know 'bout me? I heard how that nigga got yall livin' and you ain't been thought bout yo ol' MAMI." She said breaking my heart once more. "Well, I didn't think you wanted to see me." I confided. My mom looked at me like I was the devil, and walked off.

I thought she wasn't coming back so I walked down the hall to find her. I was determined to finish what I had come for. I opened her bedroom door and I couldn't believe my eyes! My mom sitting with her back to the door with a needle in her arm! I slowly backed out the room. I leaned against the wall to catch my breath. I couldn't

65

T.E Cooper

believe this shit! My-moms a junkie! I got myself together and calmed down. I knew from that moment on until my mom got her life together, she would never see my sisters. "MA!" I yelled, ready to be on my way. "MA!" I yelled again. Still no response. I ran down the hall to her room, bust open the door and ran to her. "MA!" I yelled, frantically shaking her. "What the fuck you doin!" she yelled at me all of a sudden. "Ma what are you doing? This ain't you! What's going on?" I said before I knew it. "Look. You always thought you was better than me. Tryin' to take my men, takin' my children! I hated you since the day you was born! So get the fuck outta my house, fore I have ta' cut ya' ass like a stranger." She said real leathal. I was crushed. I mean no matter how bad I thought my relationship with my-moms was. I always thought deep down she loved me. But I guess I was wrong.

"That's fine mami. I just need you to do one little thing for me, then I'm outta ya life forever." I said coldly. "I knew ya prissy ass wanted something. Well to get anything in life ya gotta pay for it. How much ya got." The woman I used to call mother said. "Fine. What's your price?" I said. "Ha, if it's getting rid of you I should do it for free, but you don't deserve that. Gimme a hundred." She said proud of herself. "Here you go. Now sign these

66

papers." I said giving her a crisp hundred and the paperwork that would forever change my life. She signed the papers without even asking what they were. As I was leaving she said some words I will never forget. "Don't forget mamasita, the road you chose is the road you will live. Ya ain't gonna get no free rides from no one, no matter what they tell you. You are a beautiful girl, use it to your advantage. You smart too, like ya daddy was. Use it. Take care of my babies, cause I can't. And Memorie, I really do love you." With that she slammed the door. That was the last time I saw my moms.

What happened at my-moms really shook me up. When I got home, E was there waitin' on me watchin 'Shark Tale' with the girls. He looked up and knew something was wrong. He excused himself from the girls and took my hand guiding me upstairs to our massive room. Once there, I broke down. I just couldn't stop crying. When E asked me what happened I told him every little detail. How the house looked, what the neighbor said and of course, what happened with my mom and all she had said. "You ain't going back." E said pissed. "I knew I shoulda went with you. That shit wouldn't a went down like that. Don't even think 'bout it no mo'. You got me and the girls and our little girl to think about. I don't want you stressing

67

while you got my seed in you. Ya hear. I got you mami, 'til the end. Now the only thing I want you to think about is getting fat wit' my seed and planning our wedding. Sky's the limit wit me and you ma." He said kissing me like he saw the world in my eyes.

Welcome to My Hood

9. A new life.

Well since I was already 3 months pregnant, E wanted to get married fast. He said he ain't bringin' no bastard kids in the world. Ya gotta love him. He even got his lawyer to start custody proceedings so no one would ever take my sisters away. This man was too good to be true. Well, you know the saying.

We decided to get married on June 12, Father's Day, you know, 'cause of me being pregnant and all. I wanted an outside wedding, cause the weather was just perfect, so E did what I wanted. He hired me a wedding coordinator and told her we were in a rush but to make sure it was what I wanted. Kyra was there through the whole thing and helped me pick out all the arrangements, as well as the color scheme. It was beautiful.

We only had a few people so I was a little confused when a young woman with a little boy walked in and sat down. "Who is that? Some family I haven't met?" I asked Kyra. "Hell, I don't know, but she don't look nothing like E. Anyway,

69

girl I am so happy for you! I can't believe you hit pay dirt. You best count yo blessins and thank God for that baby, cause girl you set." Kyra said, always looking at the money aspect of things. "Ky, I really love him." I said. "That's just a bonus." She said laughing. "Well, it's time for you to walk out there and stun everyone, cause girl you are truly the beautiful bride." My best friend said, with a tear in her eye. "Well here goes. From a girl, to a woman, to somebody's wife. I can't believe it. I'm finna be a mom, and a wife and I'm only 17." I said solemnly.

"Girl, you been all of that for some time now; this just makes it official." She said and opened the door to the backyard.

Everything was so beautiful, and just the right people. My sisters were walking down the aisle and dropping flower petals on the lawn and my man was standing there looking good enough to eat right there. I couldn't believe my luck, and at that moment I was the happiest person on earth. Then I walked pass the young lady from earlier. I looked over at her and saw nothing familiar, and then I saw her son and almost fainted. There sitting beside her was a mini version of Eric. I was crushed. No wonder he wanted a girl when most guys cry for boys. Should I run? No, I'm going to continue walking down this aisle with my head

70

held high. I'm the one he chose, I'm the one he's marrying. Even though I knew at that moment that my man wasn't faithful, I kept it moving like a good little soldier, a good little wife. The ceremony was beautiful, we had both wrote our own verses, cause E said the one everybody uses don't express how he feel. That nigga is a poet and I am his biggest fan.

When we were all headed towards the house for the reception, I saw the girl and mini E walking towards the front gates. "Wait a minute!" I yelled, looking around for E, but I didn't see him. "Can I talk to you for a minute?" I said as I caught up with them. "Sure, what's up?" she said with a bit of an attitude. "I'm Memorie, I don't think we've met before. And your name is?" I said as polite as I could. "First of all, you don't need to know my name. Ask Eric. Only reason I'm here, was cause I had to see it with my own eyes." She returned with much attitude. "Listen you are at my home and I just wanna know who you are; and who is this boys daddy?" I barked back. "Ha! You think you know so much. Well this here is Eric Lavar Watts, Jr.! Is that what you want? I hate that mutha' fucka'! And you best tell him not to come back our way, cause he ain't welcome!" With that she snatched Eric Jr. up and walked off.

71

I was stunned. I couldn't move or talk. "What up girl?? Everybody wanna know where the blushin' bride is... Hold up, what's wrong Meme? Talk to me." Kyra was saying, but at the time I just couldn't say anything. "Is this about that chick we saw earlier? Look Meme, bitches are haters, this yo wedding day so fuck that jealous hoe." My friend said like a true best friend. "That was his son." Was all I could say. "Damn." I heard Ky say under her breathe. "Look, Meme; you the one here with him, not her. If that is his son, talk to him about it later, not today. If you saw her, so did he and believe you me, that nigga gonna bring it up before you. If not, then fuck it. You got it made and you about to have a baby, yo' damn self. So don't let these bitches rain on your parade. You my sis' and I won't tell you nothing wrong." Ky was saying trying to make it better. "You know what, you right. That's my man in there and I do love him unconditionally. That just threw me for a loop. Let me get myself together and I'll be right in." I said hoping that would convince Ky that I would be alright. "Okay, don't make me come looking for you again. I'll let E know you coming." With that she was on her way to the house, leaving me with my thoughts.

Well if it is his son, and by the looks, he is, there isn't much I can do. The boy has to be at least 1, so maybe this was a broad he was messing with

72

before we got tight. Yeah, that's it. They was together before we got tight. I was trying to convince myself so I could have a good time at my reception. I couldn't drink or smoke so I had to be cheery. I did all the usual rounds and throwing the bouquet. I did all I could to keep my mind off of E's little boy, but couldn't. His little face just kept replaying in my mind.

We were going to Jamaica for our honeymoon. Jamaica! I couldn't fathom the thought. I couldn't believe we were going to Jamaica. My sisters were at the house with Ky, and my mind was anywhere but on Eric's little boy. I was beside myself. "Is it going to be okay? You know the baby." I said sounding a little worried. I wasn't really worried about the baby; the doc had cleared me for the flight. It was the flight! I was terrified of heights. I couldn't let him know, so I faked being worried about the baby. "Girl, the doctor said it would be okay. So stop worrying. We 'bout to have a ball girl! I got you, remember?" He said with that killa smile. "You right. I trust you." I said, still a little nervous. The flight was wonderful! E got us first class tickets! I just couldn't believe it. The stewardess was really nice, and when she found out I was pregnant, she 'bout broke her neck to make sure I was comfortable. I felt like a queen. I was flying first class to Jamaica, with the man of

T.E Cooper

my dreams, life couldn't get any better.

Oh, but it did! When we got to the airport, E had a stretch Hummer waiting! I couldn't believe it, and that wasn't all he had in store. I couldn't believe my eyes! He had rented us a bungalow on the beach. It had three bedrooms, a patio, a private pool and all the amenities to make me feel like I was the most special woman in the world. "Oh, E, I love it! I can't believe you went through all this trouble." I said excitedly. "Trouble? Girl, what you talking? You my wife, and nothing but the best from here on out." He said as if he already wasn't giving me the best. "Baby, you are too good to me. I love you so much. What did I do to deserve you?" I told him pulling him close. "You didn't do anything, God blessed me with you, so I gotta do the best by this beautiful angel, that I now call my wife." He said kissing me deeply. This was the beginning of a honeymoon of bliss.

We stayed in Jamaica for a month! Can you believe that a whole fuckin' month! This shit was too good to be true. By the time we left Jamaica, I'd gotten a slight tan, and a lot of love and rest. I was so satisfied with my life at that moment that I had completely forgotten about Eric; Jr.

Kyra and the girls were waiting at the airport when

74

we arrived. "What did you get us?" I heard from everyone. "Oh, I got all of you something. Wait 'til we get home and I'll show you everything. Right now, I just want to go home." I said sounding exhausted. I had a wonderful time in Jamaica, but I was ready to go home. I missed my sister's and my girl Kyra. I had a lot to tell them, as soon as I take a nap. I was out like a light. When I woke up I was at home. "Wake up sleepyhead." I heard E say. "Wow, was I sleep? We at home already?" I said yawning and stretching. "Yup, and you slept all the way." E helped me out of the car (cause I had gained a little baby weight to say the least) and walked me towards our double doors.

"Wow, girl you and that baby coming along ain't cha?" Kyra said with a smile. "I know. I just blew up overnight. One day you could barely tell and the next, Bam! I hope I don't gain too much weight. I don't want to turn E off." I said thoughtfully. "Chile please! That nigga ain't goin' nowhere. I think that nigga love you for real. You don't have to worry about the weight; he wants you to eat all the time! He told me so. He wants you and that baby to pig out. You should see the kitchen. This nigga went all out. I think he bought the market or something cause I ain't never seen that much food, unless it was at the market." Kyra told me. "Huh? How did he do that? We've been gone for a

75

month." I said confused. "Girl, when yall would call to check on the girls, he would tell me what to do to have everything ready for you when yall got back. You won't believe all the shit he did to make you comfy while carrying his seed." Kyra said matter-of-factly. "Are you serious? Like what?" I asked curious.

" Well for one, the girls have a nanny, you have your own personal chef, he switched yall's bedroom from upstairs to downstairs, the frig is packed with all kinds of fresh fruits and fresh veggies, no caffeine, no red meat,... should I go on?" Kyra said with a smile. "Are you serious? He did all that for me? I can't believe it." I said starting to run around to see what changes my new husband had cooked up. I couldn't believe it, it was just like Kyra said, with a few left outs. I was astounded. "All this for me? I just can't believe my luck. This has got to be too good to be true. No one has it this easy." I was saying to myself in total wonder.

"Well you do." E said from behind me. "You are just, just..." I was at a loss for words. I couldn't think of anything to say except, "Thank you, thank you E. You are too good to me." I said as humbly as I knew how. "No, thank you. You carrying my seed, my soon to be daughter. I love you." E said,

76

with so much passion in his voice I had to look up at him. "Why so serious?" I asked. "Baby, let's go in the room so we can talk." He said, still looking serious. "Baby, what's wrong?" I asked; concern creeping in my voice. "There's nothing wrong, we just need to talk 'bout some stuff. You know, clear the air, and figure things out. You might not love me as much when you hear what I have to say." He said, this time looking like he was about to cry. "Baby, what's wrong, there's not anything you could say that would make me love you less. I'm here for good, so you better get used to it. I love you, you are my husband, and I take that seriously. No matter what you have to tell me, we will work it out." I said, sounding a lot braver than I felt.

"Okay, it's time I tell you something. Remember our wedding?" "Of course silly it was our wedding." I said thinking I knew what this was about. "Well there was someone there that is real important to me that I want you to one day meet." He said, still hesitating. "Go on." I said since I already knew. "Well….. um…. Well…I kinda have a son. He's one going on 2. This November; on the 4th." He said, like it was the toughest thing he had ever done in his life. I said what any wife who loves her husband no matter what would say. "Baby, I already know, and it's okay. Even if you were messing with somebody else, it was before we got

77

tight. I love you baby, and any part of you." I told him. He looked at me with such surprise, I was stunned. He really thought I would leave just because he had a son. "But I will tell you this. Just because I will accept your son, and believe me I will, doesn't mean you can do this again. We are married now and I want my husband faithful. No fucking around with his mother. If yall is over, let it stay that way. And if yall ain't then yall need to be. And by the way, I saw her at the wedding; I even spoke to her, that's how I knew about Eric Lavar Watts, Jr." I said. He was totally stunned. I mean he hadn't said a single word. "Eric, are you okay?" I asked. "Yeah, it's just that, I thought you would leave me for sure for not telling you before. I really should have. And yes, it's over with his mom, I don't want her. But because of it, she's tryin' to make it hard for me to see my son. I didn't know you talked to the bitch though." He said, finally out of his astonishment. "Yeah, and you are right she is a bitch. Cause I wasn't even being mean or rude, I just walked up and introduced myself, cause I had seen lil' E. and she just went off. She did say to tell you she hates you and you should stay away. Look, that's your situation, but I am here. Just don't ever cheat or lie to me again, cause I will leave without looking back." I told him in a way that he knew I was for real. "I promise baby, no more secrets, and thanks, I think I'm going to need it when it comes

78

to that bitch, Lala. I hope I don't have to fuck that bitch up 'bout my son." He said, in a way I knew he was for real.

T.E Cooper

10. And baby makes 5.

Things seemed to be finally settling down and me and my sisters had finally come to terms that, this was our life. I was getting big as hell! Does being pregnant really do this to your body? I didn't even know I could stretch like this. I was beginning to see what my mom was talking about. "Damn, Ky, my ass is tired of caring this damn baby. I sho' will be glad when the day comes." I said out of misery. "Girl, what you talking? For someone that could give birth at any moment you look damn good. Shit, I hope if I ever get pregnant I look half as good as you." She said with a smile. "Whatever. I'm just ready to drop this load. I'm ready to meet my little, Diamond." I say, thinking of the name her daddy had dubbed her.

When we found out he was getting his wish, the nigga went crazy! I ain't never seen so much shit in all my life. One things fo' sho', this little bundle of joy ain't gonna want for a damn thing for the first year of her life. "Yeah. Me too. Cause I'm gonna spoil her rotten. And you made me the godmother! The Godmother! I just can't believe it! That's just

80

like having my own, without actually having to be pregnant. No offense, cause you do look good sis, I'm just saying. Ya know. Anyway, I can't wait for little Diamond to get here. I already went to Tiffany's, and got her the cutest set. Wait 'til you see it." Kyra was saying proudly. I didn't mind the comments 'bout being pregnant, 'cause I really did understand where she was coming from. I was just happy to know my first born was coming into the world, and unlike a lot of these trifling nigga's, her daddy loves her already. Yeah things were going just fine.

Damn, I think I just wet myself. Oh well, it ain't the first time since I been pregnant. "Oooouch!" I screamed. Oh shit! "Kyra, E, come quick please somebody help me!" I was panicking and that wasn't good. "What...Oh, shit! Meme you havin' this baby?!" Kyra said, coming running into the room. "That's what it looks like, now where the hell is E!" I snapped at her. "Okay, calm down now. We gonna have to call him from the hospital, cause he left 'bout an hour ago. You was sleepin' so he didn't wake you. Come on, let's get your stuff together and the girls and we out." Kyra said, rushing me out of my room. "My bags are in the foyer. Have been for some time now, and I don't think it would be a good idea to bring the girls. They'll be fine with the nanny." I said, a little calmer since my best

81

friend arrived. "Oh no you not. We are going!" said Jewel and Sapphire in unison. "Girls, this is not the time. I'm having the baby and I can't watch you." I said gently, trying not to hurt their feelings. Then another contraction hit, and I almost passed out. "It's time to go. Come on girls, I guess you in for the ride." said Kyra while getting me out the door.

Off we went, flying in my CLS. I thought we were gonna die before we got to the hospital. "Did you call E?" I asked in between pains. "Yeah, he gonna meet us there. And so is the doc." Kyra said. By the time we got to the hospital I was in so much pain I didn't know which way was up. All I could do was scream, "Give me some drugs! Now!" I told the nurse who was taking me up to my room. "Baby, hey, how you feelin?" E surprised me, I didn't see him come in. "Fuck you! If you ever touch me again, I will kill you!" I screamed. "Hey where is the doc?" E said sounding concerned. "He'll be with us in a minute. There are some things we have to do to make sure the baby is safe and this is a normal delivery. So let's get her to her room and get her settled." The nurse said with kindness. "Drugs, drugs, drugs, don't you hear me?! I need DRUGS!!!" I was in hysterics by then. I could not believe I was in so much pain. "Is this normal? I mean she seems to be in a lot of pain." E said getting upset. "Don't worry, it really is normal.

82

Now Memorie, is it? Let's check and see how much you've dilated." The nurse said looking at my pussy. "Oh my." The nurse said. "What!?" E and I said at the same time. "Oh, excuse me I think it's time I bring in Dr. Williams." the nurse said hurrying out. "E, what's wrong?" I said getting upset. Just as E was about to say something, Dr. Williams walked in. "Hello, Meme. Let's see what we have here." Dr. Williams said. "Somebody get me a glove pronto!" Dr. Williams shouted.

"Now Meme I want you to push one good time for me okay?" Dr. Williams said. Push? Was it time already? "I'm scared." I said. "Don't worry about a thing. This little girl is ready to meet her momma." Dr. Williams said assuredly. "Now Push!" I did like the doctor said and my little girl popped right out. When I looked at E, he was crying. The doctor asked him if he wanted to cut the umbilical cord and as he did it he balled like a baby.

When the nurse finally brought me my baby girl, I was ecstatic. She was 6 lbs. and 1 oz, she was very light, and had this little bald head, well not all the way, but close to it and she was the most beautiful person in the whole world to me. I never did believe in love at first sight, but after I saw my Diamond, I knew I was in love. I told the nurse I was breast feeding and I wanted her to sleep in my

83

room. The nurse said okay and they took me to my private room. When I got there it was the second most beautiful sight of the day (my daughter being the first).

E had all kinds of balloons and flowers and he even went out and bought Diamond a special basinet to sleep in while we were in the hospital. I couldn't believe my luck. I sat there for a minute and just thanked God. I stood up out of the wheel chair because my actual delivery was very easy. Diamond slid right into the world, literally. She gave her momma no stitches or hemorrhoids, like some other unfortunate females. I walked over to the closet and got out one of the gowns I was to wear during my hospital stay, and walked into the bathroom and took a shower. Once out of the shower, I dressed, pulled my hair into a ponytail, put on my slippers and walked to the nursery. I told the nurse who I was and showed my armband, and told her I wanted my baby. E was standing at the window in awe. It was like he had never seen a baby before. E turned and looked at me and said, "I love you so much, thank you for such a beautiful gift." And hugged and kissed me. "Well, the same to you. 'Cause if it weren't for you, I wouldn't have my beautiful gift." I said, and hugged him back. The nurse notified us that she was about to take Diamond to the room, so we walked with her.

84

Diamond was born on Dec. 22 and I was home by Christmas Eve.

Christmas was wonderful and full of food and presents. Diamond didn't even know what was going on but she had the best Christmas of all. I thought that nothing could destroy my happy world but I guess the old saying "What goes up, must come down." was dead on point. One day me and Kyra were sitting in the den with Diamond, Jewel, and Sapphire when the doorbell rang. "Who that?" Ky asked. "Beats me. I'll go get it, watch Diamond." I said, getting up and going to get the door. When I opened the door, I got a big surprise. "Hey there, Mrs. Bitch." Lala said. "What the fuck do you want? You ain't even s'posed to be at my house! And if you don't leave now you gonna see what Mrs. Bitch can do!" I screamed back. By that time, Kyra had come out to see what all the hollerin' was about. "Who the fuck is this trick?" Kyra said letting me know she had my back.

"This here's E's baby momma. But what I wanna know is; what the fuck do you want here?" I said. "First off, just cause E married yo stank ass, don't mean you the shit. And secondly I'm here to drop off his son, 'cause he can have his bastard child! And last but not least, tell that mutha fucka I had the abortion and I'm telling the police everything I know!" With that, she handed me Lil' E and stormed off. I was stunned. Not that she left Lil' E, but cause she said she had an abortion. "Did you hear what she said?" I asked Kyra. "Look forget that bitch. The baby cryin' and this bitch done left him. Let's go back in the house, and call E. And don't even think on what that jealous and obviously crazy bitch said. She's just mad, E wit' you and not her." Kyra said boiling mad.

We took Lil' E in the den with the girls and introduced them. "Jewel, Sapphire, come here a sec. This here is Lil' E, and he's going to be staying with us a while and I want you to make him feel welcome." I told my sisters. "Hey cuttie pie. Come over here with us and let's color." Jewel said to Lil E, while taking his hand. He took her hand, looked back at me and walked off with my sisters. "Girl, I just got off the phone with E, he said he on the way home now. So don't worry when he gets here he'll straighten everything out." Kyra said. "Girl, you sho'll got a lot of faith in that nigga. But right now I'm pissed. I told that nigga I didn't care about Lil E, but he had to stop fucking with that bitch! And he got her pregnant! I'm gonna wring that nigga's neck!" I said fuming. "Calm down. Of course I have a lot faith in him. Look where we stay! Look how good he's treated not only you but your sister's and

86

me. That nigga got mad love for you and I know you know this. Think Meme, just think. Don't go off on him; find out what's going on first." Kyra said trying to calm me down.

Just then, E walked in the room. He got there so quick you would have thought he was in a plane. "E, what the fuck is going on?" I yelled off the bat. "What's up? That bitch crazy, I told you this." He said defensively. "You still fuckin that crazy bitch. You stupid mutha fucka! You got her pregnant again! What the fuck where you thinking? I told you I would leave if I found out yo ass was fuckin around!" I yelled crying. "Look, baby, calm down! Please calm down. The kids are in the other room. Come on baby, let's talk. Kyra, can you please tell her to calm down." E said in a panicky voice. "Meme, come on let the man explain. Calm down. Look at yourself; you know the girls can hear you and so can Lil' E." Kyra said. "Okay, let's talk." I said thinking about my sisters and my baby and now my baby's brother. "First, let me say, I'm sorry. Yeah I fucked up and ain't no excuse, but you can't leave, I love you." E said, with tears in his eyes. "So you admittin' to fuckin her, huh?" I said shocked. "Look, I can't lie and expect us to get over this, so I gotta keep it real wit' you. Yeah I fucked her, but I realized what I was doing and left. Then she told me she was pregnant so I told her to get an

T.E Cooper

abortion. I'm sorry baby, I'm sorry. And I don't know where she is now, and she just left my son! I could kill that bitch!" E said. I couldn't even speak. I didn't trust myself to say anything so I just walked off. I heard E calling me to come back, but I just couldn't.

I couldn't believe this nigga! He damn sure got some fuckin nerve! Yeah, he fucked her but he was sorry. How many nigga's used that line? I walked past the den and checked in on the kids. They were getting along just fine and the baby was sleeping in her bassinet with the nanny watching. They looked so peaceful, not a care in the world. If I left what would become of my children, cause my sisters were my children too. Where would we go and what would I do? Damn! What the fuck do I do now? I can't believe this nigga, but then again, yeah I could. He is, after all a nigga, and they all want their cake and want to eat it too. I just couldn't get over the hurt. At least not yet, I wasn't ready to let it go. I'ma let this serve as a reminder. No matter how good I think things are going, they can always change in the blink of an eye. That bitch threatened E with the police, so I better start getting prepared just in case I gotta do this on my own.

Sure as shit stank, that bitch went to the Feds on E. Spots started getting popped and E was more

Welcome to My Hood

jumpy every day. I had let go of the little incident from a few weeks back, cause I saw that shit was about to hit the fan. "E, we need to talk." I said one night after he got home. "Sure, what up boo?" E said. "Baby, wi't all the shit happening, and you not being able to find Lala, what the fuck are we gonna do?" "Don't worry, I got it handled. You straight. I got you and the kids. We gonna make it through this." E said, not convincing me one bit. "Check it, how much money you got put up, just in case?" I asked. "Shit I don't know. I never thought I would have to worry about this type of shit." E said. "Well baby, it's time for me and you to do this thang Bonnie and Clyde style. If you get popped we gonna need a helluva lawyer, not to mention, we got 4 kids to think about. It's time to go hard, and go strong. I got cha back." I said, telling him in detail the things I had in store. Even though I was playing wifey and stay at home mom, I was from the streets and I knew how to get down if I had to.

11. Go Hard Or Go Home.

Me and E went crazy in the streets of Charlotte. Whoever owed money had to pay up, whoever had a boomin' spot, had to give it up. No holds barred, and takin no shorts. That's how I grew up, and that's what me and my boo were enforcing now. I mean, we took Bonnie and Clyde to a whole other level. These cats didn't know what hit 'em when we came through. E already had Tanglewood on lock, so that wasn't no problem. Me, I had B. Ford and Hidden Valley. I had some folks I was down for back in the day who was already controlling the Valley and would do anything for me, so that was a no brainer. We was getting doe like never before, wit' the Feds watchin and all. Ain't no other way to go, but hard when the Feds on yo ass, so that's what we did.

I mean we sold hard, soft, boy, and all kinds of exotic weed. We had it all, until that day when the Fed's came bustin' up our party. It was about 3 in the morning! Those bastards came in there deep. Like they were huntin a serial killer or something.

Welcome to My Hood

Wasn't nobody there but me, E, the kids and Kyra. They had us all in cuffs, all except the kids, they were hollerin like crazy too. All I wanted to do was calm them down. "Look man, my girl and her sister ain't got nothing to do wit' this. This 'bout me and yall. Can you please take off the cuffs in front of the kids?" E was sayin' real calm. I wanted to say something, but E had already schooled me on how to act when they came. Say nothing. Period. So all I could do was watch and listen to my husband end his life.

The Feds put a Federal Hold on E, and he got no bond. So of course, I was out of my mind. I was so lost, Kyra had to calm me down. "Girl, you gotta get it together. You got kids and some shit you need to take care of, before you ain't got nothing." She was right; there was some shit I needed to get together; so me and the kids would be straight. "Okay, let me think. First off, we gotta get another crib. We ain't gonna be able to stay here." I said getting into motion.

I had to get rid of the nanny and get out to the backyard. When shit started to hit the fan; me and E decided to burry some stash money, just in case. No one knew about the money, but me and him and I didn't want the nosey nanny knowing anything. Then, I had to find somewhere to stay. A

91

T.E Cooper

hotel would do for now, but that will be temporary. We had about 3 mill buried in the back and I was planning on flippin' that. After we told the nanny she would no longer be needed, and helped her pack and out the door. I said, "Okay, KY, you won't believe what I'm going to tell you so just keep quiet 'til I'm done." I said preparing her for the 3 mill I was about to disclose to her. "Shit, I hope it ain't no bad news. I done had all I can take." She said frowning. "We ain't ass out you know. I got something up my sleeve. Don't worry girl, we survivors and I refuse to go out without a fight. Now let's get the kids out of here and then we'll come back." I said going to get the kids ready. As I was packing small bags for the children I thought about the nanny. Damn, I shouldn't have let her go so soon. "Hey, Kyra! See if you can stop that damn nanny from getting on that flight! I just thought about it, we gon' need her!" I yelled. After getting all of the stuff I deemed necessary for the kids. I loaded them in the new Cadillac Escalade, E purchased for me about a month before.

"Did you catch her?" I asked Kyra, referring to the nanny. "Yup, and I had to put in a little extra doe, cause she said we was playing wit her." Kyra said. "That's fine, we can afford it. You drive the Benz, 'cause after we get the suite, me and you got some work to do." I said getting in the SUV. "A'ight, I'm

92

right behind you." She said hopping in the CLS.

And off we went, first to the airport to pick up the nanny and then to The Ritz, Downtown Charlotte. I had called ahead and reserved the Penthouse so we could all stay in the same room. Once we got to the hotel and had the children settled, it was time to go back to the house. "Okay, Clara, I'm going to be gone for a while, but I will return tonight. Don't deter from your usual schedule with the children. Act like everything is normal we are just in a different setting. Eric won't be with us for a while so I'm asking you, do you think you can be in this for the long haul with me? I mean do you love my children enough that even if I didn't have the money to pay you, you would still care for my children?

This is important, 'cause if you don't think you can, then we can end this tomorrow. I will pay you for a day and night's work and then take you to the airport. 'Cause I can't honestly say that I will always be able to pay you, even though we have an agreement." I said pointedly to the nanny, who didn't seem too much older than me. She had been with us for a while and I had never heard her talk of family or a boyfriend. She never said anything about anything she saw or heard around the house, but I had to be sure. I had to make sure I

93

T.E Cooper

had her loyalty to my children, if not to me. "Miss Memorie, I love your children like they were my own. I was heartbroken when you said you no longer needed me, which is why I asked for extra money. I wanted to be sure you were serious. You don't have to worry about my loyalty to you or the kids because you've had it for some time. You are a young women, and girl you be doing yo thang! I admire you, cause in this type of bullshit you holding strong, and it will be my pleasure to help with the kids, free of charge. Just consider me your friend and let's get it Popppin!" Clara said giving me dap. That was all I needed. I had my best friend by my side and someone who cared for my kids and was down wit' me. Look out Charlotte, here we come.

Welcome to My Hood

12. The Trial.

E's trial came quick, that was on account that E didn't wanna be sittin' in no Charlotte County. He knew he was lookin at life, but he wouldn't snitch, when they came at him with that Kingpin charge. He took that shit like a man and kept it movin. He had one of the best defense attorney's in Charlotte, Mr. Eddens. Now Mr. Eddens was a bad dude, he didn't play in the courtroom and he wasn't playin with E's case either. He was tired of young black men facing life in prison for what society ultimately breeds most of them to be. Well, Mr. Eddens got E's time reduced to 15 yrs. Not much, but considering the evidence and the fact that E wouldn't give up no names, that was all they could get. I was devastated to say the least. I couldn't believe I had just lost my husband to the system.

E's lawyer arranged for us to talk after the negotiations were through. I couldn't stop crying. "E, what the fuck am I gonna do without you?" I wailed. "Listen beautiful, I know this shit fucked up right now, but you gonna bounce back. I'ma get

95

my lawyer to draw up divorce papers, so you won't feel tied to no nigga locked down. As for Lil' E, I'm tryna' to find his moms so you won't have to take care of no kid that ain't yours. I love you, and don't you sit around cryin over me, cause I knew this was coming. One more thing before I go, I kept this pad over on the North side, you ain't know bout it. I had my lawyer draw up papers long ago and it belongs to you. No strings attached, no feds involved, all legit cause I made it that way. This is the last thing I'ma be able to do for you and my family, cause yall my family. It's a few cat's that owe me some money, I'ma get Big Hurk to go get it for you, so you don't have no problems. If anything jump off, call Big Hurk, he'll know what to do. Now baby, go get my kids out of that hotel and take them home." Eric said attempting to turn away.

"Wait! You just said a lot of shit and I'm not sure I got it all, but first off let me tell you this. Ain't nobody; getting no fucking divorce! NO DIVORCE! And secondly, if that bitch Lala come anywhere near my fuckin son, I will kill the bitch. That's my son! Do you hear me? I don't know what the fuck is going on wit' you, but you better get it the fuck together! I don't need you breaking down on me, or trying to fuckin' divorce me! I got a lot on my mind, and it damn sure feels good to know that

96

somebody out your fuckin' crew got my back. Now, turn the fuck around and give your wife a hug and fuckin' kiss, cause I don't know when we gonna be able to do this again." I said, taking control of the situation. Eric turned around, and smiled that million dollar smile and came to me. "Baby, I love you." Eric said giving me the most passionate kiss I'd ever had in my life. After that it was time for him to go, and with him, at the time, I thought my life. But life goes on........

13. Doing It on My Own

Eric's attorney came over to the hotel the next day, and brought a whole bunch of surprises. First, it was he, not Big Hurk that would be delivering money owed from the streets, second, he pulled out papers that officially made me Lil' E's mom, then he pulled out the papers for me to sign saying that the house E was telling me about, was mine. He handed me a book bag and the keys and said good-bye. I asked him when I would see him again, and he told me, when it was time for some money. He told me not to lose or forget his number, cause E was a good friend and he would always be there if we ever needed him. With that Mr. Eddens left.

"Ladies can we have an adult meeting?" I asked my sister, Jewel. "Okay, kids you know what that means we have to go to the other room. Come on." Jewel said ushering the younger kids in the separate room and holding Diamond at the same time. "Don't drop the baby." I said watching her wobble. "I got this sis." Jewel said with a grin then she went in the room and shut the door. "Okay

Welcome to My Hood

ladies. Now is the time, if anyone wants to back out." I said, looking at my two closet friends. "Chile please; ain't nobody goin' nowhere, so come on let's get the kids and go see the house." This coming from our friend; nanny Clara. "A'wight, let's go." I said and we called the kids out and got them together and off we went to our new home.

Now when E told me it was a pad on the North side, I didn't know what to expect. We had both hung tight on the North, but I had never heard of the street before. Thank God for navigation. We hit 85n and got off on Sugar Creek and made a left. We took Sugar Creek all the way to W.T. Harris and then we crossed over and kept on until we crossed over David Cox. "Damn, girl where this damn house at?" Kyra asked baffled. "Look, here come's our turn." I said pointing to the subdivision on the right. KINGSLEY PLACE. The sign read. "Wow, these are nice as Hell!" Kyra said getting excited. Then the navigation directed us to make the next right. And when we did we were amazed. There was only one house in the cul-de-sac, and it was gorgeous. It wasn't the mansion we just left, but it definitely was something to write home about.

It was pretty big, I guess he wanted us to have enough room, seeing how it was 7 of us. We pulled into the driveway, and just sat there for a minute.

99

"He still taking care of us." I said more to myself than anyone else. "Yes he is sista, yes he is." Kyra said, giving me a hug. "Can we go in, please?" Jewel, Sapphire, and Lil E said at once. "Of course, let's go." I said. Once we entered the house it was evident that E had been planning this for a long time. The entire house was furnished in some of the most beautiful stuff I had ever seen. "Wow, he did all this without you knowing huh?" Clara said, as I took Diamond out of her arms. "Yeah, looks that way. Look at this place. It doesn't look like the mansion at all. I mean the way it's decorated. You know, the mansion looked like a man lived there, if you know what I'm sayin, this place though, this place looks like something out of a fairytale. Like the perfect place to raise my babies." I said, loving my husband more than ever before. Well we got settled and the girls started going to the public school around the corner, and I even put Lil' E and Diamond in daycare.

I wanted to get my children in a routine and settled before I started thinking about running the streets to ensure our future. Once I felt comfortable with the way things had settled down, I called a "Grown up Meeting".

"Okay ladies, what do you think? Should we just chill or do I go out there and go hard and stack

100

some more doe?" I asked both Kyra and Clara. They were my girls and we were in it together. "Well I think we could chill for minute. I mean you are E's girl, and no matter what the Fed's gonna be looking to make sure you really didn't have nothing to do with that shit. Plus, I think you should go ahead and get that paralegal thing you was talking about. Get some legit shit goin' before you just jump back in the game. And if you ask me you don't need to be in the game anymore. You set." Kyra told me. "Well what about you, Clara what you think?" I asked, "I think, I'ma go with Kyra on this one.   You should just go to school and chill. Shit, we all can get right with the way YOU livin'!" she said laughing. "Well yall know what's mine is yours, so this is how WE livin', and I don't want yall to forget." I said seriously. With that I decided they were right, why should I be out on the streets hustling, shit we set, for life if I play my cards right.

T.E Cooper

14. A New Path.

It took 6 months for me to get certified as a paralegal, and while I was goin', Kyra decided to take some Medical Transcription classes. We both finished up about the same time, and CPCC gladly gave us our certifications. We were on top of the world, then one day while we were sittin at home smoking some weed, I received a phone call. "Hey, Memorie, it's me Mr. Eddens. I wanted to know if it was okay if I stopped by." Mr. Eddens said. "Of course, you are always welcome, you know that. I ain't going anywhere. Just sittin' here with Kyra; celebrating getting my cert." I said toakin' on the blunt. "Okay, I will be there in about an hour." He said and hung up. "Who was that?" Kyra asked. "Mr. Eddens, he's coming over. I guess he got some more money. Damn, at this rate I won't have to use my cert. If I did, it wouldn't be for the money, that's for damn sure." I said; high as hell.

Me and Kyra had moved on to the kitchen, we had a serious case of the munchies. That Purp can do that to you. "Damn, so much shit in here I don't even know what the fuck I want." Kyra said,

102

looking in the fridge. "Well, it don't matter just get something." I said, sitting down at the island in the middle of the kitchen. Just as Kyra was making us some sub sandwiches, the doorbell rang. "I'll get it; it's probably just Mr. Eddens." I said, getting up to answer the door. I made my way and opened up the door. Something about the way Mr. Eddens was lookin' made me wanna shut it back. "Hello, Mr. Eddens, how's it hangin?" I said tryin' to put some light in what I could tell was about to be a heavy situation. "Hello, Memorie, is there somewhere we can talk?" Mr. Eddens asked, making me think this was even more serious than I thought. "Sure we can go into the den. Kyra! Come into the den for a minute." I yelled, wanting someone else there just in case I couldn't take what I was about to find out.

When Kyra came in Mr. Eddens told us to sit down. Uh Oh. I thought. "Memorie, I have some bad news. Have you talked to Eric recently?" Mr. Eddens said, trying to stall. "As a matter-of-fact, no. He usually calls, but I haven't heard a thing from him in about a week. I was going to take the kids this weekend. I even tried to call and see what was up, but they wouldn't tell me nothing. He's probably been fightin' or something." I said, getting more nervous by the second. "Well, I'm sorry to tell you this, but Eric is dead." He said with more

103

emotion in his eyes than I could have thought a man could have for another man. "WHAT! You lyin'! Why would you say something like that! GET OUT!" I was screaming. "Memorie, calm down. Sit down." Mr. Eddens was saying. I was out of control. I was crying and screaming so loud, Clara came running in. "What's going on?" she asked worried. "He DEAD! He DEAD!" I cried. "What is she talking about?" Clara asked, getting worked up herself. Kyra was just sitting there stunned, she was speechless. "Mr. Eddens, what is going on here?" Clara asked the only sane person in the room at the time. "Listen, Clara is it? Well, about 3 days ago the guards at the prison found Eric dead in the showers. They didn't call me until today, I just found out like yall. I came straight here. I don't know what to say, I don't know how this happened. He didn't give up any names and they still came after him. I don't know what to say." Mr. Eddens said shedding a tear. And there it was, he was gone for good and wasn't shit I could do about it. Gone!

We found out that somebody paid big money to get rid of E. They didn't care that he didn't tell on nobody, they just wanted him gone, just in case. From the moment they put E in the ground I had made up my mind that whoever did this to my husband, the father of my children, the only man I

104

will ever love, was gonna pay.

With E gone for good, I was lost. I mean I was out of it for a month. I just couldn't take it. I felt like a part of me died with E in that prison and I didn't know if I could resuscitate it. Everybody tried to make me feel better, even though they were grieving in their own way. Clara took special care not to let the kids bother me and Kyra just catered to me like she was my maid. Everybody was lost, and at the time I didn't know how to find our way. "Look Meme, it's me KY, I know this is hard but you gotta bounce back. You can't stay like this forever, E wouldn't want that. You know that nigga always wanted you to look your best. And look at you sitting here, in ya' own stank feeling sorry for yo' self. You got way more than most bitches and you only 19. Now, I'm tryin to be nice, but yo' ass gotta get the fuck up!" KY came at me one day. "I'm sleepy, leave me alone and close those fuckin' blinds." I said, pulling the covers over my head. "Hell no. Look girl, yeah that nigga gone, and don't get me wrong, E was my nigga, but you my sista. You the one I gotta look out for. E gone Meme, ain't nothing we can do." KY said, and walked out the room.

I thought about what Kyra just said and for the first time since we buried E, I felt something. I

105

mean, I felt shit all the time, but this was different, it was like E was in the room with me. I can't explain it, it just was. So I started to talk to him. Lord knows what I would have done if he answered, but that's just what I did. "E, if you can hear me, baby I need some help. I don't know if I can go on without you. I love you so much, and I miss you like you just left yesterday. Baby, what do I do? I wanna kill those nigga's that did this to you, and I want revenge on the mutha-fucka' that put the hit out on you, but how? I'm lost boo, and this the first time I done felt like this in a long time. I'm supposed to be strong for the kids and my girls, but I don't think I can do it. I need you and I miss you." I said really breaking down and crying for the first time. Now I had cried since E died, but not like this. This was like someone had let the waterfalls loose and the storm was raging. I cried for my dead husband, I cried for my mom, and I cried for all the abuse I suffered at the hands of no good nigga's in my lifetime. I had never in my whole life cried like that. I released. I think I cried for at least 2 hrs. I needed it. I had never really broke down about anything that happened in my life, cause I always thought I was supposed to be strong for everyone else. After I cried and mourned, I finally got the strength to come out of my room.

"Mommy!" Lil' E screamed. That was the first

time he had called me mommy, I was ecstatic. What was I thinking, sitting in that room for a month? I put it in my mind that from that day on nothing would make me go there again. I had my kids and best friends depending on me to be strong. "Hey lady, how are you feeling today? It's nice to see you out of the room." Clara said with a smile. I had to give her a hug, cause even though Kyra was there and loved my kids, I know Clara was the one to really look after them. "Thanks, what was that for?" Clara said, caught off guard. I ran over to Kyra and gave her a hug too, cause she the one who told me to get my ass out the room. Then I called my three oldest and grabbed my baby. "Listen, I am so sorry for being out of it for so long. I just couldn't seem to find my way back. But something happened today that made me see it was time to let it go. I will always love Eric, but it's time I start my life again. Thanks you guys for putting up wit' me and taking care of the kids. I am in yall's debt. And Jewel, Sapphire, and you too Eric, mommy will always be here from now on. I will never leave you again. Okay." I said to everybody.

"Mommy not gone; mommy in da rum." Lil E said. I couldn't help but smile. "So Meme, you okay now? I was worried, but Clara and Kyra told me to let you alone." Jewel said looking unsure about my

T.E Cooper

mental stability. "Yeah me too." Sapphire said. "Sorry girls, I wasn't myself cause I was missin' Eric so much. But I promise you, I will always be here for yall from here on out. Can you please forgive me?" I asked my sisters, my daughters. "Yeah; we wasn't mad, just worried. We glad you feel better." Jewel said. "Well make me a promise. No matter how bad I'm feeling or acting; if I'm ever hold up in my room or a house or anything, you will come in anyway and tell me you love me. And in return, I will be the best big sister, mommy you could ever dream of." I asked of my sisters. They looked at each other and agreed in unison.

After that I got everybody together and we had a little cook-out of our own in the backyard of our house. We had a ball, and it reminded me of everything I almost gave up on. Sure, E was dead, but I wasn't, and I had to live if for nothing or nobody else, my kids. That became top of my list. First, was making sure these 4 would have the life I never had and the one E wanted to give. Second, finding out everything I could about the people responsible for taking my baby away from me. Even though I decided that it was time to come out of mourning, I still had to have my revenge. I would make them mutha-fucka's pay. That was my word.

Welcome to My Hood

15. The Plot.

After that day, life became a little easier. I had gotten a job with a really good lawyer's office doing paralegal work. Kyra had also gotten a job, and of course Clara was at home with Lil E and Diamond, while Jewel and Sapphire had gotten established in school. Life was good and everyone thought I was getting over E's death fine. Little did they know, I was using my connections from the firm. I had mad info 'bout the bastard's that were responsible for E's death. I just had to figure out what I was gonna do wit' it. I had a private detective to look into the boss. I told him, I wanted to know everything 'bout dude from what time he takes a shit, to when he lay his head down. I wanted it all, and the P.I. delivered. I stayed at work late that night, so I could go over all the information I had just acquired. I had to put a plan together.

When I got home that night the kids were already in bed and Clara and Kyra were in the den drinking daiquiris. "Good evening ladies. I see yall relaxin'. Got any more of those?" "Sure, come on over here and take a seat. You sure worked late tonight. That lawyer got some big case or something?" Kyra was saying while fixing me a daiquiri. "I was working, but it had nothing to do with work." I stated taking a sip of my drink. "Ladies, I have something to ask yall, and hear me out before either of you say anything. What if I told you I know who had E killed? And..." I said holding up my finger to tell Kyra not to interrupt. "Not only do I know who it was, but I know everything 'bout the dude. Everything. Would yall be down for a little revenge?" I finished looking at two very stunned faces. "First, who is it?" this coming from Clara. "Fuck who it is, I'm down no matter!" Kyra said, getting excited. It had been a long time since me and KY got down on some revenge shit, and she knew what was poppin'.

"Well Clara, do you know many people here in Charlotte?" I asked trying to see what the deal was. "Well, I know a few to get around if you know what I mean. And I know some pretty underground characters. Maybe the nigga is someone I know, maybe it's someone I can get help wit. But good as you and E been to me you don't have to worry 'bout if I'ma be down. That's a given." Clara said. "Good. Well, the nigga ain't no nigga first of all. He a Mexican." I said, and paused, so what I said could settle in. I watched both of

110

their faces, to see what type of reaction I would get. "Okay, what the fuck some Mexican got to do wit' E? And I don't give a fuck what he is. He gotta pay for that shit he did." Kyra was, saying pissed off. "Wait a minute KY, we gotta move careful on this shit. Them Mexican's don't play, and if he had the money to pay for E to get offed in the Fed, then this mutha-fucka' got doe. We gotta' be careful. Now, Meme, tell me everything you know, and I hope it's a lot. Like where he stays and what's his name?" Clara was saying, taking it all in. "Okay girls, let me fill you in." I said, giving them all the information that I had gotten from the P.I. After I filled them in, I let it all sink in, all we had to do and all that would get done. "Well ladies?" I questioned. "Shit, let's get this shit done!" they both said in unison.

T.E Cooper

16. Revenge.

After that day, we starting mapping out just how we was gonna get next to that nigga, well Mexican. And we all decided on one thing. Pussy! That gets 'em every time. I don't care what color or sometimes gender, pussy speaks volumes. And between myself, Kyra and Clara, there was a damn good chance we could get this shit done. Since I knew his daily routine, it wasn't hard to put ourselves in the right place at the right time.

We heard about this party, Carlos (our intended victim), was having at Club Amnesia, so we decided that we would be there. "Girl, we gotta get going, so we can get some stuff for this party. We are gonna be the finest bitches there, and Mr. Carlos Gonzalez, won't be able to resist." Said Clara; all excited. "That's what I'm talkin' 'bout. Meme are you sure we're his type of girls? 'Cause them Mexican's is funny 'bout they women." Said Kyra. "Girl, look at us. Do you think we ain't his type of women? Get real. We're every man's type. And we are gonna make that nigga, Mexican, wish

112

he never had a dick." I said, visualizing my plan. "Well girls like Jeezy say, 'Let's get, get, get it!'" Clara said with a smile. That was a moment of change. I had set my mind to getting some revenge, and what better way to get it, than being with my girls. I'm finna' show them what a ruthless bitch can do.

Ever since we decided that we would get that fuckin' Mexican, we can't find the mutha-fucka! We done been to every party and club in Charlotte, and this mutha' fucka' ghost. That was, until we got a little tip. "Yo, I heard them Esse's having a party at club Stir. What the deal?" Kyra said. "Man, I am so tired of going to clubs and parties I don't know what to do. Maybe this shit ain't meant to be." Clara said. "Shit, it's meant. And I don't give a fuck how many parties or clubs, that nigga' gone be found." I said. "Okay, cool. We're goin' to Stir this Saturday." Kyra said. Well that proved to be just what we needed.

We got to the club, and it was jumpin'. I didn't even know the Esse's partied like this! I mean, we was going to the wrong shit looking for this nigga'. We got in the club, and it wasn't what we thought, you know a bunch of Mexican's drinking Coronas with cowboy hats. Naw, these were NIGGA'S, just a little lighter. "Okay girls we splittin' up. Yall

113

know the drill. Let's scope this shit out, and find out some useful info." I said, giving orders. "That's what's up. I see something of interest right now. Check yall later!" Kyra said making her way over to one of the finest Mexican's I have ever seen. "Well, I'm out too. Have fun." Said Clara. They had left me with no problem, so I figured what the hell.

I started to walk around the club myself to see if I saw anything. And sure as shit stank; I found what I was looking for. There he was, sitting up in V.I.P, looking like a million bucks. Well, this might not be so hard after all; at least this mutha-fucka is fine. He had a small crew wit' him, so I felt like I could get on their set easy. Before I went over, I went to the bar and ordered an Incredible Hulk, swallowed it down and ordered another. I needed to at least be tipsy when I went over. After about 3 drinks straight to the head, I was ready to perform. I sauntered over and pretended to be looking for my girls. "Excuse me miss, but this is a private section. No outsiders." said a bulky looking Mexican guy. "Oh, sorry, I was just looking for my friends. You know, I got ditched." I said, with what I called my killer smile. "Hey, what we got here, Tony?" Carlos said, walking over. "Oh, just some girl that's lost. I was getting her to go, boss." said Tony, the bodyguard. "Oh sweetness, you in a hurry?" Carlos asked, while undressing me with his eyes. "I was

114

looking for my girls, but what you got in mind?" I said, as alluringly as possible. "Shit, come sit down, and we can talk 'bout it. What you drinkin'?" Carlos said, pulling me over to the table, that was occupied by 3 other Mexican guys and a couple of chicks.

"What did you say your name was?" Carlos asked while sitting me down in the booth. "Damn, you bringing strays around and don't even know they name?" this coming from a girl, who was obviously jealous. "First of all, I'm far from a stray, and secondly don't come this way mami, cause this ain't what you want. Now, we can get along while we here or not. The choice is yours." I said back, with much attitude and the feeling that there was more to this pretty face. "Yo', chill. If you don't like it, then beat it. I don't give a fuuuck. Right now the only thing on my mind, is getting to know this fine ass momaseta. Now what did you say your name was again?" Carlos said. The girl looked heartbroken, but, oh well bitch.

"My name is Jewel." I stated, lying my ass off. I didn't want this nigga to know who I really was, not just yet anyway. "Jewel, that fit's you. What are you, if you don't mind me askin'? 'Cause I can't tell." Carlos said, mesmerized by my eyes. "Well actually, my mom is half black and half Spanish.

115

And my dad was mixed with so much shit; we just called him a mutt." I said, with a smile. "Yo, you funny. Well, what 'cha doin' here? This a private party, invitation only, and I don't remember meetin' you, much less and invite." Carlos said. "Well, like I said, I'm here wit' my girls. One of them is friends wit' somebody you know. You know, Charlotte is a small place." I said quickly. "Fo sho'. Well mamasita, What's up?" Carlos asked. "What 'cha mean?" I asked innocently. "You know, what you doin', after the party?" He asked. "Why; you askin' me to leave wit' you?

I don't know you, and I ain't in the habit of leaving wit' folk I don't know." I said. "That's cool. We can just chill for now, but yo, I wanna get wit' you. Just letting you know. I always, get what I want." He said, with way to much confidence. If this mutha' fucka' only knew, what I had planned for his ass. Ha! He wouldn't wanna get wit' me, he'd probably have me killed.

I sat in the VIP with Carlos and his crew until everybody started letting out. "Yo; where yo' girls at?" Carlos asked. "They probably lookin' for me, so I guess it's time I go." I said, getting up. "Cool, I'ma walk wit' you, so we can talk." Me and Carlos got up, and started walking towards the exit. "So how I'm gonna get up wit' you? Where you live?"

116

he was saying. For a moment; I contemplated on telling him where I lived, but only for a moment. This mutha-fucka' was fine as hell, I gotta keep my head in the game. "Well, let's take it a little slower than that. How 'bout I give you my number, and I take yours and we do the call 'thang." I said, smiling and takin' out my phone at the same time."A'ight ma, that's cool. But, I'm telling you I want you, and I always get what I want." He said, with a chuckle. As we finished exchanging numbers, Kyra and Clara walked up.

"What's up girl?" Kyra asked, scoping Carlos. "Oh; hey yall. This is, Carlos. Carlos, this is Sapphire and Money." I said, introducing everyone, making sure I put emphasis on the fake names I just passed out. "Hey." Kyra and Clara said. "Well, I'ma let you go beautiful; I'll talk to you tomorrow." Carlos said, giving me a peck on the cheek. "Okay, talk to you tomorrow." I said, blushing. With that, he walked, no, sauntered off. I was to say the least, gone. "Girl, I know that look." Kyra said. "And don't you even think 'bout it. That's the nigga that ordered a hit on E, and we in this for revenge, revenge only. Ya hear me?" Kyra said, bringing me back to reality.

"Yo, I'll do Carlos if you want. That nigga is FINE!" Clara said, as we got to my car. "Yo, chill. Now don't get me wrong, that mutha-fucka is fine',

117

but we got a purpose, and yall both gotta keep ya' heads." Kyra said, seeming like the only one who wasn't mesmerized by Carlos. As we were getting in the car, guess who pulled up? Carlos. "Yo' ma'; you're ridin' flyer than me." He said, with a smile. "Well, a girls gotta' take care of herself, don't she?" I said back, flirtin'. "Fa' sho'. Listen, my boys wanna' holla' at 'cha girls; if that's okay?" He said, still cheesin'. As he was smiling and givin me all types of complements, his friends got out the jeep and walked over to Kyra and Clara. Now I knew we were 3 bad ass bitches, but these niggas, mexican's was clockin' us like we was some celeb's or something. After everybody exchanged number's we were on our way.

"Yo, what's up with the names?" Clara asked. "Well, I don't know if he knew who I was or not." I said. "Girl, that nigga don't know you. If he did, he damn sho' didn't seem like it." Clara said, and I could tell, she had had one to many. "Girl, shut yo' drunk ass up. That nigga got loot. Ain't nobody gonna tell him they real name. Shit, he been done found us out, and had us offed. Shhhit, Meme did right. Good lookin'." Kyra said, before I could even explain. We rode over to the IHOP, got something to eat and went to the house. I couldn't believe our plan was finally coming together. I thought about all we had to do, and revenge would be ours. I

118

decided, to talk to E. "E, I know you wouldn't approve of what I was doing, well at least not how I'm gonna do it, but it's the only way. I love you so much, and he gotta' pay for what he did. He gonna pay for what he did. He took you away from me, and the kids, and that shit was fucked up. I'ma be careful, and don't worry, this mutha-fucka' gon' pay for what he did to you, to us." And with that, I went to bed, dreaming of how my plan was coming full.

For the next few months, me and Carlos got to know each other. Well, at least I got to know him; he got to know Jewel, not Memorie. The two of us started getting kinda' comfortable with each other and it seemed he wanted me with him all the time. I didn't want him to know where I stayed or worked, so I went to the extreme. I rented a penthouse in Downtown Charlotte, and took a leave of absence from my job. I told them, there were some things I needed to tie up, and that I still needed some time to get over E's death. My boss was glad to be of assistance, and was very sorry for my loss. I told him he could e-mail or fax me any work that needed my direct attention and I would handle it. I told Carlos, I ran my own business and that I had no kids. God will forgive me for that fib, cause Carlos didn't need to know. I filled Carlos in on every detail about Jewel's life, from childhood

119

'til now. He was very impressed. He couldn't believe I had made something of myself after all I had been though. Poor Jewel. Ha! If he only knew. I did tell him some truths with all the lies, but I found it best to keep my real life totally separate.

I would stay at the penthouse during the week and visit my kids on weekends. During which visits, I tell even more lies to Carlos about where I go. One Saturday, we were sitting in the living room and Diamond came crawling in. I loved the sight of my daughter. She looked just like her daddy, only with my eyes. I couldn't help but notice how big she had gotten during my absences. I picked up my daughter and hugged her tightly. "Yall, this has got to come to an end. I can't take being away from the kids like this. I'm missing their lives. I'm supposed to be here for them no matter what, and I don't think this is good for them." I said.

"Look, Meme. We know this is hard, but girl it'll be over soon. Jesus was telling me some interesting stuff the other night." Carla said. "Like what?" "Well, you know how some nigga's is when they in tha' bed. He be drunk too, can't remember a thing the next day. Well anyway, he kinda' told me all about Carlos' operation." She said looking like the cat that ate the canary. "Spill it, Carla" Kyra said,

120

looking just as interested as me. "Well, I know when and where they get their shipments, how much is coming, what it's coming in and where it'll go once it gets here." She said matter-of-factly. "Well I'll be damned. You ain't no fuckin' nanny! You the shit! Girl; how you get all of that out that Mexican. You know they're tight lipped 'bout they business." Kyra said. "Well, I have my ways." Clara said with a wicked grin. Well with the information we had we could bring down Carlos' whole operation. Now let's see how ruthless a bitch can really be.

We started with the most devious plan of all, how to knock off Carlos and his business, at the same time. And I believe we had the perfect solution. All we had to do, was tip off the jack boys and 5-0. This was some shit we could do, 'cause like I said before, me and Kyra from the streets. So shit went down like this. Once we knew exactly where the dope was being delivered, we decided to change a few things. Since Kyra was fuckin' the nigga who was gonna deliver the dope to the spot, she was gonna' drop a little birdie in his ear about how the drop was changed. Now you would think after his being around Carlos for so long he would have gotten suspicious or called Carlos. Not him, he just took it as though she was telling the truth. So the dumb son-of-a-bitch did it. That was too fuckin' easy.

121

Now one thing I know 'bout these Mexicans, they don't pick up no dope after it was first dropped, they let it sit and wait to make sure the FEDS don't knock 'em. So after the drop, we had 2 weeks to get things moving. First, I went to the spot to see just what we were workin' wit'. And man, was I surprised. I thought it was 'bout two keys or something. Boy was I wrong. Man I wasn't gonna be able to get this shit out in no damn car! I was gonna have to get a van or something, cause this was way more than two keys. I called Kyra, and told her what was up, and she said she would get a van and be right over. Shit, I couldn't get all this shit by myself, I was gonna need some help. Once Kyra got there we parked the van in the back and started loadin'. Hell, after we got through I was scared to drive the van, cause of all the shit inside! But I did.

I gave Kyra the keys to the rental I had. (didn't want anybody to see my car). And I told her to meet me over to E's cousin; Big Hurk's house. Shit, I didn't need this dope, but I'm quite sure they could get past ON with this shit! I didn't even call the nigga's cause I knew it wasn't no need. Once Kyra got there, 'cause of course she didn't follow me, we knocked on the door. "You sure these nigga's here?" Kyra asked, just as Big Hurk opened

122

the door. "What's up Meme?" Big Hurk said, giving me a bear hug. "Damn, we ain't seent you in forever." He said letting us in. "Yeah, I know. Just tryin' to get by you know." I said, giving him a look that said everything. "This my sister, Kyra. Kyra, this Big Hurk." I said. "Hey where is everybody at?" I asked. "YO nigga; somebody is here to see us!" Big Hurk yelled towards the back of the house. His brother, Cas came out. "Oh; what up Meme?" He said, giving me a hug. "Who this?" he asked, admiring Kyra. "This my sis, Kyra." I said, smiling. Cas always thought he was a ladies man.

"Listen yall, I got some business fo' yall. So, let's sit down and talk." I said, seriously. I told them all about who put the hit on E, and how I found out. I told them everything. After I was through I asked, "So yall down?" "HELL YEAH!" they both shouted, at the same time. "Okay, now you know what got us here, let's set down some rules." I said. "Hol' up. How much coke we talking?" Big Hurk asked. "Shhhit, I don't even know. I ain't even count the shit; I just put it in the van. We can do that in a minute. I want yall to know that no matter how much you wanna touch that shit, don't. I mean, for real. Yall can't start slangin' that shit, until after I finish this wetback off. 'Cause if you do, I can't be responsible for what will happen to yall. This muthafucka' is big, and I gotta finish shit off,

123

before he discovers the shit is missing. Yall understand me? Cause it'll be dangerous for all of us. This shit is serious yall, this wetback is big yall." I said, and let all of what I said sink in. "Well yall?" I asked. Getting kind of worried; 'cause they was quiet for a minute.

"Okay, let me get this straight. The Mexican who had E killed; thinks you his girl, and yall ripped off his drop, and you plan on killin' him and getting his crew popped?" Cas said, seemingly in awe. "Yup, that's 'bout the 'jest of it." I said matter-of-factly. "Shhit, cool 'wit me! Let's get this shit in here and see what we working wit'." Big Hurk said, jumpin' up going in the backyard where we had the rental parked.

It took us about 45min to get all that shit in their crib. And to be honest, I didn't want to weigh it up. "Look, yall. Fuck them scales. I ain't weighing all this shit up. We gonna assume each package is a key, and go from there. Let's count how many packages we got." I said, and everyone agreed. We counted up 3 thousand packages. I was dumbfounded. I couldn't believe it. "Yo, I gotta' go get rid of this van, and I have to take somebody else some of this shit." I said getting up. "Cool, Hurk, you gotta find somewhere to keep this shit until we can touch it." Cas said, getting up.

124

I asked Kyra to help me put a thousand keys in the van, so I could take them to my cousin. I thought since these was E's cousin's, they deserved more and plus I knew my cousin Bam was straight without this shit. I just thought, hell, that's my cuz. After I was packed up, Kyra said, she was taking the rental back, and that was out of town, so she was probably gonna be gone for the rest of the night. We decided that I would take the van back the next day, 'cause it was even further out, and said our see you laters. I headed for B-Ford, and Kyra headed for South Carolina. On the way to my cousin's, I kept replayin' the day's events in my mind. Trying to make sure I hadn't missed anything, and thinking should I have given them niggas that dope.

I mean, I probably should have given it to them after I finished off Carlos, but oh well, what's done is done. As I rounded the curve going to my cousin's on Celia, I got the feeling like this was home. You know, that feeling that you get when you ain't been somewhere you love in a long time. I looked around and everything was the same, like it was frozen in time. All the duplexes were the same, the same people, just a little older and the same feeling of home, my territory. I started to think of my mother and almost came to tears. But I couldn't

125

afford to cry right now, I had business to do. Yeah, I missed my mom, but wasn't nothing I could do 'bout how she decided to live her life. I pulled up in my aunt's drive and hollered at Bam who was at the neighbor's; Miss Johnny Mae.

"What the deal?" Bam said running over to the van. "Man, I ain't seen you in forever. What is up cuz, damn I was beginning to think you had fell off the face of the earth. Ain't nobody seen you." He said rambling. "Hey, I missed you too. It's just, you know, life kinda gets away from us sometimes, and you lose track of time and the people who you loved. But, I'm here now and I brought a gift." I said. "Now see, that's what I'm talking 'bout. You bringing gifts? Let me see what you got?" Bam said, knowing the deal. Little did he know, this little gift was a lot bigger than anything else I had ever brought. "Well, I hope you can handle what I'm bringing." I said, going to the back of the van. When I opened the door my cousin said "Damn! You wasn't joking, was you? Shit, that's a big gift." "Well, I recently came into some money and I wanted to spread the love." I said with a grin. "I 'sholl 'preciate it too. I love when you come into shit, it just makes my day." He said, and called some young guns over to unload the van. "Now, don't go telling where you got that shit and if you can help it don't fuck with it for about 2 weeks. Ya

126

dig?" I said. Bam gave me a knowing look once again and said, "No problem. Shit, I got enough stuff, not to have to touch that shit for 'bout a month. Since you said that, you know I ain't touching it no time soon.

Cuz, you know I love you and if you ever need me for anything, you know I'm here." Bam said, giving me a hug while I got in the van. "Yeah I know, but for now I'm straight. But best believe, I will call if I need you and even if I don't need you, I love you cuz." I said giving him one last hug before driving off. I felt a little better about what I had planned, 'cause so far things were going as planned, but I still gotta' keep my mind on the prize. Carlos, Dead.

I pulled into my crib and parked the van in the garage; I didn't want anybody to see it. I would be taking it to Florida, when Kyra came back tomorrow. I was tired as hell, and all I wanted to do, was get some sleep. I had a long day tomorrow. The house was dark and quiet as usual, so I was as quiet as I could be. I went to the kids rooms one at a time, and took my time looking at them in their sleep. It won't be long now before I finished off the man that killed the man they all knew as daddy, all but Diamond. If I didn't kill him for no other reason, it will be because he took my daughter's

127

father before she could get to know him. And for that, he would pay. I didn't care about his family, I didn't care about his friends, all I cared about when it came to him, was taking his life. And, I would do just that. Men could be so predictable and just plain dumb. They think with their dicks and that is usually their downfalls. Carlos had a wife and children, but yet and still he wanted me. Well, he would pay for his infidelity with his life, so I hope the pussy was worth it.

I finally went to my room and tried to sleep but couldn't. Something was wrong, and I wasn't sure what it was. Today everything went off without a hitch, and no one had followed me, I'm sure. But, I just couldn't shake this feeling. I know sometimes things go wrong, so I called Kyra to be sure she was safe. Ring, ring, ring! No answer. Let me try again, cause she know she supposed to answer the phone, 'cause something could have happened. No answer again, now I was worried. Kyra always answered the phone for me, no matter what. If she was sleep, fuckin' or suckin', she was gonna answer my call. This ain't right. I got up strictly from instinct, and went to Clara's room. She was sleeping soundly, and I was sure sorry I was gonna wake her up, but we had to get out of there. Even if Kyra didn't tell whoever got her; anything, they could still show up here. It was time to bounce.

128

This was the main reason I never told Carlos anything about my family, or where I really stayed. "Clara, we gotta go." I said softly. Clara was a light sleeper, which was one of the things that made her the best nanny in the world. She could hear the kids under any circumstance. "Where's Kyra?" she said getting up and dressed. "She didn't call when she was supposed to, and she ain't answering her phone. So, you know what that means." I said. "Damn. You sure she ain't just sleep?" Clara said, as we went to the children's rooms. "I sure hope so. I hope she calls me in the morning like, where yall at? But, until then, we gotta go. Is the jeep packed like we planned?" I said, as I got Diamond out of her crib. "Yeah." Clara said, waking up Jewel, and helping her get dressed.

We got the rest of the kids up and dressed, and was 'outta that place like yesterday's news. I didn't want anything to happen to my kids or Clara. Who was turning out to be, the nanny of the year. I didn't even know where I was going; we never got that far with the plan. I had left my cell phone, cause I couldn't risk using it again. Damn. What the fuck was I gonna do? I had the kids and Clara, although I think she could have taken care of herself just fine. But damn, I got her into this mess, and I had to at least get her out. I couldn't think of

129

anything else to do so I jumped off the highway and stopped at a store to use the pay phone. I called my cousin Bam, and told him I needed him bad. He said no prob' and told me to meet him in Kannapolis. He didn't say exactly where on the phone, but I knew where he meant. So, me, Clara, and the kids headed to Kannapolis in hopes my cousin could help. Now don't think I was broke, 'cause that we were not. I made sure of that. But we needed to be underground, until I killed Carlos. And kill him I will.

We got to the K and made our way over to Bam's honeycomb hide-out. No one but three of us knew about the place. We never took anyone there. I never took or told E about it and Bam wouldn't be caught dead with one of those hoes he be fuckin' wit' up in here. So, I felt we was kinda safe. Even if I had thought about it sooner, I wouldn't have been able to get in, it had been so long since I was last there, I can't even remember where I put the keys or what the code to the security system was. Thank God for Bam. He met us there, and let us in before he started asking questions. "Damn, girl, you hang around the finest mutha-fuckas. But yo, are you sure she can be trusted up in here?" Bam was saying, referring to Clara. "Bam, I don't know what I would do without Clara right now. Trust, she's straight. I'm just worried 'bout Ky. She still ain't

130

called me. This shit is fucked!" I said, and walked over to the bar to fix myself a good drink.

"Well, the kids are fast asleep again. And not even a question about what was going on. Thank God. I guess I can tell them something in the morning." Clara said, walking in the room. "Clara, this is my cousin Bam, Bam this Clara." I said, introducing them. "Okay, cuz it's time to start talking. I knew, I should have asked some questions when you brought my little, "present"." Bam said, smiling. "Okay well, ask questions, and I'll answer 'cause I don't even know where to start." I said, taking a long swig' of my drink. As I said this, Clara walked over to the bar and fixed herself one too. We needed them, 'cause we both knew we were in for a long night.

17. And So It Begins.

After we filled Bam in on what was going on, all we could do was wait. We wasn't sure what we was waitin' on we just knew we had to wait. And, we were right. About a week into our stay, one of my neighbors called to tell me that something terrible had happened to my house. It had blown up. The neighbor said; they think it was a gas leak and hoped I had insurance. I knew it wasn't a gas leak, and the last thing I was worried about was insurance. It had started, and I knew the only way it would end, was if I put an end to it.

I had children to think about, and running forever, was not an option. I had to think, just how I was gonna finish up my plan, and get this mutha-fuckin', Carlos. If it was the last thing I did in life, I was gonna kill that son-of-a-bitch. He had taken so much from me, and I never did deal well with things being taken from me. He had to die, and I was gonna kill him. That much, was for sure. I just had to figure out a way to get his ass alone. And I knew just how to do it.

That muthafuckin' Carlos had taken so much from me and now, it was time I showed him just how it felt. I went through my phone, and made some real crucial phone calls. Like I said, being buddy buddy with a bunch of niggas, was gonna pay off real good. I knew these jack boys, Ant and Shak. They were good, plus they both owed me big favors, so it was real simple. I told them what the deal was, and what I wanted them to do. I gave them everything they needed to know about Carlos, and all his top associates. I told them where they hustled, and where they kept they stashes. I told them niggas everything about them Mexicans, and what all they had. The niggas was like, "Hell yeah, we'll do it." Just that simple. I wasn't worried 'bout them niggas getting hurt, 'cause they could hold they own. These niggas some professionals; for real. So with that covered, I waited again. I knew it was only a matter of time, before those two would get to work. They wasn't gonna rush it, they was gonna take their time and make sure they had they shit straight.

Since they only worked together with no one else, I wasn't worried bout nobody else finding out. Plus I knew they was gonna do it right, 'cause I told them I ain't want nothing from the takes. Those nigga's, was down for real. That's why I loved that

133

I knew nigga's like them, cause sometimes I ain't even have to raise a finger.

 I decided that for the time being there wasn't anything I could do, so I decided to take a long bubble bath to relax. I couldn't believe how my life had taken yet another drastic turn. Man, who woulda' thought. As I sat in the tub and relaxed, my cell phone rang. Who is that? I wondered. I tried to think of all the people who had my new number, and could only come up with a hand full of people. All of which, I would need to answer it. I sat up, and dried my hands and pulled my cell out of my pants. I looked at the number, and it was blocked. Okay, not good. What do I do? Should I answer it or just let it go to voicemail? I hadn't recorded any message on my voicemail, just so no one could be sure if this was the right number. Still ringing, I knew if I didn't pick it up by the tenth ring it would go to voicemail. Still debating I flipped it open and listened without making a sound. I wanted to see if I heard anything before I said something.

"HELP! MEME, HELP ME!" I heard Kyra screaming. Oh God! She's Alive! What the fuck is going on? "Kyra! Is that you? Where are you? Kyra are you there?!" I was screaming into the phone and jumping out of the tub at the same time. Clara

134

must have heard me cause she came busting into the bathroom. "Kyra? Is she on the phone? Is she okay?" Clara said, frantically. I listened into the phone, "Kyra? Kyra? Are you there? Where are you?" I was saying into the phone. And nothing; just a dial tone. "Clara, we gotta get the kids outta here like yesterday." I said, putting back on the same clothes. "Okay. What the fuck is going on Meme?" Clara said, as we rushed out of the bathroom towards the kids' room. "Girl, all I know is, that was Kyra on the phone, and she was screaming for me to help her. Now I don't know what kind of fuckin' games Carlos is playin', but he done fucked up now. First we gotta get the kids someplace safe that nobody knows about.

Kyra knew 'bout this place and whoever has her is probably on the way here so, we gotta bounce. Like now." I said, as I was putting on Diamonds coat. Jewel and Sapphire had already gotten up and had Lil E dressed, and ready to head out the door. "Thanks girls. I promise, when this is all over, I'm gonna treat yall to a vacation. How that sound?" I said, to my sister's, never having been more proud. They never once complained, or got on my or Clara's nerves. They would even keep Lil E company and play with trucks, and cars with him. I loved them dearly and once all this was done, I planned on showing them how much I appreciate

135

everything they were doing. "No sweat Meme. We trust you and we know you got some stuff going on, so we cool. And just so you know, we wanna go to Disney Land in California." She said with a smile. "You got it. That's my word. I'm going to take yall as soon as I handle things. Now this time when we get where we going, I ain't staying. How yall feel 'bout that?" I asked them, hoping for the best. "How long you gonna be gone?" Sapphire asked. "I'm not sure, and I wanna be honest with yall. I might be back tomorrow or I might be back next year. I don't wanna leave yall for no amount of time, but right now it's the only thing I can think to do to keep yall safe." I said seriously, as my Cadillac Escalade ate the highway up.

We were going up north, back to my old home, Philly. No one knew I still kept in contact with my folks up there. So I felt that would be a good place to hide my kids, until I could be with them safely. They were both quiet for a while before Jewel spoke. "You know, we don't want you to go. We don't want nothing to happen to you, but we also know that, no matter what, you coming back for us. So, if you gotta go, go, but hurry up and come back to us, and don't let nothing happen to you. You hear?" When my little sister said that, I was more than touched and proud. She was growing up so fast, and she understood so much. I loved my

136

sister's, my daughter and my son. They didn't have to worry, I would be back. "Okay I hear you. I'll stay safe. But yall gotta' promise me something too. No matter how long I'm gone, don't forget me, and don't let Diamond or Lil E call nobody else momma. Yall watch out for them, 'cause they gonna need yall. And no matter what happens, or what anybody say, always remember I WILL BE BACK." They nodded their heads and that was that. We were on our way to my old hood, so I felt if nothing else, my kids would get much love.

T.E Cooper

18. The Road to Redemption.

I felt a little better. As I drove north on 85, I glanced over at Clara, who was sleeping. I couldn't believe this girl was down for me, like woe. God did me justice, to send a friend like her my way. I was blessed. And thinking of good friends, my thoughts drifted back to the phone call, and the way Kyra sounded. Like.... she needed me and like she was scared shitless. That, just didn't happen. Kyra, was the strong one, and she let nothing or no on scare her. This was bad. As I looked in the back seat and glanced at my kids, I could only pray to God, I would return to them. I had so many thoughts going through my head, I didn't know if I would ever be really sane again. I drove that night, like I was on a mission. In all reality I was, I had to get my kids to safety then go back and handle my business.

It was daylight when we arrived and I couldn't help but smile. This was my old hood, and it still felt like home. I looked around to see if anything had changed, and not much had. The two high rises were still there, and the flats. The piece of shit playground, that didn't have a damn thing to play on and it still had the benches between the high rises. Home; yeah, I was finally home. No matter how long I stayed in North Carolina, Philly was still in my heart. I steered the jeep into the parking lot, and pulled in front of my mom's old friend, whom I affectionately called, Aunt Johnnie Mae. This was Sandra's mother. When I called I didn't really go into details about why I was coming, so I hoped I could tell her what was going on, without telling her what was going on. I tapped Clara on the shoulder to wake her, and let her know we were here. She yawned, and looked around and said, "This looks just like the projects I grew up in." "Really? Well, this is my second home. Come on; let's get the kids up and out of the car." I said. Together we woke each of the kids up, and got Diamond and Lil E out of their car seats.

"Were we at?" asked Sapphire." In Philadelphia. This is where I used to stay as a kid. Sapphire, you and Jewel were born here." I said. "For real?" they said in unison. "Yup; this was home before we moved to Charlotte. Now let's get in the house, there are some people that haven't seen you in a long time, and I need to introduce D and Lil E." I said, carrying Diamond towards the duplex in front

139

of us. As we walked in the door there was the familiar smell of fried chicken, corn on the cob and all the fixins', for a home cooked meal. My Aunt Johnnie Mae was like that, she somehow knew that we would need some real food when we got there. I looked around the kitchen, dining room and saw that some things never change. There were the puzzles my aunt used to do all the time. They were all over the house. There was the same table, still in the same place, by the window. Nothing had changed much in looks here; the only thing that seemed to have change; is me. I was nothing like the nerdy little girl who used to follow behind her daughter. Here stood a woman by all means and one who had seen a lot and done a lot.

I walked up to my aunt and gave her a hug. "Hey, auntie; long time no see." I said, with a smile. "Chile', let me look at you. You all grown up now, and so pretty, just like yo' momma. I'm so glad you came. Now, who are these little ones?" She said, her attention going to the children. "Well, you already know two of them. My sisters, Jewel and Sapphire." I said, motioning towards my sister's. "Oh my God; I don't believe it! The last time I saw yall, you was in diapers. Look at yall. I can't believe it. How old are yall now?" she said, totally entranced with my sister's. "They're 10 and 11. Jewel is the oldest." I said, as if I was really their

140

mother. "Well, that's 'bout right I guess. Now, who are these two over here? Are they your's?" she asked, Clara. "No auntie. This is Clara, a very good friend of mine, and those two angels belong to me. I'm a mom. The baby girl is my Diamond, and the little man, is Lil Eric." I said. "Well, I never would have thought of you being a mom. Ain't that something!" Aunt Johnnie Mae was saying. "Well, I know yall hungry, so go ahead and get comfortable, so yall can eat." She said. "Meme, this is home to you, so you know where everything is, ain't nothing changed. Yall can stay in Sandra's room, she away in Africa doing missionary work for the church. I'm going to play the lotto; I'll be back in a little while. When I come home, we can talk. Nice meeting you Clara. See yall in a little bit." Aunt Johnnie Mae said, walking out the door.

I looked around for a minute before going upstairs. My aunt had a 4 bedroom flat in the projects. It was upstairs, and it had a living room that no one really went into. I made my way up the stairs, and when I came to the top I turned left. Sandra's room was the first one on the left then clockwise it went; the oldest brother, the two youngest boys and then my aunt's room, right at the top of the stairs. I opened the door and looked around. This used to be my sanctuary, when I was a little girl. I remember how Sandra used to play in

141

my hair and scratch my scalp. Sometimes, I wonder, if I would have lived with them would my life be any different. Not wanting to reminisce anymore, I called for Clara to bring the kids up. Once we got everybody out of their coats, and washed their hands and faces I took everybody downstairs, so I could feed them. Once I had the kids settled, and my and Clara's plate fixed I decided to talk to the kids. "Well what yall think?" I asked. "It's cool here. I like the puzzles all over the place." Sapphire said, with excitement in her voice. "Yeah, she seems really nice. So, how long do you think you gonna be gone?" Jewel asked trying not to sound concerned. "Oh baby, I wish I didn't have to go at all. It's just that, right now, this is the safest place for yall. I trust auntie and my play cousin's beyond all other, so I know they gonna take care of yall. I promise to call every day, and I'm gonna get a line just for yall to call anytime you want; morning, noon or night. I hope what I have to do, doesn't take a long time. But even if it all happened in a day, I still couldn't come back to yall to soon. I don't want anybody knowing where yall at, or if you even exist. I love yall too much to lose yall. I'm through losing so, I gotta fight. I gotta fight for us to have a life. The life that yall deserve. So don't worry, only death can keep me from yall. You hear me?" I said, letting her know without saying anything else that I was coming back.

142

"Well, I think I could like it here, as long as we don't have to stay forever. It seems like a good spot to chill 'til you get back." Jewel said, trying to sound like a big girl. "Yup." Said Lil E. That was his favorite thing to say. It was a stage. "Is that right lil' man?" I said, pinching his cheeks. I loved him to death. "Yup." He said, and smiled at me. "Well Clara; what you think?" I said to Clara, who had been quiet for some time now. I was getting worried. "Well, it seems like the perfect place to hide the kids, it's just that; ain't it kind of rough?" she said, concern for the children showing on her face. "Well, didn't you say you grew up in place like this? Besides, everywhere is dangerous now a days but I really think this is the best place for them right now. No one knows anything about my family up here, 'cause I ain't never told them nigga's anything 'bout this spot and they gonna love the kids like we would. They gonna be straight." I said, suddenly trying to convince myself as well as Clara.

"Well, I just wish I could stay with them. That way I know they're straight. I hate all this, and I'm ready for it to be over with." She said, close to tears. "Listen, you can't cry, 'cause then I'ma cry and that ain't what we need right now. We know what we gotta do, and we know the kids need to be safe

143

T.E Cooper

while we do; so this is how it goes. We gotta both be strong for the kids, cause we don't want them to worry." I said patting Clara on the shoulder. "Girl, you right. I know they gonna be safe here. You got mad love when we pulled in. I'm just ready for this to be over. We got so much to do." She said. I started thinking about what Clara said and was almost lost. What the fuck were we doing? Going up against one of the biggest drug dealer's in Charlotte. Could we do it? Could we pull it off? I wondered. So far, we've been able to get his ass where it hurts. But that wasn't enough. He killed the love of my life, the only man that would ever hold my heart. He would have to pay. That much was so. The only question was; could I really do it? Could I be ruthless enough to cut his throat? Hell yeah! And when I do it, it will be with a smile. So far he had taken so much from me. I got my kids hiding out, Kyra was still missing and my house was gone. Yeah this mutha-fucka was gonna pay, if it was the last thing I did.

The next morning it was time for me and Clara to leave, and it was the hardest thing we ever had to do. I knew I was gonna dread it, but I had no idea it was gonna be this bad. I couldn't believe Lil E was screaming and saying, "Mommy, come back!" and even though my sister's didn't chase me, I saw the look in their eyes, and it was too much. Even

144

though we talked about it, it was still the hardest thing to do. The only thing on my mind when I hit the highway going back to Charlotte, were my kids. All I wanted to do was dead this Mexican spick, and get back to my kids. I damn sure hope this don't fuck them up. I gotta get my mind right, so I can get back to the matter at hand. How to get his whole crew popped, and how to kill his ass. That was the ultimate goal, to kill his ass. After all, he was the one who ordered the hit on E. This nigga was gonna feel me; Fo' sho'.

During the ride; me and Clara talked about everything but what we were going to do. I guess we thought if we didn't talk about it then we wasn't 'bout to do it. Well once we got to Virginia, I said we needed to talk. We needed to make sure our plan was full proof, and that we would be the only ones to walk outta that mutha-fucka'. First, Clara made a call to her cousin, who was a sheriff in Charlotte. She gave her a tip, and told her we would tell her more once we arrived. With that in place, we made a few very important phone calls. The first, to the Mexican that Clara had been fuckin' with. We knew he was pussy whipped, but we also knew he would tip Carlos on us coming back to town; which was what we wanted.

See, word on the street was; Carlos had bounced

145

after all that shit went down. He was trying to distance himself from the bullshit. Well, you can't hide from a good hit. I knew he wouldn't be able to stop himself. See, even though he had a price on my head, he couldn't resist the temptation of coming to town to do it himself, or watch some other mutha-fucka' do it. As long as I was at his feet begging for forgiveness. But that shit wasn't happening. I don't know who he thinks he's dealin wit', but cuz' got me fucked up. Ain't no fuckin' beggin' fo' no fuckin' forgiveness unless it's him, begging me. That shit's fo' sho'. He fucked my life up, and now it was time for him to pay with his life; period, point, blank.

19. Getting Shit Done.

Now word on the streets of Charlotte; was that if I ever returned, that somebody was for sure to take me out. Like kill me. Ain't this a bitch? These the streets I grew up on, and now they turn they back. But that's okay, 'cause I'm not the bitch to complain, 'cause I know how the game goes. One minute they love you, the next, you're yesterday's news. That's how it was, that's how it is and always gonna be. Ain't no sweat off my back. I would just show them who they fuckin' wit'. These muthafucka's must not know, I'm a Dondatta in these streets. Watch me work.

My first stop was my old hood. I knew no matter what was going on, Bam had my back. And of course, I was right. "Yo' cuz, where you been? I went to the spot and yall was gone. What gives?" Bam said coming out of my great-aunt's apartment. "Shit. Shit was getting thick and I didn't want you all up in my shit. You know I can handle me. You know I just didn't wanna leave no trail that leads to you. You my cousin, and I love you and I don't

147

want anything to happen to you." I said giving him a hug. "Well you ain't gotta worry 'bout that. No matter who these niggas is, they know who I am, and they ain't stupid." He said, laughing like he just told a joke. Truth be told, he had a helluva' reputation, and not many nigga's or Mexicans would cross his path. I just didn't want him involved; that is until now. I knew he had access to everything I needed, guns, soldiers, and then some. My cousin had it all and I knew all I had to do was ask.

I told my cousin that we needed to go into the house to talk. He made a joke 'bout me not staying out in the open too long. I knew I was safe with Bam. Ain't nobody gonna act stupid on his turf. Once inside my aunts' house I began to tell Bam what I was planning to do. I told him I had a connect in the Police Department and they were waiting on the warrants from the judge to be signed as we spoke and I told him about the Mexican that was coo-koo for Clara and how we could probably get him to unknowingly, bring us Carlos. I asked him what he thought and what he thought I needed. He kept it real, "I can't help with no snitchin' shit cuz. Now, I'm all for you fucking him up but snitching; can't do it. Tell me about the part that don't involve the boys and we on." "Cool cuz; I feel you. But yo; I got's to get this nigga like

148

by any means necessary; no matter what. I don't care how I get him, I just gotta get him. Now you ain't gotta be involved with that other shit, just handle a few loose ends. That's all I ask. I got the rest and you know me, won't nobody know you was involved. Just me, and you know I got you." I told Bam. He was much more willing to work with me once he found out he didn't have to deal with the police. We talked about what needed to be done and when things would jump off.

Once the police started hitting spots; I was sure Carlos was gonna be looking for a safe spot to crash. That's where Clara's Mexican came in. Although he didn't know it, he was gonna bring Carlos right to me, where I was gonna kill him. If things went as planned we would find Kyra and take this nigga down. I desperately wanted to find Kyra. She was after all, my Best friend. And I couldn't lose her. I didn't care if it was just her body, I still wanted her home. And that's what I planned to do. Around 3 o'clock the police started hittin' Carlos' spot's. It was beautiful. They did it all at once and those mutha-fucka's didn't know what hit them. The police caught them doing all types of shit too. And just as I suspected, they found Kyra in one of the dope houses. They had her chained to a bed naked. The police said, it looked like they were using her as their personal sex slave. I was broken. I

149

couldn't believe they had done that to Kyra. But that was okay; 'cause I was gonna make Carlos pay, if it was the last thing I did. Clara called to tell me that everything went as planned and Carlos would be arriving at the destination in about 1 hour. Perfect; I was ready for the bastard. This mutha-fucka' had taken my life and turned it upside down then flipped it in ways that nobody should have to experience! He took my husband and almost took my best friend, ain't no telling what type of counseling Ky gonna need after this shit and ain't no telling when things will be okay for me to go to my children. Oh yeah, this mutha-fucka' gonna pay. That's my word.

I waited on Carlos at Clara's Mexican's house, thinking about everything that was happening and couldn't believe that this was my life. Life's a bitch and then you die; you just gotta roll with the punches and keep it rollin'. "Yo; where you at Tony!" Carlos yelled, out of the blue. He was early. He must have driven like a bat outta' hell. "Yo Tony, we gotta get the fuck outta here. Shit's crazy! The fuckin' police done raided everything! Ay, where you at Tony?" Carlos said, looking around the condo. I was sitting in the den when he came in. "What the fuck! Bitch, I'ma kill yo' ass!" Carlos said, charging at me. "Please, I suggest you sit the fuck down, before I kill YO' ass!" I said, holding a

150

Desert Eagle at his chest. "Oh and I know you ain't got no gun, so don't front, and sit yo ass down. There's a lot we gotta' discuss." I said, sitting back down on the couch. "What the fuck; we gotta talk 'bout bitch?! When this is over, my people gon' kill yo ass! I suggest you put that fuckin' gun down, and let me kill you. At least that's all I'm gonna do; now if my people get hold to yo pretty ass, they gonna treat you worse than that bitch friend of yours. Ha, ha." This punk mutha'-fucka' think I'm playin', don't he? POW! I shot his ass in the leg. "Now, like I was saying, we got a lot to talk about, so I suggest you shut the fuck up and listen." I said, standing up and walking around.

"Bitch! You just shot me! Is you fuckin' crazy? Where the fuck is Tony? What you do to him? He was supposed to be here. What the fuck?" Carlos kept yelling. "SHUT THE FUCK UP!" I shouted. "Goddamn, you run yo' mouth like a fuckin' bitch! Now, who the bitch Carlos? Huh? That looks like a nasty wound you got there. Do you think you gonna bleed to death? Huh? Well before you do, let me tell you who the fuck you fuckin' wit'. Now, I was gonna be easy on yo ass, and kill you peaceably, but fuck that! You gonna suffa'. Do you know what those nasty muthafuckas did to my girl? My best friend? Well, let's just say it's gonna take some time for her to recover. But..." POW! I

151

shot his ass again, this time in the other leg. "What do you want? Please, don't kill me! I didn't do anything to you. Why are you doing this?" Carlos asked, begging for his life. I thought it was time I enlightened him on a few things. First I started off by telling him my real name then I proceeded to tell him who my husband was. I told him that he had my husband killed for nothing, 'cause he wasn't no snitch. I told him, that he took the whole blame in court and didn't deny a thing. While they couldn't even help with his defense, he still stayed loyal to him. I told him, what he had taken from me, starting with that day. I told him it was time he pays for what he did to me and my family. Then I emptied my gun in his body.

I stood there for quite some time after I had killed him. I wasn't worried 'bout no police, 'cause these Mexican's some noisy mutha-fuckas, so they always sound proof their cribs. Maybe that was their mistake, but my good fortune. Clara had taken care of Tony days ago, and they still didn't know he was missing. So far, it looked like things where looking our way. After about an hour, I got myself together. While I was in the condo, I made sure that I kept gloves on, and I also wore my hair pinned up and in a hat. I didn't want any hair fibers turning up at any time. I walked over to the front door and if Carlos had been paying attention

152

when he came in, he would have noticed the 3 gas cans sitting in the foyer. I proceeded to pour gasoline all over the condo. After the last can was empty, I went into a back room and dropped a book full of lit matches, and walked out the door.

T.E Cooper

PART II. (A DIFFERENT LIFE)

Damn! I'm late again, picking up the kids. This has got to stop. I mean, I know I'm the only reliable person at the office, and this is a big deal we are trying to close, but enough is enough. I mean ever since I've been working at Time Warner Cable as their Senior Manager of Customer Service, life has been hectic. But I love it. I can't lie. This life is so far from the life I used to live; that I can't help but love my life and be proud of myself.

Me and my family live out in Ballentyne again and things are really looking up for us. As I said, I landed a hell of a job with Time Warner Cable; well it was more luck than anything. One day, I was at Starbucks downtown, looking through the want ads in the Charlotte Observer and this gentleman walked up to my table. He asked if I was really looking for a job and I told him I was. He gave me his card and told me to come and see him the next day, which was a Wednesday. I was surprised to say the least and I didn't even ask him why he came over, 'cause that much was obvious. He

Welcome to My Hood

couldn't keep his eyes off of me. Well whatever, 'cause if he try something while I'm at work then you know what I'ma do, Lawsuit! Ha, ha, ha. Well anyway, he turned out to be the V.P. of Human Resources at Time Warner Cable. I was thinking it was a scam at first, 'cause I knew the only reason he approached me, was 'cause of my looks. But dude was for real, and he hooked me up. Now I'ma be honest; he did try to holla once upon a time and no I didn't sue; I just put him in his place real nice and so far, haven't had a problem since. Well that was the beginning of my now 5 year relationship with Time Warner Cable.

I have been here for 5 years and still can't believe it. I have come so far. Not to mention my girls and me are still tight. We didn't live together anymore but we were still the 3 musketeers. Kyra was now living in a place called, Seigle Point. It used to be Piedmont Courts, one of the worse hoods in Charlotte. They decided to tear it down due to all the dope and teenage pregnancy among other things. So like everything else close to downtown, they put up condos. Kyra was working at University Medical Associates, as a Medical Transcriptionist. She was still going to therapy for all that had happened but she was coming along good. It had been five years and of course she still had her demons. I asked her once; how they had

155

T.E Cooper

caught her when we had planned everything to a T? She said; she didn't want to talk about it, so I left it alone. I'm sure there are things that happened to her that she will never talk about. I always felt responsible for what happened to Kyra, that's why I bought and paid for her condo. She objected at first; 'cause she was afraid to live alone but her therapist said it would be good for her. So, that's what I did. It took her a while to actually start staying there but now she's feeling better. I'm glad; she deserves to be happy. Oh and Clara ain't doing too bad herself. Miss thang is now a Clerk of Superior Court. She said she always wanted to work in the court system, without being responsible for putting people in jail. She was now staying in a beautiful house in the University area. She said she wanted a big house cause she wanted the kids to come over as much as possible. Of course, I didn't mind. I purchased her house for her as well, it was the least I could do, don't you think? Yeah, it was.

In the five years since that night, we have all changed and grown into productive citizens and never looked back. My kids were all getting big, Jewel was now 16 and Sapphire was 15. They were both growing into beautiful young women and I couldn't be more proud. Jewel was a basketball star with model looks and she was sure to get a

156

scholarship to someone's college (even though she doesn't need one. She said she wanted one so I wouldn't have to pay for college. She thinks I do too much. But I don't, I do what I have to because I love them.) cause they been looking at her since she was in the 9th grade. Next year will be her last year in high school and I can't believe it. She's always gotten good grades, and as far as I know (and we're pretty close) she's only had one boyfriend, whom she promptly dumped when he started asking for sex. Well, at least that's what she told me. Anyway, she's beautiful and I'm really proud of her. Now Sapphire, won't be outdone in anything, she's very competitive. She's in the 10th grade and she's into everything. I mean everything. She play's volleyball, basketball and runs track. She's a sprinter. The girl is fast; so fast as a matter-of-fact, she was chosen to run in the Junior Olympics next spring. I couldn't be more proud. She and Jewel both, have always maintained straight A's. Sometimes I'm just amazed at how well they turned out.

As far as Diamond, she is now 7 years old and a mess if I ever seen one. She inherited my grey eyes and she has the most gorgeous mound of hair on her head. She might not have had a lot when she was a baby but she sure was making up for it. She was in 2nd grade and as far as I can tell she loves

157

T.E Cooper

school. She's not into sports like my sister's; she's more of a girlie' girl. She loves dress up and stuff like that. She says she wants to be a model. I can dig it. As far as Lil E goes, he's now 9 and looking more and more like his daddy every day. Sometimes I can't believe how much that boy looks like his daddy, it's just amazing. He loves football of course, what nine year old boy doesn't. He play's for the PAL League over off of Oaklawn. He's the quarterback. That boy can throw too. He wants to play pro, we'll see. After college, I said. My life was coming together pretty nice and I really didn't have any complaints.

After all the shit that went down a few years ago, I stopped working for the lawyer I used to work for. Too many bad memories; it was time to keep it moving.

When I reached the kids school, I was in a pretty good mood. "Hey yall; how was your day?" I asked. "Oh mommy, guess what! I'm running for class president." said Diamond. "Oh really; well that sounds nice. How did that happen?" I asked, with a smile. Diamond was always a people person and I knew one day she would do something great. "Well Timmy; you know him the boy I don't like but he likes me, well anyway he said that I should run." Diamond, was saying. "You like him, you just

158

don't want mommy to know." Lil E said, picking with his sister. "Shut up big head, you don't know nothing! Well anyway, mommy the teacher said, we get to put up posters and stuff, so I wanted to know, would you help me." Diamond said. "Of course sweetie; we're gonna make the best posters ever." I said. "Mommy' where we going?" Lil E asked. He noticed that we weren't headed towards our house. "Oh, I thought we would go and see Auntie Kyra. I haven't talked to her in a couple of days and I wanted to check on her." I told the kids as we got off on Davidson. "Yeah, I haven't seen Auntie Ky in a long time and I bet she got something for me." Diamond said, happily. "Yeah me too, she said she was gonna get me that new Vice City game." Lil E piped in. "Now yall; you know I don't want yall askin' Auntie Kyra for a whole lot of stuff. Yall got enough stuff as it is. And I don't know about that Vice City game, it's kind of violent. You know how I feel about those games anyway." I said to the kids pulling into the parking lot of Kyra's condo complex.

After I found a parking space, we got out then headed to Kyra's condo. It was on the top floor, the Penthouse. Of course I had to put my main girl somewhere special. I loved this place and if I didn't have the kids, I would have had a place here myself. It was in the perfect spot too, right

159

T.E Cooper

downtown. Plus, I loved the color scheme, it was beige and brown and a little red; those where my color's. As we entered the main hallway and walked to the elevators, I looked around the lobby. It was just beautiful. I wonder how they keep those flowers in bloom all year 'round. I would have to talk to the supper, 'cause these arrangements where bangin'. The elevator arrived after a short wait and we were on our way. This elevator led directly into Kyra's penthouse. When the doors opened, they opened up to a foyer that led to the main door. We got off the elevator and proceeded to the front door or the main door to the living room.

We knocked and knocked and Kyra didn't come to the door. So me being me; used the spare key I kept on my key ring. I opened the door then me and the kids went in. I told the kids to go to the kitchen to fix themselves a snack and proceeded to the backroom where I assumed Kyra was. I walked to the bedroom and knocked on the door. Even though she knew we were coming, I didn't want to walk in on anything. "Come in Meme." I heard Kyra say. I walked in the room and almost fainted. There was Kyra, sitting on her bed, with a gun to her head.

"Kyra what are you doing?" I asked, trying to mask the panic in my voice. "I can't do it no more Meme.

160

The lies, the pain, the memories! I can't do it anymore. I love you, you know that and I would never hurt you on purpose. I just got caught up and didn't know what else to do but now I can't take it. You so good to me and I ain't been nothing but a piece of shit to you." Kyra was saying, crying. "Listen Kyra whatever it is; we can get through it. Please don't do this. The kids are with me. Please Kyra don't do this. Imagine how it will affect the kids." I said, staying where I was, by the door. I didn't want to make any sudden moves to scare her and possibly make the gun go off. "Listen Meme, you don't know that. Once you find out, you might take this gun and shoot me yourself. I deserve it, and soon you gonna think the same." Kyra said.

She turned around on the bed and faced me. She sat the gun on her lap. Good; okay, I can do this. This is my best friend and I wasn't gonna lose her, no matter what she was talking about. I wasn't gonna lose her, not like this. "Ky listen; you know I love you; you're my sister. What I'ma do without you? Me and you have something no one else has; true friendship. And I know, that we're both strong enough to handle anything. You always had my back and trust, I got yours." I said pleading with her to put the gun up. "Okay, well since we're like that then here it is. Lil E is my son." She said, and looked at me deeply. "What are you talking about?

161

Lil E's momma is that bitch Lala; we both know that!

Listen Ky; let's put the gun up and talk. You wanna call your therapist? That might help, 'cause this ain't the way." I said, moving a little closer, so I might be able to snatch the gun. "No, you got it all wrong. See, when we first met I was pregnant. Remember? What did you think happened to the baby?" Kyra asked. "What you talking 'bout Ky, you got an abortion. Remember?" I said getting really worried. Kyra was really losing it. I wonder what happened when Carlos' boys got hold to her. I was thinking my girl might need to spend some time in Behavioral Health.

"No I didn't. I just told you that. I was too far along to get one, so I had to keep the baby. Do you remember when we went to my cousin's birthday party; out at Celebration Station? And it was the first time I had seen my mom? You remember how I was so broke up after not seeing her for about six months. Well, if you will recall I left with my mom and was gone for about 3 months. I had the baby and gave him to my cousin Lalandra aka Lala." She said. I stood there and thought about all that she had said. I tried to replay the events she was talking about in my head. "But that would mean; you knew Eric before me?" I asked, feebly.

162

"Look, this is how it went down. First of all, you ain't the only one that noticed that E was a keeper. Yeah, me and him had met before you and him started kickin' it. And the baby was planned on my part. Then he met you and all of a sudden he ain't wan't no baby. So me being me, had to find out who you were. I already knew Miracle, her moms and mine went to college together, so it wasn't hard to wiggle my way in. Then I met you and you was cool, you know. I was like, dang she a'ight. And I didn't know what to do. Hell, by then I was already too far along to get rid of the baby and I damn sure wasn't about to take care of no kid by myself. So, my mom's hooked it up with Lala to keep him. It was supposed to be temporary but like I said; I ain't wanna be no mom. Then you and Eric got all close and shit and the next thing I know, yall married. Now, why would I go and get a baby and the nigga done up and married you. Shit, I told him to tell you but he said I betta not say a word. So I kept my mouth shut. Shit, he was still taking care of Lil E and me at the same time. So why blow up my spot. Then Lala pulled that bullshit and yo' I swear, I didn't know he was fucking her too. That nigga was a dog. But you never did see; so who was I to kill your flow?" She said, matter-of-factly.

Before I knew it I had snatched the gun, threw it

163

on the floor and commenced to whuppin' up on Kyra's ass. I couldn't believe what she had just told me and had me feeling sorry and shit for her stank ass! This bitch gonna get it! I snuck her in her mouth and before I knew it; it was on. She grabbed a handful of my hair and punched me in the face. I swung around and punched her in the stomach, which made her double over. That was all I needed. I grabbed her head and put it in a headlock quick. She didn't know what happened. Before I knew it, we had torn up her bedroom and she was bleeding like hell. "Mommy! What's going on? Why are you and Auntie Ky fighting?" Diamond said, crying. I looked up and saw my children standing there, looking scared as hell. I was standing there with Ky in a headlock that looked like I was breaking her neck. I could have. "It's time for us to go kids." I said, letting Kyra go. "Mommy, what's going on?" Lil E asked. "Baby, here take mommy's key's and go take your sister and get in the car. Mommy will be down in a minute." I said, handing Lil E my keys. He did as he was told and drug his sister off and out the door. I made sure they were both gone before I finally turned back to Kyra.

"I don't know what would make you do something like this. I was your friend. All you had to do was tell me. I probably wouldn't have even fucked with the nigga if I hadda' known. But no,

164

the two of yall wanted to play with my life. Well one thing's for damn sure. YOU AIN'T LIL E'S MOTHER! I AM! You heard what he called me; MOMMY, so don't get any bright ideas about taking my son from me 'cause, I will kill you. And you know what, I'm taking this fuckin' gun too, cause you won't say, I was the reason you killed yourself. And for the record, there are lots of ways to do it without using a gun. If you were serious, you'd think about it. And Kyra, don't ever call me again. I don't give a fuck what happens; don't call me." I said walking out on my friendship.

I couldn't believe how stupid I was. How the fuck could he? I should have known. If the nigga had money, then no doubt Kyra fucked him. I just couldn't believe they had done me dirty like that. And all the while, acting like they ain't knew each other and shit. I hated that bitch! I reached my car and jumped in and took off like a bat out of hell. I couldn't believe it, I just couldn't believe it. When I stopped at a light, I looked back at my son and took a good long look at him. And sure as shit stank, he had that bitches features. I guess I had never noticed it before, 'cause he still looked just like his daddy, except now I noticed he had her nose, and her mouth. He also had her eyes. I couldn't believe it. I should have known, I should have known. As I drove through downtown Charlotte; me and the

165

kids passed McCormick's and Schmitt's, the seafood restaurant. "Mommy, can we get something to eat?" Lil E asked. He loved seafood. Just like Kyra, I never noticed. "Sure baby. Just let mommy go to this CVS to get some stuff to clean up a little bit." I said, pulling to the curb in front of the drug store.

I was sure I looked a mess, after fighting with Kyra. I told the kids I would be right back and ran in. I quickly went to the makeup isle and picked up a few things. I paid for them and went into the bathroom. I was glad that I had let my hair grow back out. If for no other reason, but it looked a damn fool. I brushed it back into a ponytail and washed my face. I had gotten a washcloth, and some dove soap. After I dried my face off, I applied some light makeup and gloss on my lips. I looked at myself in the mirror and decided that I looked decent enough to go to dinner with my kids. As I left the store I only had one thing on my mind, the betrayal of the two people I loved and trusted most in the world. How they had played me for a fool. I walked over to the car and told the kids to get out; we would walk down the street to the restaurant. It was only a block away and it was a nice evening out. Summer was approaching fast, that you could tell by the warm weather we were experiencing. We got to the restaurant and I asked the hostess if

166

we could have an outside table, being it was so warm. She told me that it would be an hour wait for whatever table we wanted. It was a popular spot. I conversed with the kids and decided that we would put our names down and be back in an hour. That would ensure we had a table when we returned, and that way I could pick up Sapphire and Jewel from practice.

Me and the kids proceeded to the car and drove through downtown, to the highway. It had changed so much since when I was a kid. It was looking more and more like a big city. I chuckled to myself. "Mommy, are you gonna tell us why you and Auntie Ky were fighting? Was it over me?" Lil E asked. I looked at him, wondering how much he had heard, before I realized they were there. "Why you ask that Eric?" I asked, fishing for answers. "Well, I thought I heard my name is all." He said, being flippant. That in itself told me, he had heard more than what I would have wanted. "Well Eric. I guess you heard what we were talking about, huh?" I said. I was scared as hell. What do I tell my son? I just have to let him know I'm here. "Don't be scared. You're not going to get into trouble." I said, sensing his hesitation. "Well; I think I heard the whole thing. See Di wanted some of Auntie Ky's grapes, and you know how she loves her grapes. So, before I let her get any I told her I had to ask, so

167

T.E Cooper

I came back to ask about the grapes." He said, then paused looking at me to see if he should go on. "He ain't lying mommy. I did want some grapes and he wouldn't let me touch 'em. Said he had to ask. Tell him, we don't have to ask at Auntie Ky's house, mommy." She said, obviously still miffed about the grapes. "Mommy will buy you some grapes at the restaurant. Now, go on Eric."

"Well I don't know if I should, 'cause I'm not sure I understand." Lil E said. "Go ahead baby; I'll try my best to help. Okay?" I said, encouraging him to get it off his mind. "Well I think I heard Auntie Ky say that... I'm her son. Is that true, mommy? Is Auntie Ky my, real mom?" Eric said to me with tears in his eyes. I didn't know what to say. Should I tell him the truth or should I let him think he misheard? I was really at a loss for words. We were approaching the school so I told Eric that we would finish after we picked up his sisters. I was trying to think of what I was going to tell my son. Because he was my son, by all rights and purposes. I didn't want to say anything that would damage him, or the security that he felt in a loving home. "Well, Eric I really don't know what to tell you. I don't want you to be hurt." I said, looking at my son. "Mom, just tell the truth. That's what you tell us to do; the truth, mom. I wanna' know." He said. Just then Jewel and Sapphire walked to the car. "What's

168

up everybody?" they said. "Mommy and Auntie Ky had a fight, and Auntie Ky said that E is her son." Diamond spit out. "Huh? What's she talking about Meme?" Sapphire asked. "Okay everyone, we will talk more at the restaurant. You okay with that Eric?" "Yes ma'am." Eric said, looking solemn.

We arrived at the restaurant, and were seated. I guess it's time to talk to my baby, and get it all out in the open.   "Well, Eric you heard correctly. Your Auntie Ky did say that she was your mom." I said, and paused looking at Eric to see what type of reaction I would get. He looked at me solemnly and said, "Well, if she's my mom, then how come you my mom?" he asked, confused. It was time, I told him the truth. Well part of the truth. He needed to know, and I knew that as long as he had me, we would get through it. "Well baby it's a long story, but I will tell you the most important stuff. Okay." I said. "Okay." He said. "Well, first of all, let me tell you that I had no idea, until tonight. Just like you. I had no idea. I thought your mom, was a young lady named Lalandra. And, at the time; me and your daddy didn't think she was able to take care of you, like we could. See, your daddy told me all about you and I wanted to love you as much as I could, so your daddy decided that you would come and live with us." I said, looking at Eric to see if he was following. He was staring at me intently, so I

169

figured that he was.

Just then the waiter came over to take our orders. We placed our orders, with me making sure that Diamond got her grapes. The whole time, I was looking at Eric to see if I could read his thoughts. "Okay, so I came to live with you and daddy? How old was I?" Eric asked. "Well sweetie, you were only 2 at the time. And you were so cute; I just loved you to death. I mean, you always were my son, so I just kept it like that. I loved you, from the moment I laid eyes on you. And I promise that nothing is going to change. You are my son Eric and don't you ever forget it. Okay?" I said, to my son hoping he wasn't too hurt to understand. "I know ma, I just wanted to know the truth. I mean, Diamond kinda look like you and you always said I looked like dad, so I never said anything. I love you mommy, you told me the truth and you didn't have to. I don't care if Auntie Ky say she my mom. You are my mom." He said, and gave me a winning smile and started to dig into his food like his life depended on it. "Well, I love you too, baby." I said, with a smile.

I started to eat my food and just as it was getting good my cell went off. Now who is this? I don't feel like talking to anybody. I looked at it and it was Clara. Oh boy, I guess she talked to Kyra. Did I

170

really feel like listening to somebody defending Kyra right now? No, not really and I know that's what Clara was gonna' do. I knew she meant well but I just wasn't in the mood. I didn't want to be reminded of how long we had been friends and so on. I'll just call her back later. Me and the kids finished dinner then decided to take in a movie. What the hell? It was Friday and we didn't have anything else to do and I felt like spending some time with my kids, just us. We hoped on 85 and headed towards Concord Mills. That way, after the movie, we could do a little shopping. Shopping always made me feel better. Me and the kids decided to see Madagascar. I liked the Disney movies; they were usually funny and enlightening. After the movie we decided to walk around the mall. I wanted to see if there were any good sales and the kids, of course wanted to see what new games they could talk me into getting.

By the time we left, we were all exhausted. We put the bags in the trunk and piled into the car. The kids were dead tired, by the time we hit the 485 loop, both Diamond and Eric were gone to the world, with Jewel following suit. "Are you okay Meme?" asked Sapphire. "Sure baby, why do you ask?" I said. "Well, I know how close you and Ky were and I know you have got to be hurting right now. I'm a big girl you can talk to me if you like."

171

T.E Cooper

She said, I just looked at her, and yes she had grown up and was a young woman but I didn't want to bother her and have her worrying about me. "Well, a lot has happened to us these past few years and I thought that me and Ky would always be tight but you know stuff happens. I will be okay though, don't you worry." I said, giving her a smile. "Okay." She said and closed her eyes.

That gave me time to think. I thought about all the good times, me and Kyra had as teenagers and all the shit we went through to get where we were today and couldn't believe it. Why didn't she tell me she was pregnant by E? I mean, at the time me and him wasn't even that serious and I thought we was better than that. Then I started to think of how could she be around her son every day and not say something? I just didn't understand. As I got off on the Rea Rd. exit, I was more confused than before. I just couldn't fathom that E, of all people would keep something like that from me. That lying bastard, I couldn't believe him. He told me all of those lies about Lala. And not to mention he was fucking her too! I wonder how many bitches he had on the side. Was I that dumb, or was I that in love; that I couldn't see the obvious. Because as I think back on it; there were definitely signs of his infidelities. There were times that he wouldn't answer his pager or his phone. And there were

172

times when I would call and he didn't answer then Ky would call and he would pick right up. Were they fucking in my house; the house that we had turned into a home? I couldn't think about that, 'cause if I did, I might be tempted to go back to Ky's house and jump on her again. OOOH, I was so mad! I was hurt, and confused. I just couldn't believe it. Before I knew it I was pulling into my driveway. I had gotten here pretty quick. Well my mind was occupied.

I hit the automatic garage opener and pulled the car inside then turned it off. I let the garage door down and opened the backdoor to my car, where my children were sleeping peacefully. My Eric was a big boy and growing bigger by the day. He was a lot more understanding to the situation than I thought he would be. You know, you hear those stories of adopted children turning out to hate their adoptive parents. Well I put it in my mind that, that would never happen with us. No matter what I had to do, Eric would know that I loved him dearly. Just like Diamond. I woke the kids up then helped Eric and Diamond to their rooms. The bags could wait until tomorrow. After they had gotten in their pajamas and I had them tucked into bed, I headed downstairs to my den. I had a lot on my mind and I needed a good drink.

173

T.E Cooper

As I got halfway downstairs, I decided that I needed to take a shower so I could relax. Instead of going back upstairs to my room, I decided to take a shower in the guest bedroom. Ky spent the night sometimes, so there was clean towels and stuff in the bathroom. After I got out, I put on the Ralph Lauren; terry cloth bathrobe that hung in the guest closet. I went into the guest bathroom and decided, why not sit in the Jacuzzi. The guest bathroom tub was also a Jacuzzi. I looked in the cabinets and found some Calgon. I started the water and turned on the jets. While the water was running I ran downstairs and fixed myself an Apple Martini; light on the apple and heavy on the tinni'. As I settled down and let Calgon take me away, I cried. Not loud but before I realized it; I had a steady flow of tears, racing down my cheeks. It was the first time, I felt hurt like this. This was different from when E was locked up and it was different from when I found out he was dead. This was the type of hurt you felt, when someone who you loved like your own flesh and blood betrayed you. Now, if it hasn't happened to you then you might not be able to relate. But this was, deep down in my soul. Kyra was more than my best friend. She was my sister, my confidant, my world, other than my kids. And, she betrayed me. How can I trust friendship again, after something like this? Was I destined to be betrayed, by those who claim to love me the most? I

174

didn't have the answers to any of those questions, I only had more questions.

I finished up my martini, turned the jets off and washed up. Sitting in the tub, turning into a prune wasn't giving me any answers. As I dried off, I heard my cell phone and this time it wasn't Clara. It was Kyra. They each had different ringtones. I froze immediately. What did she want? Didn't she know that our friendship was over? I had nothing to say to her, so I ignored the phone. As a matter-of-fact, I picked it up and turned it off. There. That should send the message, that I had nothing to say to her. I continued to dry off then I put on the robe. I always liked how snug robes felt when you had them on and therefore I made sure there were at least 4 in all the bathrooms in the house. I decided that I needed something else to drink because Kyra calling really was unexpected. I went into the den and lit the gas fireplace. Even though it was warm outside, I liked the ambiance it gave off; comforting.

I then went over to the entertainment center and turned on the cd player. I looked through my cd's and decided on some India Arie. I loved her music. It was mellow and comforting. I could relate to what she was singing about. Her songs always had something to say. And at that moment I needed to

175

be soothed. I walked over to the bar and decided on a Blue Motorcycle.

I had plenty of liquor in my den. It was where I chilled out. You know me and my girls. And we were always trying new shit. We went to Borders bookstore and got a book on how to make mixed drinks. We decided that we could make our own drinks just as good if not better than the bartender at any club. 'Cause we all knew their drinks were watered down. And they be having the nerve to charge an arm and leg. Shit, I sat and reminisced on many a night me Clara and Kyra sat in here getting tore up making our own concoctions. The thought made me smile and brought tears to my eyes at the same time. I started to think of all the shit we had been through and survived. I mean, came out on top. And now this. Why did it have to be this way? And once again, I found myself crying. I couldn't imagine why I was crying so much. Shit, I should be happy I found out what type of person Kyra was. Maybe it's the alcohol. I don't know but whatever it is; I just want it to go away.

Welcome to My Hood

20. Getting By.

Of course I woke up, with a major hangover. Damn! I know better than to be drinking like that. What the hell was I thinking? Then, it all came back to me. Everything that Kyra had disclosed to me; came rushing back like a tsunami. I just sat there, in my bed and wallowed in what had become of my life (or so I thought) of friendship. I had to get out of here. I got out of bed and threw on my robe. I wonder if the kids are up for a road trip. I walked downstairs to my kitchen, where all of my children were posted up. "Good morning." I said, while fixing a cup of coffee from the automatic coffee maker. "Good morning, mom. Hey what are we doing this weekend? Ain't this family weekend?" Diamond, was asking.

"Well I was just thinking about that. What do you guys think about, a road trip? We could go down to Atlanta and do some shopping. You know, just chill. What do yall think?" I said, looking from one to the other for a response. "Shoot; that sounds good to me. I need some new stuff, anyway. Are we gonna go to Lenox Mall?" Sapphire said. "Yeah,

177

I wanna go to the Louis Vuitton boutique. And, I think that Gucci store is calling my name!" Jewel said with full enthusiasm. "Cool, can we go to the Underground? They gotta a game store, that's off the hook. I love going to Atlanta." Eric said. "Well I guess that's settled then. After you all eat, clean the kitchen and start to pack. We can leave, as soon as yall are ready. You know what, don't pack. We gonna take showers and hit the road. Anything we need we can buy when we get there." I said feeling a bit enthused myself.

I finished my coffee and went to my room to take a shower. I went in my room and went to my gigantic closet that definitely didn't need any more tenants and started looking for something to wear. I decided on a pair of Bebe jeans and matching short sleeve sweater and some Nine West ankle boots. I was going to be chillin' with the kids this weekend; I didn't need to look fancy. The jeans, sweater and boots were all a combination of my favorite colors, beige and brown. The jeans were a chocolate color and the sweater had different shades of the same chocolate and beige. The boots were all beige with a slight wedged heel. I stepped out of the closet and walked over to my dresser. This dresser was just for my lingerie. I mean I had loads of the stuff; all matching too. I sifted through the drawers searching for something comfortable, yet cute. As I

178

looked in the third drawer, I found just what I was looking for. A set of' Joe Boxer undies. They were made of cotton and the bra didn't have any underwire. I set everything on my bed and headed towards the shower. I was still a little uptight and my head still hurt, not like it was but still a little throb. I decided against the Jacuzzi, thinking that I might get to comfortable and fall asleep. So I headed over to the shower.

I loved my shower. Not all the showers were made like this in the house, I had this 'specially designed. It had 20 shower heads and a steam setting. It was big enough for at least 5 people. I reached in and set the setting on all 20, with a massage. Yup, by the time I get out of here, I should feel like a new woman. That was how it always made me feel. Today I decided on some Cucumber Melon body wash from Bath and Body-works. I loved the smell of their products. I lathered my loofa and began to scrub. With the massage on and all those sprayers, I was starting to feel better all ready. I washed from head to toe, at least 4 times before I finally shut the shower off and stepped out. Aww, that was refreshing. I walked into my room and got dressed. After I was dressed, I went into the separate vanity to fix my hair and apply a little makeup. I went light today, 'cause I really didn't feel like much makeup. I sprayed on

179

T.E Cooper

some Usher for women and was ready. I went into my pocketbook closet and found the pocketbook that matched my outfit and switched all of my important items to it. After this, I was ready to go.

I left my room and went downstairs to the game room. Sure enough there was Eric, fully dressed and playing his WII. I asked him where his sisters were and he just shrugged it off. He had no interest in where his sisters were. I looked at him and chuckled and walked into the living room and there they were. Jewel was doing Diamonds' hair and Sapphire was watching BET. "Yall ready?" I asked. "Yeah, just let me put this last ponytail in D's hair and we ready." Jewel said, while doing the last ponytail on Diamonds' abundant head of hair. "Dang girl, you got too much hair." Jewel said, pushing Diamond off her lap. "Now ma, you sure you don't want us to pack something? Cause ya know, we can shop." Sapphire said putting on her light, Gucci leather jacket.

"Naw, yall straight. I told you, we gonna do some serious shopping. And we gonna have fun doing it. Now, let's hurry up so we can beat any traffic. I wanna get there in time today, to do some major damage." I said, grabbing my Dolce and Gabana purse. I yelled for Eric to come out of the game room and come on. "Dang, I'm always the only

180

boy. Why I always gotta be the only boy? Huh, ma?" Eric asked, while putting on his lightweight Ed Hardy jacket. "Well sweetie, some men love to be surrounded by women. You should feel lucky." I said, giving him a peck on the cheek. We headed out the door that led to the garage and were on our way.

I decided against taking the Lexus 470 jeep. It was cute but not a lot of room. I decided on the Escalade that E had bought us years ago. It was big and roomy plus it always reminded me of E. Even though, at that moment I didn't want to think about him or Kyra. As we pulled out of the garage and out of the driveway, my cell phone rang. I looked at the caller I D and decided to answer it, cause it was Clara. "What's up?" I said, as I maneuvered my way out of my neighborhood.

"What's up? Is that all you have to say? Why haven't you been returning any calls, or answering the phone for that matter? I know that shit that Kyra told you was fucked up but come on. Yall been friends for way to long, for a nigga to come between yall. I mean, if you woulda' noticed the signs, you wouldn't be going through this right now. 'Cause honestly, I could tell, just by the way they acted at the house." Clara said, matter-of-factly. Wait a minute, this bitch knew

181

what was going on and didn't tell me! What the fuck is this? Conspire to keep Memorie in the dark. Stupid little Meme; who didn't know that her husband was fucking her best friend! I hung up. I didn't even respond to what she said. I just hung up. I couldn't think about all that right now cause it was a distraction and I was driving all of my kids with me. I needed to keep my wits about me.

I turned off the phone and put it in my purse. If I needed it, it was there. Now to focus on the 3hr drive to the A. Me and the kids always liked to take road trips with each other. Even though Eric acted like he hated being the only boy, he really loved all of his sisters. He enjoyed our shopping trips, just like us. He just couldn't say, 'cause it wasn't manly. He just made me laugh sometimes. Jewel started singing along with the radio, while everybody else played the game. I got a PS3 hooked up in the jeep just for these occasions. I was watching the traffic and thinking about all I had been through and what it took for me to get here. I couldn't believe it. As I concentrated on the road I really listened to Jewel sing. That girl had talent; with a capital T! I wonder why I never heard her before around the house. She could really sing, I mean like professionally. Me and her gonna have to talk later. As we continued to drive, the scenery started to look like a forest. I mean the scenery between

182

North and South Carolina going down to Georgia was just beautiful. If I were an artist I would just pull up on the side of the road, and paint. That was one of the reasons why, I loved this drive. The other was, of course, the kids. I loved being with them. Sometimes I just thanked God, for all my blessings.

Then, I started to think about Kyra. I mean, I know for most people, they would have just cut her off and not think another thing about it. But it was different for me. I don't know why, maybe it's that loyalty thing I have going on. I don't know but whatever it was, I wished it would go away. I didn't want to think of all the reasons why she did what she did, and I didn't want to think of how long we had been friends. I sure didn't want to think about why she would just abandon her child, 'cause the nigga didn't want her.

That shit, was trifling. And, I just couldn't forgive her for that. I might be able to almost forgive her, for fucking E but just abandon her child? Naw, I don't want no parts of that girl no more. She just wasn't the person I thought I knew. It was time for me to move on and if Clara couldn't understand it, then oh well. Right now I don't want to talk to her 'cause all she gonna do, is tell me how long we been friends and shit. Shit, that's the point I was trying

183

T.E Cooper

to make. Look at how long we were friends! I misread her by a long shot. I started thinking about what my cousin told me a long time ago; to watch her, 'cause she was grimy. Boy, was that an understatement.

I got to thinking about Bam and decided to give him a call. I turned on my cell and dialed his number. "Yo, who 'dis?" was the greeting I got. "Hey cuz, it's me, Meme. What you been up too?" I said, in a cheery voice. It felt good hearing Bam's voice. I was always close to him. "Hey cuz! Where you at? Long time, no hear from. How's the kids?" Bam was saying, with just as much enthusiasm. "Oh the kids are fine. We're on the way to Atlanta, to do some shopping. I just wanted to hear your voice, 'cause I was feeling a little down." I said, letting him know that something was wrong. "What's up cuz? Ain't nothing going down like last time, is it?" he asked, sounding a little cautious. The last time he helped me, he didn't like how things turned out. He ain't want no police involved but at the time, I saw no other way.

"Naw, ain't nothing like that. It's just that....well do you remember that warning you gave me about a certain somebody?" I asked, being vague, cause I didn't want the kids to know who I was talking about. "Umm... let me think. Well, was it a girl or a

184

guy?" he asked, sounding confused. "A girl." I said simply. "Uh, oh. You found out 'bout cha' girl. Didn't you." He said, more as a statement than a question. "And you know it. I just can't believe it." I said, still not wanting to say too much. "Well, I told you that girl was foul. It just took you a little longer to see, that's all. Ain't no crime in that. Shit, the bitch had me fooled too for a while and then I found out just what type of person she really was. That bitch ain't right in the head. I hope you watch your back from now on, since you know." Bam said. That bitch better not, think it! "Shit, they know what the deal is. Look, let me call you back when I get to the hotel. I got the kids with me, you know. I'ma call you, 'cause no matter what you know, it ain't shit like what I found out." I said. "Aight. Then I guess I'll talk to you later. Yo and cuz, be careful." He said and hung up. I loved my cousin and I couldn't wait to tell him all about what had happened between me and Kyra.

I looked up and the sign said that Lenox was the next exit. I have to pay attention, 'cause the highways in the A are crazy. They run all which a ways. I saw my exit and got over to the far right lane 'cause the two lanes actually went to two different places and if I wasn't in the right lane, ain't no telling where we would end up. I stopped at the light and studied my navigation to see just

185

T.E Cooper

how far we had to go, to get to the hotel. I was tired of driving and I know the kids were tired of riding. I saw that we were only two blocks away from the Ritz Carlton and woke the kids up. Everybody had fallen asleep on me. As everyone was waking up, I pulled into the hotel and up to the valet parking. After all the kids were awake; we got out and I handed my keys to the valet then got my ticket. We entered the hotel and I went to the front desk, while the kids wandered around the lobby. It wasn't their first time there, so they knew where they were going. After I got the keys to our suite, I rounded up the kids and headed towards the elevators.

As we were walking I thought I saw a familiar face. As I studied harder; I realized; it was Leo. I knew Leo, from a few runs I had made to the A when I was younger. He was one of the sexiest brothers I had ever met. He had a caramel complexion and some of the most gorgeous eyes I had ever seen. They weren't any particular color, just gorgeous. I believe it was the way they were shaped and those long eyelashes. His eyes looked like, they belonged on a woman. While I was daydreaming about Leo, he noticed me then walked over. "Hey, Meme; long time no see. How you been?" he asked, with that sexy A drawl.

"Well you know, I been around. How you been?" I

186

said. "Well you know a brotha 'aight. Who are these cute kids?" he asked, turning his attention to the children. "Well these are my rug rats. This is Jewel, this is Sapphire, this is Diamond and this is Eric. Kids this is an old acquaintance of mine, Leo." I said, introducing him to my children. "Well, I see somebody been busy. I remember you wouldn't even give a guy like me the time of day. Must be one helluva' guy. Where he at? I would sure like to meet him." Leo said, looking around like he was expecting someone to show up. "Well, my husband died about 6 years ago. So it's just me and the kids now." I said starting to feel like I was doing something wrong, by talking to Leo. For some reason, I just couldn't think of another man the way I had thought or felt about Eric. I just couldn't.

"Oh; my bad. You know it's been a long time since we saw each other. I didn't know, or I would have come to the funeral." He said, with genuine concern. "Oh, we're okay. You know, we get by. I believe we gonna be alright." I said. "Well, what brings you to the A?" Leo asked, changing the subject. "My momma gonna take us shopping." Diamond said, with much enthusiasm. "Oh, is that right? Well, from what I remember your momma could shut a store down." He said with a chuckle. We had actually missed at least 3 elevators, while standing there talking to Leo, but for some reason I

187

didn't care. I could have stood in that lobby all night and talked to him and looked into those gorgeous eyes. "Well, Leo, it was nice seeing you and I hope to run into you again while I'm here. You take care." I said, moving towards the elevator that the kids had already entered. "Sure. We should get up while you here. You know, for some drinks or something." He said, with a grin. "Oh, okay. That sounds nice. How do I get in touch with you?" I asked, taking out my cell. "Well how 'bout we get each-others numbers, that way if anything happened we could call and tell the other." He said taking out his cell. We exchanged numbers and said our goodbyes.

"Wow. He was cute!" Jewel said, smiling from ear to ear. "I hear that sista'!" chimed in, Sapphire. "Really? I hadn't noticed." I said to the girls, not wanting them to think the wrong thing. "Well I did and that man is fine, with a capital F. I sure hope you gonna call him. I can tell you this; if he was my age, I would be all over him." Jewel said. "Girls, it ain't like that. We know each other from a long time ago; he just wants to be friendly. He probably won't even call." I said, trying to convince the girls to give up this conversation, cause I swear if I thought about Leo anymore, I would probably cum. Thinking about it, when was the last time I had this coochie tapped? Damn! I can't even

188

Welcome to My Hood

remember. Now that's bad. I been trying so hard to give the kids a good life, I had forgotten all about my own needs. Damn! He is fine.

We arrived at our floor and exited the elevator. It wasn't hard to find our suite, 'cause there was only two on the whole floor. We opened up the door, and went in. Of course, Eric went straight to the television; that boy. Me, I went over to the bar to see what they had to offer. I usually didn't drink before I took the kids out, but I needed a stiff one to calm my nerves. I couldn't believe it. That nigga had me trippin', just like when I met E. Naw, couldn't be. Aint' no nigga ever came close to making me feel like that; or maybe not. Well, I wasn't gonna think about it. I couldn't think about it. After I fixed myself a light drink, I went into the master bedroom. The suite we were in had three bedrooms. I figured while we were here the girls could share a room. I know Eric wasn't gonna share a room, with any of them. I looked around and decided to take a little nap. I was tired from the long drive and I needed a nap, bad. I walked back into the living room to tell the kids that we would go out after I had some sleep. "Hey yall; I'm tired, so I'ma' take a little nap before we go. If yall leave the room, come and tell me first and Jewel, Sapphire, watch out for your brother and sister." I said. "That's cool. We ain't going anywhere, we

189

kind of tired too. We gonna chill and watch a movie 'til you get up." Sapphire said, kicking off her shoes. I nodded at them and headed to the bedroom. I was beat. I remembered that I was supposed to call Bam back and decided that could wait til later. Then I laid on the bed and crashed.

I don't know how long I was out, but when I woke up I felt like a new woman. I got up, went to the bathroom and washed my face. I'ma have to visit the nearest Wal-Mart, cause I gotta get some Dove soap. After I was finished in the bathroom, I went to check on the kids to see if they were also still sleep and if they were ready to go. They were all in their rooms knocked out. I decided to let them sleep and go do some mandatory shopping by myself. I found a notepad and wrote them a note telling them where I was going and that they could order room service if I wasn't back in a little while. I then grabbed my purse and keys and was out the door. I walked out of the suite feeling, refreshed for some reason. I guess I needed that nap a little more than I thought. As I was on the elevator I checked my phone to see if I had any missed calls. And of course I had 15 from Clara, and one from Leo. I just stared at the phone. He called. I wonder. Naw, he just wants us to do some catching up. I wonder if I should call, after all, I do need to do some serious shopping tonight if we want to go out

190

shopping tomorrow. I decided to call Leo anyway. Shit, he might wanna go shopping with me. Like that'll ever happen. Well anyway here it goes.

"Hello." A deeply sexy voice answered. "Uh, uh, hi. It's me, um, Meme." I said, stammering feeling a lot more nervous than I thought. "Oh, hey Meme. What the deal, shawty?" he said, when he realized who it was. "Nothing much; just about to go and do some necessary shopping. Me and the kids came with nothing but the clothes we got on." I said, with a laugh. Leo laughed and said, "Well you know, shopping is a necessity for all woman, no matter what the occasion. So where do you plan on going?" he said, with a certain amount of interest that I couldn't pick up on. "Well, tomorrow I was planning to take the kids over to Lenox Mall. But for tonight, I really don't know. I do know, I can't come back to the hotel wit' no bull, 'cause my two oldest, ain't goin' for it." I said, laughing again. I had reached the valet parking and was waiting on my jeep. "Well, how about a little company? You know, talk about old times and all." He said, crushing any hope of maybe getting some.

"Sure why not? I'm just about to leave the hotel. I'm waiting on the valet to bring my jeep around. Where you at?" I said. "Well, how 'bout we ride in my car? I'm around the corner from the hotel and I

191

could swing by right now, if you like. That way, you don't have to worry about directions." He said. Wow, I wonder what he was doing on this side of town. As a matter-of-fact he was in the hotel earlier. "Sure, I can tell the valet never mind. How long will it take you to get here?" I asked. "Give me 'bout 15 and I'll be there." He said. "Cool, see ya' then." I said, hanging up. I walked over to the valet just as they were pulling my truck around. I told him never mind to go and re-park it then gave him 50 dollars for the trouble. I went over and sat on the benches they had outside for guests, and called Bam. Since I wasn't around the kids, this was the perfect time to talk.

"What up?" I said when he answered. "Yo, cuz. I see yall made it to the A safe. Huh." He said, always looking out. "Of course; I'm about to do a little shopping and the kids are upstairs sleep. I thought they had slept enough in the car, but I guess ain't nothing like a soft bed. Well anyway, guess who I ran into." I said. "Don't know, tell me." "Leo." I stated. "Yo, that's my nigga! Where you see that cat at?" he asked, sounding just as excited as I did when I saw Leo. "He was at the hotel when we checked in. I couldn't believe it. It's been so long since I saw him, I almost didn't recognize him." I said, being evasive about the fact that he was on the way to get me. "Yo, if you see him

192

again, give him my number and tell him I said hit me up. Now what happen wit' that bitch, Kyra." He said getting right to the point. That's what I loved about Bam; he was as straight up as they came.

"Lil E, is Kyra's son." I said simply, feeling the tears welling up. Boy not now. I really don't wanna cry. "Yo say what? Cuz' what you talkin' 'bout? Lil E, as in; your son Lil E?" he said, not believing, just like me when I first found out. "Yup and the bitch was still fucking my man and living with me at the same time. Hell, if I hadda' known that, I woulda left the bitch with Carlos boys. The bitch Lala is her cousin. She gave Lil E' to her cause E wouldn't leave me and he was also fucking her cousin Lala, and had that bitch pregnant too." It was all coming out in a rush. I could always confide in Bam, I knew he would listen, no matter what.

"Damn." Was all he could say. Yeah that's what I thought. "Damn, cuz, I'm sorry 'bout that shit. What, all of a sudden she want Lil E or something?" he said, thinking way off. "Hell no! We went over there the other day and she didn't answer the door, so I used my key and me and the kids went on in. I told them to go to the kitchen and fix a snack while I went to see what Kyra was doin'. Well anyway, when I got to the room the bitch in there with a gun to her head. Now, you know I

193

didn't know what was going on, my dumb ass. All the bitch wanted to do was, confess. She wanted to get some shit off her chest and chose to be dramatic 'bout the shit. To say the least, I beat that bitch ass. I mean, what else could I do? And the kids walked in on us, so I stopped. But guess what, Lil E heard her. And he says he understands, but I don't know cuz." I just let it all come out. Like I said, Bam was gonna listen, then he was gonna comfort me, which I needed right now. Not somebody reminding me how long we were friends.

"Well, cuz; you gonna be alright. You know you straight; fuck that hoe. I don't believe she pulled that shit on you. And didn't you buy that damn condo she staying in; that shit got me mad for you cuz. So what up wit Lil E'?" true to form. "Well I told the bitch, not to come anywhere near my son. I meant that shit too. E is my son. I got the papers, and I'll kill that bitch before I let her get him. Anyway, the trifling hoe don't even want him, so fuck her." I said, looking up and seeing Leo pull up to the hotel. "Listen cuz, I'ma call you back. My car just got here." I said, quickly. "'Aight, you call me later. Love you and cuz, fuck that bitch." He said and hung up. That's why I loved Bam; he was always in my corner.

"Well, hello there." I said to Leo, admiring his

194

Pearl White Phantom. Damn! This nigga livin' Large! The interior was a Peanut Butter with wood grain out the ass. He had a specially designed tv that was made into the middle column. To say the least, his ride was fly. "Well; look at you; looks like somebody been doing good." I said, teasing him about his whip. The man wasn't looking too bad himself. "You know, a nigga gotta eat." He said, with that sexy smile. Damn, just looking at him was making my pussy wet. I'm damn glad I got on black, 'cause if I stand up, everyone will know that I just nutted all on myself! Damn! This nigga was fine! How come I never noticed how damn fine his ass was? "So where to?" he asked, bringing me out of my daydream. Good thing too, 'cause if I woulda kept that up, I probably would have raped his ass. "I don't know. I know I plan on doing some major damage tomorrow, so probably somewhere I can get some cute stuff, that's comfortable at the same time." I told him looking at the bulge between his legs lustfully. Well, it has been 5 long years since I had some good dick. Well, if you talking about real good dick then 6; since before E got locked up. Damn, I might have to invest in some vibrators.

21. A Fresh Start.

Leo was whipping the Phantom on the highway in and out of traffic, like he was driving a Honda. "Well, I think I know just the place. It's a little ways out, but it's worth the drive, when you see what they have to offer." He said, with a seductive grin. I think he saw me staring at his dick. "Cool, I'm in your hands. I trust you." I said, and laid my head back against the headrest and closed my eyes. I wasn't tired; I just didn't want to keep staring at his dick. "That's good to know. What, you tired? I thought you just woke up?" he asked. "Oh, I'm not tired, just enjoying the ride." Okay, not that kind of ride. I heard him chuckle and opened one eye to look at him, "What's funny?" I asked. "Nothing; so tell me, what makes a woman pack up four kids, no excuse me, no packing and just come to the A? What, life in Charlotte not treating you good? 'Cause you know, the A always welcomes you." He said, and that time I caught the hint.

"Well, you know some stuff went down wit' my girl and I just wanted to get away. Away from the

196

madness, ya know." I said, feeling comfortable enough to talk openly. "I hear that; so tell me something else. Was your dead husband your kids' father?" He was fishing, trying to see if I got any crazy baby daddy's around, hiding in the bushes.

"Well, technically speaking, yes." I said, enjoying the game of cat and mouse. "Oh, I see." He said becoming real quiet. I busted out laughing. "What's so funny?" He asked, looking a little erked. "You, are what's so funny. All you gotta do is ask and I'll tell you whatever you want to know. And since you started with the kids, I'll tell you. Jewel and Sapphire are my sister's. It's just that I'm the one who raised them, so they call me mom. Diamond is mine; all me and Lil E, well he's a long story. Let's just say, my husband was his father and all his life I've been his mom." I said, putting any questions about any baby daddies to rest. "Oh, cause girl I was gonna say, you started early as hell!" He said, laughing trying to put light in the situation. "Well, I could tell you were a helluva woman back when I met you. I always knew you would be special. So, how about we get reacquainted this weekend and see if it turns out to what I want." He said, looking at me through those sexy ass eyes. Keep looking at me like that and he gonna get what he looking for.

"Just what is it that you want?" I asked, being as

197

flirtatious as I could; seeing as how I had the advantage, with my eyes. No one can look me straight in the eye. They were too intense. But this nigga, this nigga looked me straight in the eyes for a second, before he looked back at the road and said, "I don't think this is the time or place to tell you what I really want, so I'll save that for later on." I was speechless and wetter than Niagara Falls. We exited the freeway and made a lot of left turns. I never could get over how everything in the A went the same direction. Anyway, we pulled up in front of this cute little shop. Epopofassta; it read. "Hey, this is cute. How you know about this place? Your girlfriend bring you here; a lot?" I asked, fishing for some answers myself. "Nope, my sister owns the shop. And for the record, I don't have a girl or kids." He said; smiling and holding the door open for me.

"Hey big bro!" a booming voice called, as we walked in the store. "What's up Fashama?" He said, giving the littlest person a hug. I couldn't believe that all that voice came out of that little body. "What you doing here and who is this you have with you?" His little sister, Fashama with the booming voice asked, smiling in my direction. "Well, this is a good friend of mine, Meme. Meme, this little lady is my sister Fashama." He said, still smiling. "Well, it's nice to meet you. You know, he

198

don't bring any of his lady friends here, you must be something special." She said. Leo looked a little embarrassed by her comment, but decided not to say anything. "Well, Meme is in town for the weekend with her children and they need a few items." He told his sister as she ushered us around the store. The place was incredible; I mean she had everything from, Christine Laubrough, Dolce and Gabbana, Manolo's I mean everything! I was in heaven. I loved to shop and I loved to shop in a place that has all of my favorites. "Wow, you have a lot of great stuff in here. Where do you get all this stuff?" I questioned, as I looked around. "Well before I opened this store I used to make costumes and outfits for shows like The View and some of the soaps." She said, smiling. "Wow, that's great." "Yeah, I made a few good connections while I was doing that. It's just, you want your own. Ya' know? Well anyway, I got a few good contracts and here I am." She said, twirling her hand around what was obviously her prize possession. I really could feel where she was coming from. For a long time I wanted to start my own business too. I admired her for following her dream.

"Well girl, I'm getting ready to be one of your most loyal fans. Look at all this stuff and you have stuff for kids too! This is incredible." I said; with excitement all in my voice. I walked completely

199

away from Leo and his sister to explore the shop some more. Boy, she was gonna get my business all the time. I hope she has a web page. I wandered around some more and went to the children's side. It's always easiest to find Diamond and Eric something to wear. I went over to the section that was labeled Gucci for Kids. I picked out this cute Gucci jean dress with the matching boots for Diamond and a Gucci jean jacket, shirt, pants and shoes for Eric. Then I went over to the junior misses side. Thankfully, Jewel and Sapphire liked my taste in clothes so it was kind of easy to shop for them as well. It's just that I couldn't decide on whether the Dereon' outfit for Jewel or that Dolce and Gabana dress and boots. I had already decided on this cute Prada outfit with matching shoes for Sapphire. It was her favorite color, red. I continued to look at the two outfits I had picked up for Jewel and decided to get them both. Then I went and found another outfit for Sapphire and the younger kids. After I had them out of the way it was my turn to find something for myself.

I walked around for a minute before I saw this wrap skirt and shirt that I just had to have. The skirt was black and pink and the shirt was pink with a plunging turtle neck with no sleeves. It was gorgeous. When I looked at the tag I saw that it was Prada. Just my style. I found some cute stilettos and

200

was on my way to find another outfit for myself when I came across the most gorgeous dress I had ever seen. It was a dress that you would wear to a cocktail party. It was teal green and made of the softest silk I had ever felt. It hung down over one arm and gathered at the waist just a little then dropped down to about mid-thigh. I had to have it. I didn't have anywhere to wear it, but damnit I was gonna get it. When I picked it up Leo's sister came over. "It's beautiful, isn't it?" she said. "It's a Vera Wang original. There's not another like it. I also have the shoes, if you're interested." She said with a smile. "I sure am. This is gorgeous." "Okay, what size do you wear? Let me guess, a 6." She said. "You hit the nail on the head." I said still admiring the dress. "Okay, be back in a minute." She said and was off. I took my spoils to the counter with a look of pure ecstasy in my eyes.

"Wow, I thought you said a little shopping?" Leo said, laughing. "I know, sorry I took so long. It's just that your sister has the most amazing collection, I got lost for a minute. Thank you so much for bringing me. I can't wait to bring the kids. Jewel and Sapphire are gonna have a heart attack when I bring them." I said, smiling from ear to ear. "Well, thank you. I enjoyed watching you shop. You looked happy." Leo said, with a smile. "Well I don't want you to think that I'm materialistic or

201

anything, but I do love to shop." I said being honest. Fashama, came back with some of the prettiest shoes I had ever seen. Yup, I would definitely be back. "Well, is this all?" she asked. I nodded my head. "Girl, you sure know how to shop. I'ma give you a discount, since my brother likes you so much." She said, with a smile.

She totaled me up and when I started to pay, Leo stopped me. "What type of man would I be if I let you pay for your stuff?" He said, smiling and paying his sister at the same time. "Wow, girl, I don't know what you did with my brother, but I like this guy." Fashama said, laughing. "You don't have to do that; I can pay for it myself." I said shocked; cause the total was no laughing matter. "Girl, please this is chump change. Now come on, let's finish up shopping so we can go catch a movie." He said, grabbing my bags. "Well it was nice meeting you and I hope to see you again." Fashama said, giving me a hug. "Like-wise." I said returning the hug. "See ya big bro and thanks." With that we were out of the store, headed to God knows where. "Thanks Leo. I appreciate that a lot. You didn't have to, you know." I said still not believing he just spent that much money on me and the kids. He probably thinks he's getting some ass. Well, he's right! I was thinking how I could get his fine ass in bed anyway, he just made it easier.

202

"Okay, where we going next?" I asked. "Well I was thinking; Frederick's of Hollywood." He said casually. "Yeah that sounds great. Only thing though, I'ma have to go somewhere else to get some undies for Eric and Diamond but me and the girls love Fredrick's." I said, with a smile. I might just be able to pick up a little something for later on. "Well, it's settled. We'll go to Fredrick's for you and the girls and later to Wal-Mart for the kids. How does that sound?" he asked. "Fine, um, did you say we were going to the movies?" I asked. "Well sure; you do want to go; don't you? It's the premier of Will Smith's new movie, I AM LEGAND. All the big wigs will be out." He said, smiling. Thank God I bought that dress. "Oh, I thought you meant a regular movie but that sounds cool too." I said, not wanting to sound to impressed. "Cool, after we finish shopping, I'll drop you off at the hotel so you can get ready. I'll be back around 9:30, the movie starts at 11. I wanna get there a little early, if you don't mind." He said.

"That's fine with me. And Leo thanks. I really needed this weekend to unwind and it looks like you're gonna help with that. Oh yeah, my cousin told me to tell you hi and he said to call him. I'm supposed to give you his number." I said. "You mean, Bam? Cool, what's that nigga's number? I

203

T.E Cooper

ain't talked to him in ages. That's my dog." Leo was saying, with a smile. "Yeah, well give him a call. Oh my, is that Fredrick's? I mean, I've been to the one in Charlotte but it's nothing like this. It's all by itself out here." I said, looking bewildered by the large store. It had to be at least 3 levels and just huge. Wow, I was gonna have some fun in here. "Well down here in the A, we do everything big, shawty." He said, with a devilish grin. I just smiled at him as we pulled into a parking space. "You go 'head, I'ma be in; in a minute. I got some calls to make." Leo said. "Okay, I shouldn't be long though. I'ma just pick up some undies." I said, getting out the car. As I exited his whip, he called me over to the driver's side window. "Here, take this and get something sexy for me." He said, and winked. I joked with him saying, "For you or for me?" I said, with the sexiest smile I could muster. "For you to put on and for me to take off." He said, and rolled up the window smiling. I just turned and walked off. I didn't have anything else to say.

As I was walking through the parking lot, I looked down at my hand and saw what he had handed me. Oh my God! It had to be about 5 grand; at least. I stopped for a minute and looked back at Leo. He just smiled and kept talking on the phone. I just shook my head and walked into the store. Like I thought, it was huge. I didn't know where to start

204

and since it was late I acquired some help from a young lady that worked there. I told her that I had two teenagers, so I wanted some undies but not too raunchy. She took me to a section that I know my sisters would love. They had everything, from PJ's to matching bra and panty sets that were cute but not sexy; just what they needed. I told her their sizes and what I wanted. She quickly obliged and picked the stuff up in the right sizes and colors. All the while, I was looking at some perfume for myself. I told her that would be fine, and to put them on the counter. I had gotten them each 4 PJ sets, and 10 matching bra and panty sets. That should hold them both for a while.

Then I explained about my night and who I was going with, my dress and the type of affect I wanted to make on this nigga. "I have just the thing. Follow me." said the young lady. Together we walked to a back room. I would have never guessed. She walked me towards something that looked like a vault. When she opened it there were all types of lingerie in cases. They were all glittering and shinning. "Wow, what are these?" I asked, in awe of all the beautiful underwear jewelry. "This is the special vault of love, as we call it. When a woman wants to impress a man or vice versa, this is where they come. Nothing says love or seduction like diamonds." She said with a smile. By that time

205

I had my eye on something. It was a set that included the diamond studded bra and thong as well as the diamond studded garter. It was beautiful. I had to have it.

"This one." I said without further thought. I didn't want to look at anything else. I had to have it. "Don't you want to know how much it costs?" she asked, a little unsure. "Sweetie, I don't give a damn. Trust me when I say, I got this." And I meant it. The money Leo gave me only covered what I already had at the desk for me and the girls, cause I got some cute regular sets as well but this; this was the icing on the cake. And I wanted Leo to cut it. "Girl, I can't wait to be like you. Do you know how bad I would love to be able to afford something like this?" she was saying, with admiration while taking my set out of the case and finding the box it was to be wrapped in. " Really, which set do you like?" I asked her. "Boy that's easy; take a look over here." She walked me to a case across the room. If I had of seen it first; I might have gotten that one for myself. "It's beautiful, isn't it?" she said with such admiration in her voice I decided to buy it for her. "Do you have a boyfriend?" I asked. 'Cause if she liked it so much, I was sure she had someone she wanted to wear it for.

Welcome to My Hood

"Yes, I just got married last month. We didn't get a chance to honeymoon 'cause we're both still in college. So, once we graduate we're gonna take a nice honeymoon. I would love to wear something like this for him. He's so special. You know, he saved me. He literally, saved my life. He's my knight in shining armor. I love him so much." She was saying, looking wistful. Right then and there I decided not to only buy her the set but why not get them that honeymoon? Hell, I could afford to be generous. "Where would you like to go?" I asked, digging for information. "I would love to go to Aspen. You know; one of those cabins in the woods type deal. Where the waiters would come to the cabin with room service and we would sit by the fire." She said, this time literally dreaming. That was all I needed. I had a plan and I would go through with it. She was a big help and I know that this would be tippin' big time. But hey, everybody deserves a break sometime.

We got to the desk and rung up my purchases. They totaled over a mil. Oh well, it was well deserved. I walked over to my little helper. "Hey what's your name anyway? You sure was a big help and I'm gonna let your manager know it too." I said, with a smile on my face and an arm full of bags. "Kymia; Kymia Thompson." She said, with a smile and a wave goodbye. Kymia Thompson. I

207

gotta' put that up somewhere. I walked to the car feeling elated. I don't know why but it felt good to think of what I had planned for the young couple. I was once young and in love. I reached the car and Leo got out to help with the bags. "Damn, shawty, I thought you said a "little shopping"." He said, with a playful tone. "Well trust, for me, this is light shopping. Oh, guess what I decided to do." I said; excited to tell someone what I planned on doing. "What?" he asked. "I'm gonna do what Oprah always tells us. I'm gonna pay it forward. You know; do something nice for somebody you don't know." I said, smiling thinking of what I had planned.

"I hope you talking about me." He said with that sly ass smile. Damn. There go these panties. He done had my pussy melting all day. I think I might have actually cum a few times. Since I didn't respond to his question, or at least he thinks I didn't, my pussy said otherwise, he told me we were going to our last stop before he took me to the hotel to get dressed. We went to a local Wal-Mart and I jumped out while he sat in the car in the front of the store waiting for me. I saw one too many heads turn my way and the ones that were female showed straight hatin'; so the fuck what. I was that bitch. I deserved to be riding in that Phantom, with that nigga. I put my head in the air and proceeded in the store. I went to the children's section and picked out 4 PJ sets for Dee and Lil E and got them each 10 pair of undies and matching t-shirts. I proceeded to the check-out line to pay for my packages.

Then I heard this behind me, "Girl, you see that fine ass nigga out there in that Phantom! You know I gots that number." She said, bragging to her friend. I pretended to be looking at a magazine, so I could get a good look at her. Chile please! Leo wouldn't touch her ass with a ten foot pole. Satisfied, I turned back around and continued to wait my turn. "If you don't believe me; here's the paper." She said, to her friend trying to prove a point to me. I had seen them when I came in and they were the same bitches hatin'. I took out my cell pretending like I was making a call and looked up Leo's number. I studied the number as I listened to her call the number out loud. And just like I thought, the bitch was lying! That was nowhere near his number. Oh well, some bitches is just dumb. It was finally my turn and when I paid for my stuff I made sure those two broads saw that I was holdin' bank. Skank hoes. I grabbed my bags and took my time leaving. I wanted them to see me get back into the car with the nigga they would both be going home dreamin' about.

209

After they paid for their things and were headed towards the door; I put a quarter in one of those machines and got some gum then sauntered out the door behind them. I slowly walked over to the car and dramatically opened the door. I looked back to see if they were watching and sure enough, they was staring at me with hatred in their eyes. Ha! Stupid bitches! "You got everything you needed?" he asked. "Yes, thank you. I appreciate you spending your day with me. I can't wait for tonight. I plan on having a real good time." I said, with a smile. Leo just looked at me with those sexy eyes and pulled the Phantom out of the parking lot. We were headed back to my hotel and I couldn't wait.

I called Jewel on her cell to tell her that I was on the way. "Hey baby, what yall doin'?" I asked. "Oh nothing, we just ate dinner; me and Sapphire took the kids down to the gift shop and a couple of other shops downstairs in the lobby. Other than that, we chillin'." She said. "Well okay, I'll be there in a minute. When I woke up earlier you guys were sleep, so I didn't want to disturb you. I went shopping so we can have something to wear out tomorrow. I can't wait 'til yall see what I got." I said, cheerily. "I hope you didn't go to the mall without us. We were looking forward to that." Jewel said, thinking I went on a shopping spree without her. That girl loved to shop. "No silly, I just

210

went to a couple of local stores. Yall gonna like what I got. You know I got taste. Well anyway, I'll be there in about 10 minutes." I said, saying goodbye.

We rode a while longer listening to Mary J. Blige's "My Life" cd. I was enjoying the ride and the music when I felt something massaging my leg, and it felt good. I looked down and Leo's hand was slowly making its way up my thigh and towards my pussy. He went up and started to unbutton my pants. "Lift up." He said and I did as instructed. He worked his hands towards my pussy and started to slide his finger up and down my clit. Damn, that feels good. I closed my eyes and enjoyed what he was doing. He slid one finger, then two inside my hot wet pussy and massaged my clit with his thumb. He was fucking the hell out of me with his hands and I knew I was really about to cum. "You better stop before I cum all over your seats." I said in a low moan. "Baby I want you to nut all over my hands and seats." He said picking up the pace. I was fucking his hand like it was the last dick on earth and sure enough; I came so hard I totally lost all of my composure and screamed, "I'M CUMMIN'!" body shivering and jerkin'. He didn't stop until I sat perfectly still. Then he withdrew his fingers and started licking and suckin' off my pussy juices like it was the fountain of youth. DAMN!

211

T.E Cooper

"You like that baby?" he asked, bending over to give me a kiss. I was speechless and he just smiled. By the time we reached the hotel I had gotten myself together. "Now what time you gonna be here?" I asked, anticipation all in my voice. He smiled and said, "I'ma be here at 9:30 on the dot. I can't wait either." He said then leaned in and gave me the kiss of a lifetime.

He got out the car and came to my side to open the door for me. He helped me inside the lobby then got a bellboy to help me with my bags. "9:30." He said, and with a quick peck he was gone. I know I must have stood there looking in the direction in which he just left for about 10 minutes, before the bellboy cleared his throat and asked me if I was ready to go up to my suite. I said "Yes". then we were on our way. Damn, that nigga had my pussy drippin' wet, thinking about tonight. Whoa, I thought to myself, I better be careful. This nigga might fuck my head up. I had never responded to anybody like that. Not even E and he was the love of my life. Yeah, I better watch my step with this one. As the elevators parted and we headed towards my room; I couldn't help but wonder, why the fuck I never got with that nigga! I walked in the hotel and towards the elevators. I was excited about tonight and couldn't remember the last time I had been so excited. I walked slowly

212

to the elevators while checking my phone messages. My mailbox was full and I knew who had filled it. I figured it was time I talked to Clara. I dialed her number and waited for her to pick up.

"Hello? Is that you, Meme?" Clara asked, sounding out of breath. "Yeah girl; did I catch you at a bad time?" I asked. "No, I was just doing some laundry. So what's up with you? Where you at?" she asked. She hadn't started in on me about Kyra and I was glad. "Girl, me and the kids decided to take a shopping trip to the A. I needed to get out of the house and the kids did too. What you been doing?" I was starting to feel glad that I called her. I really needed my friend. "Well, you know I been chillin'. I was a little worried about you though. You know, with everything that happened." She said, easing into the inevitable. "Oh girl, I'm straight. I figure, ain't shit I can do 'bout it now. All I can do is live my life and raise my kids." I said, trying to let her know not to go there.

"I feel you girl. But I do wanna say this. Kyra is grimy, and you were right about everything you said the other day. I wanted to tell you, sorry for coming off on you like that. Shit, I found out some shit 'bout cha' girl, you ain't never gonna believe." She said, sounding like she had something interesting to tell. "Uh, oh, if I know Kyra and I

213

think I do now. I know this is gonna be a doosy. What happened, tell me." I said, while entering the elevator. "Well you ain't gonna like it but here goes. She was the one that dropped that dime on us with your boy Carlos. That bitch wasn't kidnapped at all; she was with them mutha-fuckas! And all those bruises she had; they staged that shit.I always wondered why they kept her alive, now I know; she was down with them the whole time. And the dime that was dropped on E came right out her pocket and she the reason why Carlos had E killed. She went and told them that E was talking to the FEDS about them." She said, taking a deep breath.

That bitch! She was the reason my life was turned upside down and inside out. And she was the reason E was dead. I couldn't say anything, I was speechless. "That bitch!" I voiced out loud. "How could she do that to me? I just don't understand, Clara. What the fuck is wrong with that bitch? I treated her ass like fam' and this how she do me? Well, that bitch gonna pay, you can believe that." I said, angrier than I had felt when she told me that Lil E was her son. "Oh wait a minute; you ain't heard the last of it. I think you probably wanna sit for this one." She said, being dramatic. "I'm in the elevator, so spill it." I said, anticipating the worst. "She wants custody of Lil E." she said and was quiet.

214

I think I should have been sitting down like she said, 'cause as soon as she said it, I sank to the ground. The bellboy turned around and tried to help me up, asking if I was okay. I just sat there. NO! She can't want to take my baby from me. No! "Miss, are you okay? Should I call the front desk?" the bellboy was asking me. I composed myself enough to let him help me up and I told him I would be fine. "Meme, are you okay? You know you don't have to worry about that shit right. You are legally Lil E's mother and that shit ain't gonna change. Ain't no judge in their right mind, gonna' overrule the adoption and give him to her. Just chill and everything will be alright." Clara was saying, trying to convince me. I was devastated, to say the least. "You know what, you're right. She could have spoken up a long time ago, like when Lala brought him to my house and dropped him off. That bitch said nothing, she just tried to tell me that everything was gonna be alright. Fuck her, that's my son and I dare that bitch to try and take him from me. The only way she'll have him, is if I'm dead.

I said, thinking to myself; there was no way I was gonna give up my son. "That's what I'm talking about. Don't worry. Have fun this weekend with the kids and when you come home, we gonna

215

T.E Cooper

handle that bitch. I got cha' back, 100." Clara said, and it made me feel better. "Girl, I just got to my floor, I'ma' call you back when I'm on the way home." I said. "Okay, take care and don't worry." She said, and hung up the phone. As me and the bellboy made our way to my suite, I let my mind wander, just a little. No matter what, that bitch will never get my son, no matter what. When we reached the suite, Sapphire was at the door. "I thought I heard the elevator. Daaaang, what you buy?" she said, eyeballing all the bags. "Just a little something to get us through tonight; until we go shopping tomorrow. I want yall to see what I got." I said walking through the doorway. I turned around and gave the bellboy a helluva tip; after all he did help me in the elevator and closed the door.

"Wow, mommy, what cha' buy me?" Diamond sang. "Well, look in the bags, it's all there. First, let me get my stuff out. I got yall two outfits apiece and some undies and PJ's." I told them handing over the bags. "Oh, my God! MA! This is gorgeous! Is this mine?" Jewel was asking, holding up the Dolce and Gabanna dress. "Yes, that's yours, and it has the matching boots." I said, with a smile. "Man Lil E, that outfit is fly. I like Gucci on you lil' bro'." Sapphire said, just as she pulled out her Prada outfit. "AW! This can't be mine! OH MY GOD!!! Thanks ma, thanks." She was screaming, almost

216

crying. "You're welcome baby, you're all welcome. And, you don't have to thank me for anything. I'm your mother and I'm supposed to make sure yall got everything yall need. And, at the time I felt you needed some Prada, and you some Dolce', enjoy. Oh, look what I found at Fredrick's of Hollywood." I said as I pulled the bag out. I handed them their bags that I had stuffed in one big bag and watched the looks on their faces. That's was all I needed. That made me happy.

Diamond and Eric found their jammies and were all excited too. I felt good knowing that I could provide my children with the things they needed, as well as wanted. "Yo ma, you have the sweetest taste. I swear; I love you." Jewel was saying, with the biggest smile. "Well good, 'cause I'm going out tonight and I want yall to watch the kids. I'ma pay you too; 'cause I know this is supposed to be a little vacation. And, we're still going shopping tomorrow."

"Cool, where you going and who you going wit'? Your friend, Noni?" she asked. "Nope. Remember the guy I introduced yall to earlier? Well, he's taking me to the premier of the new Will Smith movie, "I Am Legend." I said, nonchalantly. "WHAT?!" was the response I got from both the older girls. My youngest two were already in the

217

living room watching Nickelodeon. "Yes, it's no big deal; I told yall we were old friends." I said, trying to play it down. "Well, what time he gonna be here?" Sapphire asked, looking at the clock. It was already 7:45. "At 9:30." I said. "Well you better hurry up and take a shower, I'm glad you got your feet done. Where's the outfit you wearing, so we can check it out." Jewel said, as we all headed towards my room.

The girls were acting like I had never dated before. Well, I guess I hadn't dated since all that shit went down, that Kyra was responsible for. "Girls, I got this," I said, just then Sapphire found my lingerie set. "OH MY GOD, OH MY GOD!!!!" was all I heard. "Ma this is beautiful. Are you sure you supposed to wear this? Are these real diamonds?" she asked in amazement. "Yes, baby to both of your questions. They are real and I am supposed to wear them." I said, and smiled. "Well, I wish I had a set like this." Jewel was saying. "Girls I got yall. I told yall we going shopping tomorrow." I said to them. Already knowing I had seen a set for each of them. "Now scoot so I can get ready." I said shooing the girls out of my room.

They were too cute. I can't wait to see the look on their faces tomorrow when I take them to get theirs; or the young lady that worked there. I laid

218

everything out on the bed and headed for the bathroom. As I washed up in the shower, I thought about the night ahead. I wonder what he has planned. I mused. I wasn't sure what was happening, I just knew it felt good. I started humming to myself while I dried off, well, I thought, here goes nothing. I went over to the bed and started to lotion my body with some body lotion I got from Fredrick's. Mmmmmm, that smells good, I hope it lasts the whole night. I got up and stared at the lingerie I had purchased. Am I really supposed to wear this?

I picked up the bra and twirled it between my fingers and thought that it wasn't as heavy as I thought. I put it on and was like, hey, this is comfortable. I picked up the thong a little more cautiously. I really wasn't sure about this one but fuck it. I slipped them on and they were comfortable as well. Thank the Lord. I thought. I wasn't afraid to pull the garter up my leg now. I walked over to the closet and closed it so I could look at myself in the full length mirror that was attached. I turned all around, looking at my luscious curves and flat stomach. I had no stretch marks and to say my body was beautiful was an understatement. I had what a lot of women pay to get. I had a perfect set of tits and my ass was slammin'. I had let my hair grow real long; it hung

219

just at my waist, and dyed jet black and of course; my gorgeous eyes. No matter what my age, these puppies keep 'em coming back for more. Yeah, if I were a man, I would fuck the shit out of me too.

I withdrew from the mirror and finished putting on my clothes. The affect was simply breathless. Wait 'til Leo gets a load of me. I was gonna knock him dead in his tracks. I pulled out my make-up kit and pulled on my apron and got to work. Didn't have to do much, just apply some teal eye shadow then some gloss, and that was it. I never did need make-up. I brushed my hair and I was ready. I looked over at the clock and it read, 9:15. Whew, and not a moment too soon. I grabbed my clutch and headed out the door. When I walked into the living room of the suite, the kids went ballistic. "WOW! MY GOD MOM! LOOK AT YOU!" they all shouted, at the same time. "Why, thank you. Well, I'm about to head out. I have my cell if yall need me and yall be good. I love yall." I said, waving my hand and walking out the door at the same time. I felt pretty good; I was loving this dress. The way the dress hung off the shoulder on the left side was killer with the diamond studded bra I was wearing. I knew it was well worth the money I had spent today.

Welcome to My Hood

22. Oh What a Night.

When I walked off the elevator, all eyes were on me; men and women. Some guys almost lost their jaws. I tell you men are so predictable. Give 'em a pretty face and a banging body and they're putty in your hands. "Excuse me, miss but I must say, you are absolutely gorgeous, may I ask your name?" this older white guy asked. I was used to it; they came in all shapes, colors and sizes. "Memorie; thank you." I said, smiling into his eyes. He was stunned. And before he could come out of his trance, Leo walked up. "Damn baby! You are killing that dress." He said, completely ignoring the gentleman that was standing there. "Why thank you. You don't look too bad yourself." I said, admiring his Armani suit, and Gators. The suit was all white, and so where the gators. He looked absolutely magnificent. "Well, you ready to go?" he asked, offering his arm. I gladly took it and looked back at the gentleman that was still standing there, and waved bye.

"You are one fine sista'. I hope you don't mind me saying so. I can't wait for the movie premier to be

T.E Cooper

over with. I want you alone." He said, walking up to an all-white stretch Hummer. "Wow, you go all out, huh." I said, thinking it was a rental. "Well, I bought this puppy 'bout a year ago and from time to time I like to take it for a spin. Besides, I can't drive tonight; I plan on doing something else with my hands." And there was that devilish grin again. The driver opened the back door for us. It was huge on the inside. I tried not to let it show, that I was definitely, impressed. "So Leo, there's no way you got all this doing what you was doing when I knew you long ago. Tell me, what does this new Leo, really do for a living?" I asked, trying to start a conversation. 'Cause just looking at him, was making my pussy drip. "Well, you're right, there's no way the cops would let me live like this. I sell beats. You know, produce." He said, while pouring us some drinks.

"Really, anything I know?" I asked, getting more interested by the second. "Okay, you know that joint that Neyo and Fab did called "You Make Me Better"? Well, I did the beats." He said, with a smile. I could tell he was very proud of himself. Shit, he had the right to be proud, hell the nigga came from the gutta' gutta'. It always felt good to see a young black man make it. "Wow, I love that song. Are you serious? Okay what else?" I asked, eager to hear more. "Well, let me think. I did the

222

beats on that track called "Lollipop, by Lil Wayne, I also did most of the beats on Mary J. Blige's new CD." Wow, I was double impressed. Mary was my girl. I liked Lil Wayne too, but you know Mary is the shit. "Wow that's a lot under your belt. If nobody ever told you, I'm proud of you." I said.

Then all of a sudden he was tongue kissing me like his life depended on it. And he was a helluva kisser too. Damn, I think I just creamed all in these diamond studded drawers. He stopped kissing me to start kissing my neck. The next thing I knew, the brotha had his head between my legs, and was tongue kissing my pussy. He knew just what spots to hit. He started licking my clit and finger fucking me at the same time. I was in heaven. This nigga was working my pussy like it was his full time job, and he was gonna get a promotion. I started to move my hips and literally, started to fuck his mouth. I couldn't help myself. It felt so damn good, I knew I was about to nut. "Oh, shit, Leo, you better stop, you gonna make me cum." I said breathless.

"That's what I want. I wanna taste your juices. Cum baby; cum all in my mouth." He said then dived back in. well I was never one for not giving someone what they wanted, so I did just that, I nutted so hard, all over and in that nigga's mouth. Right there in the back of the Hummer. When he

223

T.E Cooper

was finished, I was still horny and tried to undo his pants but he stopped me, with a wicked grin. "You, are gonna have to wait." He said chuckling. I just looked at him. There was not much I could do other than rape him, so I sat up and got myself together.

I looked out the window and saw that we had arrived, and it was crazy. There were people everywhere! They had a red carpet down and we pulled right up to it. "Ready?" Leo asked, extending his hand. "Ready as I'll ever be." I said, taking his hand and exiting the Hummer. As soon as we stepped out onto the red carpet, photographers were everywhere. Snapping pictures and asking all kinds of questions. Wow, Leo really was somebody. We made our way into the movie theater while stopping here and there to pose for pictures. I was eating it up. I loved all the attention, posing every chance I got. We finally made it into the theater and man oh man. There were stars everywhere! And everyone seemed to know Leo. We stopped to talk to so many people, but I promised myself that I would always remember talking to Will and Jada.

I was star struck. I couldn't find my mouth, much less anything to say. Jada was asking Leo if he could have his agent call her 'cause she had a song that she wanted him to produce the beats for. I

224

couldn't believe it. Jada Pinkett-Smith wanted my date to do a song with her. This was too much. Leo finished his conversation with Will and Jada then we proceeded to the theater.

"Damn Leo. You didn't tell me it would be like this. I'm sure glad I decided on this dress. What would you have done, had I not had anything to wear?" I said playfully. "Well, I would have just bought you one on the way here. There was no way I was coming here, without you on my arm." He said, leaning in to give me a kiss. "Well, what about tomorrow? You know we gonna be in all the tabloids. Did you see all those paparazzi?" I asked, with some concern. I didn't know anything about his career and I didn't want to be the one to jeopardize it. I realized that he had a lot going on and I didn't want to be the 'cause of a scandal. "Shit what they gonna say? That I was with one fine ass lady? I ain't worried about that shit. That's the shit that nigga's be all stressed out about. Not me. I just go with the flow and let the chips fall wherever. Don't worry your pretty little head about it." He said; squeezing my hand letting me know it was all good.

"If you say so; I sure don't mind. I'm sure my girl, Clara, is gonna give me the twenty questions." I said, with a laugh. "What you gonna tell her?" Leo

225

asked. I had to look over, cause I thought I heard some seriousness come into his voice. "I'm not sure. Why, got any suggestions?" I countered. "Well, you could tell her, I'm your man." He said, dead serious. "My man? I don't know; I mean, yeah we've known each other for a while. But we just saw each other again, after what seems like a lifetime. How you know I ain't got any skeletons in my closet that might mess with your career? 'Cause you know, the public can be ruthless. Plus, don't you think we should get to know each other a little better, before we go committing ourselves to each other." I was serious. I mean, sure this nigga was fine, but how I know he ain't gonna change? Plus, there's the distance thing. How will that work out? I was truly interested, but I was a little cautious. Was I ready for another relationship? "Well, tell you what. We can take it slow. Not too slow, but I understand where you coming from. 'Cause there some things that you might not be willing to deal with. So we can feel each other out. But just to let you know, I don't wait long and I always get what I want. And right now, that's you." He said and turned his head towards the movie screen.

I sat there thinking about what he had said, wondering if it could work. I had the kids to think about and like I said; the long distance thing. But if I really wanted to, could I make this work? I sat

226

there daydreaming about what it would be like to be, Leo's woman. Could I handle it? Well I decided to think about that another time, right now I had a fine man on my arm and we had the whole night ahead of us.

T.E Cooper

23. Another Chapter.

The movie turned out to be really good. That Will can act his ass off. "So what you wanna do? Go out to eat, go to a party, or go to my house?" he said, insinuation all in his question. This man had just eaten the hell out of my pussy, and I was eager to see what else would happen but I was famished. "Well, do you have a chef? 'Cause if you do, we can head to your place. But if not, I think it would be best if we got something to eat." I said, with a smile. "Ha, ha, hungry? Well, since you mentioned it, yes I do have a chef at home. As a matter-of-fact, I'll call him now and tell him we're on the way. What do you want to eat?" he asked, with his cell to his ear. "Anything that's plentiful." I said, and laughed. "Okay, how 'bout some steak with some baked potatoes, a salad and grilled corn on the cob." My mouth was watering already. "Sounds great to me." I said and sat back and watched the night scenery of Georgia. I was always in awe of the beauty of Georgia, it felt so serine.

I think I might buy a boat. Yeah, when I get home

228

I'ma have to look into that. We drove for about 30 more minutes before we got off the freeway. We made a right, and drove on for what seemed about, 20 more minutes then we turned into the most beautiful neighborhood I had ever seen. Now, don't get me wrong, my neighborhood was nothing to sneeze at but this, this was absolutely amazing. The homes were all mansions, and the yards were immaculately kept. We drove down the first street and made a left, then we drove down that street and made another right, then we drove some more. "Dang boy; where you stay; on the river?" I asked, joking about how long it was taking to get to his home. Even though; we were already in the neighborhood. "Yeah, I know right. You think you're here, and then you still got to ride. I like it like this. See, my house really is on the river. And it's the only one on my street. You can't miss it. Keep looking." He said and motioned for me to look out the window. And he was right. As soon as we made a left, I saw it. The only way to describe it is; the Cinderella castle at Disney World. I thought the house that me and E shared was something but this, this was in a whole 'nother league. This nigga was paid; ain't no doubt about that.

"Leo, it's beautiful. Did you pick this out yourself?" I asked, still looking at the massive home as we drove up the winding driveway. "Well actually, I

T.E Cooper

designed it." He said, with a kool-aid grin. "Quit playin'! You designed this house, for real? I thought you said; you sold beats for a living?" I said, unable to believe that he designed something so beautiful himself. "Well I do, but I like to draw and this is the house I always wanted. I drew the blueprint a long time ago. You know, when I was in the game. I told myself, that one day it would be mine. And here it is. This is the house I want to raise my family in." he said, with true conviction. "Well, it's amazing, to say the least." I said, as we exited the Hummer. Once I stepped out of the truck and onto the grounds, I was simply amazed. I loved everything about the outside and I was dying to see the inside. "Come on and give me a tour." I said, pulling him towards the gregariously large double front doors. "Okay, slow down." Leo said, with laughter in his voice.

As we approached the doors, they swung open. An older gentleman was standing there waiting on us to arrive at the top of the stairs. "Good evening, Master Jones. Did you enjoy the movie?" the gentleman asked. "Yes, I did Maurice. Thank you. Let me introduce you to my friend; Memorie or as everyone calls her; Meme. Meme, this is Maurice, my friend." He said, introducing us. "Ah, Master Jones, you do me justice. I am his butler, ma'am. For some reason he refuses to see that. That's why I

230

call him Master Jones, so he can get used to it." Maurice, the butler, said with a smile. "And for the last time, please call me Leo. I don't like being called anyone's master." He said, with a scowl. I just laughed at the interaction between the two of them. You could tell that they were truly friends and that both cared for the other. Maurice escorted us towards what I assumed was the kitchen and Leo said, "Please tell the cook to set us a table on the terrace in the master suite; I'm going to give her a tour." He said, guiding me out of the kitchen.

"How long has he worked for you?" I asked curious. "Well, he was actually friends with my father and he's actually my Godfather; if you can believe that. Anyway, when my dad died about 2 years ago, he came to stay with me. He refused not to work, "for his stay" as he puts it. So I just go along. He's quite hilarious actually. He likes to pretend that he really is a butler." He said, laughing. We were walking down a long hallway with pictures on either side. "Wow, I see you're into art." I said, admiring his collection. "Well, Maurice really picked out everything, he's the art buff. He said that it made my house seem more refined." He said, looking at one picture in particular. "Why would he say that? The house is beautiful. I think it's perfect." "Well, you've only seen the outside, the kitchen and the hallway. I also

231

have a studio, a pool hall, and..." "An indoor swimming pool!" I said, taking in the magnificent pool. It was gorgeous. It had to be Olympic size and it was in the shape of a gigantic heart. "Why is it shaped like a heart?" I asked, stilling staring. "Well, I always thought that I would only occupy it with my one true love." He said, with that wicked grin again.

"Come on let's get in." he said pulling me towards the double doors that led to the pool. "I can't, I don't have a bathing suit and besides I thought we were going to eat?" I said, a little skeptical. "Don't worry, you don't need a suit and we can eat in the pool." He said as we entered the pool area. I looked around in amazement. He had this prepared all along. He had candles floating in the pool and a table set for two. It was the most romantic thing I had ever seen. He walked me over to the table and pulled my chair out. "Well, what do you like to drink?" he asked, seduction all in his tone. "Well a chocolate martini would be nice. But if you don't have one, a glass of white wine would be fine." I said smiling. I knew what he wanted. Me plastered And I was down, 110%! "Well anything the lady wants, she shall have." He said then went over to the intercom. He pushed a button and told someone on the other end that he was ready to order. "Wow, is this really your house? Or are you

232

just trying to impress me?" I said, jokingly. "Yes, this is me and yes I am trying to impress you. How am I doing?" "So far, so good but let's wait and see how the chocolate martini tastes then I can judge." I said, laughing.

Someone who could pass for a waiter appeared in the doorway then Leo motioned him in and told him what we wanted to drink. The waiter nodded his head and left the room. "How about a little privacy?" "And how are we gonna get that? The room is made of glass." I said motioning my hands around me. "Watch this." He said then went to the other side of the room. And in an instant the room went dark. It was like something had come and covered it up then the ceiling seemed to open up and show the stars. Now, this was some romantic shit. Damn! If he only knew how wet my pussy was right now. Whew! I gotta control myself. I could sure tell I hadn't had sex in a while, 'cause at this moment in time, I was horny as hell. "Well, what do you think?" he asked, pulling his chair to sit right next to mine. "I think it's simply breathtaking. I love the stars, you know. They're just so beautiful." I said, answering dreamily, trying not to focus on him so much.

"Well not as beautiful as you." He said leaning over and kissed me passionately. I almost passed

233

out. Damn, this nigga was good! Damn, this nigga Tasted, so good! He let his tongue play in and out of my mouth, liking my lips from the inside out. Ooooh. I heard myself moan. I pulled away quickly as the waiter returned with our drinks. I thought he was bringing a glass apiece but he bought the whole damn bar! Well a rolling bar actually, but still. This nigga had plans I see and damned if I wasn't down for the ride. Leo walked over and locked the door; I had noticed that when the waiter brought our drinks, he also pulled a tray in with our food. The setting was perfect. Leo placed our food on the table, side by side. He placed my chocolate martini in my hand and led the way to the table. The blinds were closed on the inside pool and the roof was open. It was a clear night out and you could see the stars and constellations perfectly. We both sat down noticing how famished we both were. We tore the food up while having the most pleasant conversation the entire time.

I had never met anyone who had actually gone to see the "Great Pyramids" or "Stonehenge". Leo said, since he had the money he wanted to see the world, not just the party spots but something that would have meaning in his life. I told him that I would love to one day be able to take my children to see those very things. I always wanted them to know that there was so much more out there than what we see at home. He shared my sentiments. I know we had to have sat there for hours talking and drinking. I was feeling pretty good then the sun started to rise and it was the most beautiful thing I had ever seen. I started to cry. I mean seriously cry. I don't know what made me do it but it damn sure came out. It was probably the alcohol. Then Leo started to kiss my tears away. And I never thought in a million years that someone sucking and licking your cheek could be a turn on but damn, did that shit feel good! He continued to kiss my cheek, then my neck. Then he stood me up and slid my dress down, while he looked at me on his knees. I looked down at him to see what was going on and I swear I saw a tear fall from that nigga's eyes. "You're so damn beautiful." He said and began to slowly and erotically kiss my bellybutton. He traveled from my navel to my inner thighs.

By this time I had sat down. He was literally making me weak in the knees. Then he found my spot and all I can say is, DAMN!!! This nigga French kissed my pussy like it was the last on earth and humanity itself depended on it! I felt myself start to rotate my hips and I started to slowly fuck his mouth. OH MY GOD! "Yeah baby, fuck daddy in the mouth, come on baby, cum. Daddy wanna taste those juices you got built up in you." He said

235

muffled by my neatly shaved pussy. And then he put one, then two fingers in my pussy and started to work my shit like his fingers were a dick! And at the same time, he was steady stroking my clit real slow with his tongue. I couldn't do anything but give into the feeling then I spread my legs and put my hands on my pussy lips then held my lips open so he could really eat my shit, and before I knew it, I felt my body start to shake, I tried to stop him so he could put his dick in while I came, but no, this nigga was for real when he said he wanted to taste all my juices. And tasted them he did. He held fast to my thighs and pulled me toward his face and sucked and licked up every drop of cum my pussy had to offer. He was licking and sucking so good, I heard slurping sounds, and that just sent me into a fury, I wanted to taste him the way he tasted me. I stepped out of the chair, my pussy still in his mouth and told him to sit down.

"My turn." I said with a sly smile. I knew I looked hot with my real diamond lingerie on and my banging ass body, I knew I was about to send this nigga to heaven. I made a show of going down on him. I slowly licked his nipples until each one stood at attention. I acted like they were his dick and they tasted so good. I slowly trailed my way down to his huge dick. Damn, it looked so smooth and I was salivating just looking at it. I slowly tickled the

236

Welcome to My Hood

head with my tongue. Mmm, just like I thought, damn he tasted good. I licked some more while holding his balls in one hand and slowly taking the whole thing in my mouth a little bit at a time. Once I got the whole of it in my mouth, I let it sit there for a minute while I played with his balls. I came back up and started licking on his large shaft like it was a lollypop. And then I started spittin' on it and sucking and licking my spit along with some pre-ejac, liked I loved the way he tasted and felt in my mouth. And I did. While I sucked and slurped on his dick I began to fondle myself. That nigga's dick instantly got even harder in my mouth. I stuck one then two of my fingers in my pussy and started to fuck myself while I sucked him off. In no time at all I tasted the salty sweetness of his juices. When I tasted it, I really started to suck and swallow everything he had to offer.

After I knew he was finished, I continued to suck away until he was rock hard again then I stood up and told him to sit back and enjoy the ride. I stood over him so I could ride this pony while he was sitting in the chair. I slid my wet pussy down on his dick slowly at first then I just went wild. His dick felt so good going in and out of my pussy, I screamed. I slowed down the ride, letting his dick slowly move in and out of my pussy. My shit was so wet; you would have thought it was title wave in

237

that bitch. I mean; I was slow stroking that dick and all you could hear was "squish, squish". "Damn baby that pussy wet as hell; I knew it would be. Damn baby, fuck that dick just like that." He said and leaned back in the chair some more giving me some more leeway with his dick. When he did that I twirled around, with his help and was sitting backwards on the dick. I went up and down real slow, twirling my ass as I did. When I would come to the top of his dick, I would just sit my pussy on his tip and let my pussy lips kiss the head of his dick. Damn that shit sent shivers up my pussy. I continued to do this until he thought he was about to cum again. "Aw hell no; I ain't cumming again without really fuckin' this pussy." He said, then stood up and bent my ass over the table, propped both my legs up on it. With my ass in the air and my legs spread wide, he proceeded to fuck the shit out of me. I don't mean he just pounded it, he massaged it and all. He played with my clit then licked his fingers and ran them down my tits, there were times he would stop fucking me just to eat my pussy from the back. He was actually fuckin' my pussy with his tongue. I mean, he let it go in and out while he licked all around my outer walls, at the same time, massaging my clit like it was a baby. Damn this nigga was good at what he did.

I couldn't take it anymore and had to turn around,

238

he didn't miss a beat. He just spread my legs more, so he could get a better taste and started fucking my pussy hole with his tongue again. When he stopped, he started to finger fuck me and smile down at me at the same time. What he was doing was feeling so damn good. I was massaging my breast, playing with my nipples while his hand took possession of my pussy then he plunged that entire dick up my pussy but I was ready, I took that dick like a champ. My pussy was so sloppy wet; he could have driven a bulldozer up my ass. I wrapped my legs around his back and did my best to fuck him back. This is what I'm talking about. I knew I was gonna like this nigga. "Baby, before you cum; pull out. I want you to cum in my mouth and on my titties." I said seductively in his ear while he was giving me the fuck of my life. "Ooohh babbbby, I'm bout to cum." He said pulling. I dropped to my knees as he finished massaging his dick while his salty, seamen shot out. I put my tongue on the bottom of his dick then let him nut all over my lips and rubbed it in my breasts as it ran down my mouth. I was sucking and licking all around and on his dick as he continued to ejaculate on me. When his fluids stopped; I sucked and slurped up every ounce of nut he had on his hands, nuts and dick. I let that nigga know what it felt like to be weak in the knees. As we lay on the side of the pool; it had turned completely daylight.

239

T.E Cooper

"Lordy, where did the time go?" I said smiling, getting ready to get up. "Wait a minute, where you going?" Leo asked, pulling me back down. "Remember, I'm here with my kids and I promised to take them shopping today." I said. "Yeah, you're right. They're probably wondering when we gonna join them for breakfast." He said with a sly grin. "Are you going with us?" I asked, getting up and putting my dress on. "Well actually, I was thinking about it but I have some errands to run. But, I did get a car for you and the kids to ride around in, so you don't have to worry about getting lost or anything, and one more thing... the kids are downstairs in the den waiting on us." He said and smiled. I looked at him incredulously. "What are you talking about?" I asked dumbfounded. "Well, I kinda thought we were going to have a long night, so I took the liberty of sending for the kids when you were asleep. They bought your clothes so you can take a shower." He said grabbing my hand. "Right this way; we never made it to the bedroom, so this will be your first time." This man was incredible. How was I ever gonna leave and go back to Charlotte?

We made our way down another long hallway. This house sure has a lot of them. We turned left and stopped in front of some double doors. The

240

doors were crafted beautifully, they had all kinds of angels engraved in them and they looked like they were made of ivory. The door handles were gold, and it looked real. Leo grabbed both of the handles and opened the doors. To say the room was magnificent would be an understatement. It was simply heavenly. And that wasn't doing it justice. For one; it had the biggest bed in the world! I had never seen a bed that big and I owned a California King. The bed was a four poster bed with blue and cream shear's hanging all around it. The room also had one of the most exquisite fireplace's I had ever seen. The mantle was made of the same design and texture as the two double doors that led to the room. All the accessories were also in gold. It had an alcove that looked out over the water. I could get lost in this room and not even try to find my way out. "Well, what do you think?" Leo asked looking at me. "Well, I can say one thing, you sure have taste; it's beautiful. Now where is the bathroom? I wanna go ahead and shower so I can eat; I'm famished!" I said planting a kiss on his lips. Leo closed his eyes and pulled me close then returned the kiss with a passion. "Come on now; if we keep this up, I'll never go shopping." I said laughing and pulling out of the embrace.

"Okay, this way; the bathroom is actually quite big. Did you wanna take a shower or bath?" he

241

asked me leading me into a huge bathroom that had two showers and two tubs as well as double sinks. I had seen the double sinks before, but never double showers. "What's up with two of everything?" I asked; my curiosity getting the best of me. "Well to be honest, I couldn't decide. I wanted a sunken tub, but I also wanted a Jacuzzi and I wanted the shower that has the 20 shower heads, and I wanted a steam bath with the shower. So I just decided to have it all in one room." He said laughing. "I know it sounds crazy, but when you from the hood and you make a come up like I did; the first thing you do, is start spending money like crazy. Thank God that faze is gone. I would have been broke in another year or two with the way I spent money my first year of getting a deal." He said reminiscing. "Well, we certainly have room. I think I'ma go for the 20 head shower. I have one at home and it soothes those aching joints." I said, smiling. I walked over to the shower to turn it on and set the sprays. I was ready for this. I swear I needed it. "I think I'ma soak in the Jacuzzi. Go ahead and take your shower." Leo said heading for the Jacuzzi. "There are towels and washcloths in the cabinet over there, and you have some shower gel. I got some for you from my sister's store the other day." He said then he took off his clothes. It took all my willpower to get in the shower, 'cause that was one sexy nigga!

242

Once I stepped in the shower and the sprays started to hit me in various places; my body started to get soothed. I stood under the spray of the water for a good 10 minutes, just letting the water take over my body. I took my time lathering up the washcloth and washing my body. The hot water felt good. Afterwards I dried off with a towel that you could use as a blanket and walked in the bedroom. Leo had already gotten out of the Jacuzzi and hopped in the other shower before I was even finished. I know I stayed in the shower for at least 45 minutes; I was refreshed now. Taking a long shower always did that for me. When I walked in the room I didn't see Leo, although my things were laid out on the monstrous bed. As I walked over to the bed; Leo came out of, what I guessed to be the closet, although it resembled a large room.

"Oh, there you are. I thought you had drowned in there." He said laughing. He was carrying some jeans, a shirt and a shoe box. "I know those kids are like; what the fuck?" I said. "Well, they've had some orange juice and muffins for now. The cook is excited that so many people are here for breakfast, I'm quite sure we're gonna have a feast." He said putting on a white tee. "Good, cause I feel like I could eat a country." I said putting on the black and pink ensemble I had gotten from his sister's

243

store. After I was dressed, I went into the bathroom and used a brush to pull my wild hair into a ponytail and I was ready.

Together we walked into the den to greet the kids. They didn't even hear us come in; they were engrossed in the theater sized movie screen. "Hey yall!" I said, walking over to the kids. "Oh; hey ma; you look nice." Diamond said. "What yall watching?" I asked. "Finding Nemo; you know that's my movie." Jewel said with a grin. "Well since you like the movie so much, we can eat breakfast in here. I'll be right back." Leo said then walked out the room. "I like him; he's nice. Guess what he said mom?" Eric was saying excitedly. "What baby?" I asked snuggling up to him. "He said that if you would let him; he could take me to see the Atlanta Hawks play the Charlotte Bobcats! It's a playoff game mom! Please can I go? Please?" he said giving me his best begging act. I couldn't help but laugh at him, he was so silly. "Well, what about shopping?" I asked. "He said, I could chill with him today, so I don't have to go. You know I hate shopping." Lil E said. When did he talk to my son? I would have to ask him. "Well, I'll see what he's talking about when he comes back."

"Hey, ma, I really like him. Did you know we were going shopping in a stretch Hummer!" Sapphire
244

was yelling. "What color?" I asked thinking it was the same one from last night. "CANDY APPLE RED!!!" Sapphire yelled even more excited. "Yeah, he said the next time we ride; I could get to choose the color. But I have to say, that red is dope!" Jewel piped in. Well, one thing for sure. I don't have to worry about him trying to take my money; he had enough of his own.

Leo walked in just then. "Well, breakfast will be served shortly. I hope yall are hungry, 'cause Cook; cooked a feast." He said, taking a seat next to me. "Leo, please tell my mom I don't have to go shopping with them and that I can go to the game with you." Lil E started in on him. "Yeah, I told him he could chill with me today and later on we could catch the game. I got a press box you know. He'll be perfectly safe." He said. "Well okay but don't complain about any of the clothes I pick out for you." I said to him laughing. "Thanks mom." He said, giving me a hug and a kiss. "Wow, you need to take him more often. Since he's gotten big; he don't ever want to hug or kiss his old mom." I said, joking. "Aw mom, I still give you hugs and kisses." Eric said, sheepishly. Just then the person that resembled a waiter came in with what was surely a feast for kings. "Wow! We're gonna gain 10 pounds just looking at all this food." Jewel said, with a smile. "Like I said, Cook is glad to be able to cook

245

for more than just me. Most of the time; I don't get to eat at home, always on the go." Leo said. "Mom I could get used to this. And wow, it's delicious." Sapphire said. With that; we all dug in to a most delicious breakfast.

"Well that was good. I guess we can head on out. Eric, are you ready?" Leo said checking to see if he had everything. "Yup, ready." Eric said, happily. I couldn't believe my son. Well I guess I could. It probably was boring for him to go shopping with his sisters and his mom. Me and the girls told them bye and headed out ourselves. "Lord have mercy; you guys were right, it is big." I said staring at the stretch Hummer; Leo had rented us for the day. "I know; I love it! I wish we could have one of these every day." Sapphire said, all excited. "Girls, now let's act civilized. We have a lot of shopping to do, so let's get going." I said, as we entered the Hummer. The inside was really nice, you know with TVs and everything. Diamond loved the fridge, which Leo had instructed them to make sure they had packed with stuff. I couldn't believe my luck. I almost don't want to go back to Charlotte tomorrow. We took in the sites as the driver took us everywhere.

And as promised I took the girls to Fredricks so they could get some diamond studded undies.

246

They were ecstatic; I figured they would be. I mean, this was the best store we had come to by far. Sure; we had hit Lenox Mall up pretty good. I know the girls spent at least 10 g's on themselves, but this was different. I don't know, maybe because it was so intimate but we loved every minute of it. And just as I thought; the young lady named Kymia, came over to help. "Well, hello. I didn't expect to see you back so soon. And who are these gorgeous girls?" she said, with a smile. "Well, these are my girls. Girls this is the young lady who helped me out yesterday. She picked out some really cute stuff for yall." I said. "Thanks." They said. "Well, what brings you back to us today?" Kymia asked. "We want some diamond studded undies." Jewel almost screamed. "Ha, ha. Well okay ladies; come this way." And we followed her into the vault. "Wow, look at all this stuff. I'll be glad when I can wear stuff like this." Diamond said. "Well you still have a little ways to go, but today we gonna get your sisters something." I said. The girls started looking around the vault to see what they liked. They each wanted to get more than one set, and I was like what the hell, you only live once.

As they showed Kymia what they wanted and asked her to get their items, I wandered around to see if the set Kymia wanted was still there, and it was. I told her I would like it and didn't tell her

247

why. I saw the disappointment in her eyes, but I gave away nothing. After she had retrieved everything that we wanted we left the safe. Kymia took our vault items to the counter and I asked her to put the special one in a separate bag. I told the girls to look around some more as would I.

I wasn't interested in buying anything else for myself; I wanted to be able to talk to my travel agent. I called her and told her what the deal was and she said cool; she gave me all the info I would need to give Kymia and told me what she would need Kymia to send to her. I was excited to do something so nice for someone I didn't even know. When I was done talking to my travel agent, I went to see the manager. I told her what I had done and for whom and asked her if she could help. She informed me that Kymia hadn't taken a day off since she had been working for them, not even for her wedding and that it would be a pleasure to do something nice for her because she truly deserved it. When I heard that; I really felt good knowing that I was doing something nice for someone who deserved it. I rounded up the girls while the manager got Kymia.

After we rung up our purchases I told Kymia I had something for her. The manager reached behind the counter and pulled out the bag containing the

248

diamond studded lingerie set. Kymia reached in the bag and pulled out the lingerie set and looked from me to the manager. "What's this?" she asked perplexed. "Well, since you have been so nice to me and the girls; I thought you deserved it. Plus, you liked it so much." I said, with a smile. "I can't take this, it's, it's, way too expensive. But thank you, thank you very much." She said trying to hand me the bag. "Oh no; I'm not taking that back, besides; you have to have something sexy to wear on your honeymoon." I said, still smiling. "Honeymoon? What honeymoon?" Kymia asked more confused than before. "Well, I talked to your manager and we decided that it was time for you to take a vacation. So Ms. Kymia, you and your husband will be taking a cruise to the Bahamas." The look on that girls face was priceless; that made me feel so good. You know the old saying, "What good is having money if you can't do something nice." Well that was my nice.

When me and the girls left, Kymia was still smiling in shock. "Wow ma; that was nice. I hope they enjoy themselves." Jewel said. "Well, she deserved it, you know. I mean from what her manager told me; she's a good hardworking person that deserves it." I told her. We all climbed into the hummer and started out. "Well, let me call Leo and see where him and Lil E are at." I said pulling out my phone. I

T.E Cooper

called Leo and he informed me that they were still at the game and that they would meet us at his house later on, so he could take us out to eat before we left. I said okay and told the driver to head to the hotel. "Well, we might as well check out since we won't be staying there anymore." I sat back and relaxed and enjoyed the ride. I started thinking about all the shit I had been through and what it took for me to get where I was. I was very thankful.

Our trip to Atlanta was really good for me. Leo and I said we would stay in touch and he said he would be up to Charlotte when he got some free time. That was cool with me, cause being with him stirred up too many emotions that I still wasn't ready to deal with. I still hadn't been in a serious relationship, or any relationship for that matter, with anyone since Eric and I wasn't sure if I ever would be. For the time being, that was how I wanted it. Just me and my kids; no man; no complications. I knew that I would have to deal with a bunch of bull when I got back, so I didn't let anyone know I was home for a few days. I knew that sooner or later Clara would call or come by the house. And I was right. When I got home from work on Wednesday, she was sitting in my driveway. "What's up chick?" she said, getting out of her car. "Nothing much; what's up with you?" I said, letting up my garage. Clara followed me in and came in the house with me. "Well nothing much, just can't believe your girl." She said, getting straight to the point. "Well, let's get in the house good before we get on that subject. How was work?" I asked, heading towards the kitchen.

"Same ole', same ole'! Different day, same shit. What's up with you though? How was the trip to the A?" Clara said, going in the fridge to get an apple. "Well, girl, you won't believe the shit we bought. We went to this Fredricks; man that thing was a mall, all by itself and the shit they had in there would make you cry." I said while taking a drink from my water bottle. "Ooh, I bet you went crazy! You gotta let me see what you bought. I know you got some fly shit." " Oh my God, you will never believe what they had! A fricken' vault with diamond studded lingerie! You know I had to cop something for me and the girls." I said, excited. "You got the girls some too? What about me? I know you didn't forget about me." She said, smiling and rolling her eyes at the same time. "Sorry, I didn't get anything for you, but you know we can go down there anytime and do the damn thing. And girl, you will never guess what else I got while I was down there." I said, with a sly smile. "What? I know you ain't get no dick! Oh my God! You did! Tell me everything! You nasty bitch! What

251

T.E Cooper

happened? Is he cute?" Clara was rushing to get everything out at once. "Hold up girl. I'm going to tell you everything; dang!" I said still stalling. You know I had to keep her guessing for a minute. "Well, come on bitch, spill it." Clara said, ready to hear the juicy story.

"Oh, okay. I ran into this guy I hadn't seen since like, forever. His name is Leo, and yes he is fine as hell!" I said, with a smile. "Well, 'bout time. Damn girl I thought you was gonna be celibate for the rest of your life. Well tell me the juicy stuff. 'Cause the way you smiling, you got some good stuff." Clara said, laughing. "Girl, I thought so too, but oh well." I said giggling. "Me and the kids had a real good time. Leo says that he'll be in Charlotte in a couple a weeks. Maybe you can meet him when he comes." I said. "Cool; I wanna meet the nigga that put an end to that dry spell you was going through." Clara said then we walked into the den to watch a movie and get some drinks. Clara stayed at the house until about 9 that night. "Well girl, let me get out of here. I gotta go to work in the morning. Call me tomorrow so we can talk about you know who." She said giving me a hug and walking out the door.

One thing I didn't want to talk about was Kyra, but it looks like I'ma have to deal with it anyway. I

252

walked through the house turning off all the lights and checked on the kids. Diamond was already in bed and E was on the way. I walked down the hall to Jewel's room to see what she was doing. "What up ma?" Jewel said, while putting on her scarf for the night. "Nothing much; just doing my rounds. What up with you?" I asked and sat down on the bed. Usually when Jewel asks me what up, that means she's got something on her mind. "Well, I was just thinking, what's going on with Auntie Ky?" she said, sitting down next to me. Now I know my kids love them some Ky, so I really didn't know what to say and since I had never lied to my kids I was truly at a loss.

"Well, it's kind of complicated. Your Auntie did some things that just came to the light, and I'm not sure what I'm going to do right now. I need some time to think." I said, playing it safe. I didn't lie, but I didn't tell too much. "Are you talking 'bout her being E's real mom?" I just looked at her. What do I say to that? "Yeah, that and some other stuff. And for the record, I'm E's mom." "Yeah, we know that. We were just talking and we were just wondering if yall was gonna see each other again. I mean, yall been friends for a long time, ma. And yeah, what she did was trife, no lie. But people make mistakes. I mean; maybe she was just confused and got caught up. You know, that happens a lot." I looked

253

at Jewel and couldn't believe we were having this conversation. She had grown up so much, seems like I missed it, sitting here listening to her. "I know what you're saying Jewel. It's just that, sometimes when someone you really love betrays you like that, well, it's kind of hard to just let it go. I need some time to think, cause that ain't all that's going on. That's the simple part, there's some much more complicated stuff going on." I said solemnly. I was thinking about the stuff that Clara was saying on the phone when I was in Atlanta. And if any of it were true, what would I do? Would I do anything? I wasn't sure and that's why I really did need some time to think.

"I guess I understand. Whatever it is, you won't be sending us back to Philly? I mean, I love Aunt Johnnie Mae, but I love you more. And we missed you when you were gone. We don't want to have to do that again." She said, looking a little scared. I looked at my sister-daughter, and almost cried. The only reason she was asking about Ky, was 'cause she didn't want to leave me. Damn! I love my baby too. I took her in my arms and just hugged her for a minute. I knew that was what she needed, 'cause she let me hug her as tight as I wanted and didn't complain. "Oh baby; don't worry. I will never leave yall like that again. And I want you to know that the only reason I left yall that time, was because I

254

needed yall to be safe. I missed yall too, but baby I would have died if anything would have happened to yall. Especially on account of me; just know this; I will always come back for yall; no matter what. If I ever feel like I needed yall to be somewhere safe, that's what I'll do. But remember; I WILL ALWAYS BE BACK." I said, with her head in my hands. I wanted her to know that I would always be there.

"I know ma. It's just we miss you when you're gone." She said smiling and giving me a peck on the cheek. "I think you should go talk to Lil E though. I think he's just a little bit confused. I mean, he knows that you're his mom. He just doesn't understand 'bout Auntie Ky. Is it still okay if we call her that?" She said. "Sure baby. As a matter-of-fact, if yall want to still call her and talk, I understand completely. Just don't expect me to have anything to say to her right now. I can't take yalls relationship with her from yall. I know yall love her and that's okay too. And I guess I probably should go talk to E. Last time we talked it was only for a few minutes. I just don't know what to say." I said; a little worried. I was scared to death to talk to my son about his biological mother. I wasn't sure if I would lose my son tonight, and I wasn't ready for that. "Ma, listen. Don't be scared; E loves you and he knows you are his mom. You my sister for real and don't nobody know, cause it don't matter, you

255

my momma for all purposes of the word. We all love you ma, so go talk to E. He needs you right now and he's really confused." Jewel said with the wisdom of an old woman. "Okay baby. You go on to bed; I guess it's time I talk to your brother." I said getting up and giving her a hug and kiss. "Goodnight ma and good luck with E."

I walked out of Jewel's room, seeing her for the first time as an adult. Because that was sure some adult advice she gave me. Well, it's time to get it over with. Damn! I sure hope he doesn't hate me when we're through. Knock, knock. "E, you woke?" I say pushing his door open slightly, so I could look inside to see if he was already sleeping. "Yeah ma; I'm woke." I walked on in the room and shut the door. Damn, I was nervous. My palms were sweating and I know I had sweat dripping down my face.

"Hey ma what's up?" E asked, sitting up in the bed and cutting on his lamp. "Well, I thought we should talk. You know, 'bout Kyra, your mom." I said, through almost clinched teeth. She didn't deserve the right to be called E's mom, but there it was. And life ain't always pretty. "What about her?" he asked, almost with an attitude. I say almost because he knows I don't play with those attitudes towards me. "Well, don't you have any

256

questions? I mean, we talked about it a little bit, but I feel like we should really talk. Ask me anything and I'll do my best to answer. I won't lie to you, so ask away." I said, preparing myself for the worst. "Well I guess I do have some questions. You promise to tell the truth?" he asked, sitting up even more. "I promise." I said holding one hand over my heart and the other in the air.

"Okay, well, how come Auntie Ky just now telling the truth? I mean, didn't she love me?" Now this was going to be harder than I thought. "Well... I think she was scared. I mean, maybe she didn't think she could take care of you like you deserved. And if that's the case, then, yes, she loved you very much. Because if she knew she couldn't take care of you and she let someone that she knew could take care of you then, that's love. 'Cause that means, she loved you enough to make sure you were safe and loved." I said then stopped and considered what I said. Maybe she really was scared. I mean, the man she was pregnant by was her best friends' man and he showed no interest in being with her for good. "Well, she been around this whole time and she still didn't say anything. I mean, if that was you, you would have kept me no matter what!" E was upset and I wanted to ease his pain but I didn't know how. "Well of course sweetie. I will always come back for you and I will always be here for

257

you. I'm glad you know this and I want you to always remember too." I said. "I know ma; you love me; I know and I love you too. I love you even more now, for some reason. You kept me even though I wasn't yours, and you loved me. Thanks ma. And as far as Auntie Ky goes, well, I guess one day I could talk to her myself. That is, if you don't mind. I don't want to stay with her, I just got some stuff I wanna ask her; that she has to answer, but only if you want me too." He looked at me and I couldn't help but smile. My boy was growing up and I liked the man he would become. "Sweetheart, anything you want. Just let me know when you want to do this and I got your back, okay. And I want you to always know that you are my son, and I love you more than life itself. I would live, breath and die for you. Remember that always, no matter what." I said giving him a hug. "I know ma. I love you too." He said hugging me back. Wow! I got 2 hugs this weekend. Life is looking up. "Okay, now it's time for you to go to bed. Sleep tight, and say your prayers. I love you baby." I said standing and turning the light off. "Love you ma. Goodnight." And with that he was off to sleep.

I don't know why I thought our little talk would result in him wanting to go stay with Kyra. Thank God, because I know that was one thing I wouldn't let happen. Sure, when my son wanted to go and talk to his mom, I'ma take him. But she damn sure better understand that; just like he came with me, he would be leaving with me.

I went to bed that night feeling like this was the quiet before the storm; I just had a feeling. I know Kyra better than anyone, and I knew if she told the truth about E, she had ulterior motives. Kyra wouldn't have told me E was her son just for clarification. No; there was something else to this puzzle; I just had to find out what it was. I would have to get with Clara tomorrow so we can put our heads together and figure out what Kyra had planned. 'Cause if I know Kyra, and I do, I know she got a plan. It was just up to me to figure out what it was before it was too late.

As a matter-of-fact, let me call Clara right now. I don't think either one of us should go to work tomorrow or any day for that matter, until we find out what this bitch is up to. "Yo Clara." I said into the phone. "Listen; something up wit' cha' girl. I know this bitch. She wasn't confessing to make herself feel better. That bitch is up to something. I think we need to skip work for 'bout a week, so we can figure out what this ho' is up to." I said, really getting pissed. I mean; the nerve of this bitch! But that's okay, cause I'm gonna figure out what the deal is, if I gotta die. "Shiiit, I was trying to tell you

259

T.E Cooper

that this weekend; skippin' work is fine wit' me. I kinda thought the same thing, but you know her better than me. All I know is, she done some pretty foul shit to us. So yeah, I'll be there tomorrow morning bright and early. Have breakfast ready." She said and hung up. I tried to think about some of the things she said over the phone this past weekend, but couldn't. Sleep was calling my name, even if I don't sleep the whole night.

The next morning we all overslept. Ha! We were beat; nobody woke up until Clara came over. We didn't even hear her come in. Thank God she got a key, 'cause she might have been standing at the door all day. "Girl, you better wake up. Ain't the kids got school?" Clara said, laughing. I was never one to oversleep and yet here I was. "Huh? Who that? What time is it?" I asked, all at once sitting up in bed. I opened my eyes to let them focus, and they landed on Clara laughing her butt off at me. "Ha, ha, ha, ha. Girl, what the deal? You're always on time. And I'm sure this will be the first time in history that the kids will be late for school." She said pulling the covers off of me. "Damn! I was tired as hell. I couldn't sleep at all last night. I got a bad feeling 'bout this bitch." I said standing up and going to the bathroom. I washed my face and brushed my teeth and came back out the bathroom.

Welcome to My Hood

"Girl, will you help me get these kids ready. I can take a shower when we get back. And please tell me you got some kind of weed, 'cause I'm sure gonna need it." I said, going in my drawer and pulling out some sweat pants. "Girl; you stupid. But yes, I got some fire. But first, let's get these kids up and out of here. I told you to have breakfast ready, ho." Clara said, laughing some more and throwing a pillow at me. "Chile' please; you just woke me up. We gonna have to stop somewhere and get the kids something to eat, you can get something then." I said pulling my hair into a ponytail. I didn't even wrap it up last night. "That's cool with me. Come on, let's get these kids up." She said, as we walked out my room.

We decided to split the kids up, two each. Clara took Jewel and Sapphire and I took E and Diamond. We woke the kids up and they were just as surprised as me and Clara; that we had all overslept. They each got up quickly and got dressed. They moved pretty quick too; I wonder if all kids are like that. After everyone was dressed I pulled Diamonds hair into a ponytail like mine. We was thuggin' it today.

261

T.E Cooper

24. Now This.

We all peeled out the house about a quarter to ten, and didn't even care. We took the jeep since it was all of us and stopped at Bojangles on the way to the kid's school. They all went to Victory Christian Center; private school. I liked it there and the kids loved it. A lot of people say that my kids are missing out on a lot 'cause they go to private school, but I don't see it that way. I feel like my kids going to the same school throughout their school years is a plus. All the teachers and staff know them and are close to them. There aren't that many kids to a teacher in one class, so there's always lots of one on one time. Not to mention it's a Christian based school, so that was the biggest plus to me.

We arrived at the school then I went in to sign them in. The lady in the office was very understanding, seeing as how they had never been late before. I gave everybody hugs and kisses then walked to the parking lot. As I walked towards my car I couldn't help but to wonder again for the hundredth time, what Kyra was up to. I got in my jeep and looked

Welcome to My Hood

over at Clara and said, "Girl, we got a problem, and we gotta solve this shit before it gets out of hand." With that I pulled out the school parking lot, with Clara silent beside me. I drove out to 485, heading towards my house thinking all kinds of thoughts. I know Clara was probably thinking the same things I was, cause she was just as silent as me. As I came up on the Johnston Rd. exit, something popped in my head. I thought 'bout what Clara had said, when I was in Atlanta. I couldn't remember it all 'cause all I remember is I didn't want to talk about Kyra. I did remember that Clara had implied that Kyra had something to do with that shit that went down a few years ago. Now, that had to be some bullshit. True, Kyra been on some bullshit lately, but I swear I don't think she had anything to do with that shit. Damn, shit was just coming together and now this. As I pulled into my neighborhood, I had to ask Clara. "Okay, what were you talking 'bout when I was in the A?" There I put it out there, now let's see where Clara takes it.

"Girl, it's so much shit; we better wait 'til we're in the house." I agreed and we rode the rest of the way in silence. The closer we got to my house the more nervous I got. After the bomb that Kyra had already dropped, I wasn't sure if I could take any more bad news. We pulled up to my house then I hit the garage opener and we pulled in. Still in

263

silence we both exited the car and went in the house. "Hey girl spill it. What the deal?" I said, as soon as the door had closed. "Well okay, but I think we are both gonna need a drink. Let's go in the den and I'ma fill you in." I believe that walk to the den was the longest walk of my life. All kinds of shit was going through my head. I knew that whatever Clara had to say, wasn't good. I knew how devious Kyra could be. I had seen it several times. Now don't get me wrong, I wasn't scared or any shit like that. I just knew Kyra, and I knew she had fucked up. When we got into the den, Clara went over to the bar. "Girl, spill it. What the fuck is the deal?" I asked while taking my drink from her. I sipped on it and it was strong as hell. It was only a little after 11 and we were drinking. This was definitely not good. I looked at Clara and couldn't read her face. She had a blank expression on her face that was unreadable.

She took a sip of her drink and took a deep breath. Whatever she was about to say must be real heavy. "Girl, I don't know where to start. Let's see, since I already told you most of it, I guess there's only one more thing to tell." She said, looking at me strangely. I felt in my bones that I wasn't gonna like what she had to say. I mean, with all the other shit that Kyra had done, the look on her face told me this was the worst of the worst. "Come on Clara,

264

Welcome to My Hood

tell it. I mean, you done already told me the fucked up shit. Damn! It can't be much worse than the woman that I thought was my friend; my sister; was fucking my man, got pregnant by him, set him and us up and now wants to take my son. Shit, what else is there?" I said. Shit I was ready to hear it all. I needed to hear it all, because I still had love for this chick. I mean no, I won't be fucking with her no more, but I needed something else to make me stop being hurt. I mean, she was my sister for Christ sake. "She killed your mom." Clara said and then she just looked at me.

For a moment I thought she was joking. I mean, my mom died of an overdose, she wasn't killed. What the fuck was Clara talking about? "What you mean she killed my mom? My mom died of an overdose; she didn't kill my mom." I said, trying to deny the truth. The look in Clara's eye's told me she wasn't joking. She really thought that Kyra had killed my mom. "Girl, I don't know where you getting your info from, but this time it's wrong." I said trying to convince myself more than anything. I just couldn't bring myself to believe that she killed my mom. Ain't no way. I mean, true, me and moms didn't get along, but shit she was my MOM! Naw, this shit gotta be wrong. "Girl, say something. Who told you that; 'cause they don't know what they talking about." I said, looking at Clara with a

265

T.E Cooper

pleading look in my eyes. I hadn't even realized that I had starting crying. Clara got up and came over to the loveseat where I was sitting and sat down beside me. "No Meme; that shit is real. The bitch killed your mom. I ain't got all the details, but her cousin Lala told me." She said, and I just knew she was telling the truth. "All Lala said was that Kyra had always been jealous of you. No matter how good to her; you were, all she ever did was bad mouth you behind your back. I mean that girl was obsessed with having everything you had. I guess when E told her fuck her, she snapped. I'm sorry to be the one to tell you that fucked up shit, but I thought it was only right that I be the one. Your cousin Bam just found out about it too."

I just sat there with tears streaming down my face; I couldn't believe it. All this time I thought my-moms died from an overdose, but the whole time it was that bitch. "Girl; you alright? I mean, you know we gonna handle this right? That hoe had you fooled, but don't worry she gonna get hers." Clara said, taking me in her arms and rocking me back and forth. I still hadn't responded; I was in shock. Then all of a sudden I was enraged! "WHAT THE FUCK WAS THAT TRICK THINKIN'?! YOU GODDAMN RIGHT THAT BITCH GONNA PAY! I CAN'T BELIEVE THIS SHIT! AWWWWWW! THAT FUCKIN' BITCH,

THE FUCKIN' CUNT, SLUT, HOE! JUST WAIT BITCH; I'M COMIN' FOR THAT ASS!" I shouted all of a sudden. I was pissed off, I was hurt, and I was ashamed. How the fuck could I miss this shit. Boy, that bitch shouldn't have let this shit get out, 'cause she just put the nail in her own coffin. Clara was looking at me with a worried expression on her face; like she wasn't sure if I was sane or not. Oh, I'm sane. Sane as shit, and that bitch gonna pay. That's my word.

"Clara, I got something for that ass. This bitch wanna keep fuckin' wit' my family, that's okay. This bitch is gonna get it. You say Bam know 'bout this? How long has he known?" I asked, a plan already starting to form. Me and Clara sat in the den making phone calls and making plans all morning. By the time it was time to get the kids we had found out some really valuable info on ya' girl. We called an end to our plans for the time being to go pick up the kids. I was going to have to talk to Jewel's coach, 'cause with the shit that's about to go down, she won't be able to stay for basketball practice for at least a week. Hopefully he'll say that I can pay him to do private lessons, at our house. I had to think of ways to protect my kids without them being shipped off. I told them that no matter what I would never send them away again, and I meant it. As I pulled up to the school I wondered if

267

my sisters would ever find out about our mom; I hoped not. They don't talk about her much, but I know there are times when they miss her. She did love them, even though she let other things get in the way. I told Clara I would be right back cause I had to talk to Jewel's coach and she said it was okay; go do what I had to do.

As I walked in the school I was thinking that maybe me and the kids should stay at our other house. No one knows about it, not even Clara or Kyra. That might be a good move. That way they could be safe and I could still be there. I would also have to take them out of the school for a while. Just until I got things handled. I knew a couple of the teachers that would love to teach privately. I figured that if I could talk to a couple of them then I could hire one of them to stay at the house and tutor the kids. I know Jewel and Sapphire are gonna be a little mad, but this had to do with their safety. As I entered the office I let the receptionist know why I was there and asked if I could speak to the principal. Their principal was someone I had gone to school with. Her name was Caprice Byrd. She was always a cute girl, real smart and dedicated, she and I were cool. We never hung out or anything, but I had a respect for her and vice versa.

The receptionist told me that the principal would see me and I walked around the desk towards her office. Upon entering her office I noticed several diplomas and plaques lined up on the wall. This chick was smart, and it showed. This was a private school, very exclusive. There were plenty of teachers and would be principal's that would have loved to work here. A while back I had spoken to Caprice and she told me that she was looking for a private school to work at. When I heard she wanted to principal, I was ecstatic. The kids were already in attendance here and their principal was leaving the next school year. I told Caprice about it and told her who to speak to at the board. I, of course, helped out a little. I never told her I put in a good word for her. I was on the board as a silent chairman, and the board pretty much valued my opinion. I said a few words and the fact that she graduated top of her class in high school, college and grad school was a plus. To say the least, she got the job.

Upon entering her office, Caprice stood up and walked over to me and gave me a hug. "Hey girl; what's up?" she asked. "Hey to you too; how's everything going? Is the staff treating you well?" I asked, starting a little small talk. "Girl, I love it here. The staff is great, and the students are even better. Of course I have a few miscreants here and

269

there, but overall this place is great. You know I'm eternally grateful for you helping me get this job. I don't ever want to leave." She said, smiling and sitting down. "Now what brings you to my office? Are the kids okay?" she asked. "Girl, the kids are good. There's just some stuff going on right now and I wanted to know if you could spare a teacher that's educated in elementary as well as high school studies. I have to take the kids out for a few months." I said. I knew I didn't have to go into detail because Caprice knew a lot about me. I had to keep it real with her cause I never knew when I would truly need her. And this time, I needed her.

"Cool, no need to say anymore. Yes, I have a teacher I can spare. She's very good; she used to teach home-school. So she's great with all kids. What about Jewel? You know she's gonna be mad if she misses any of the conference games and scouts. And Sapphire, isn't she in a few groups that need her around here? Do you really have to take them too?" she asked. I could see where she was going with this, but I didn't know. "I mean, they could stay with me until school is out. That's only a few months from now, and nobody knows me. They would be completely safe; I promise. You could even have someone keep an eye out if you like." She said, smiling. I knew she would be a valuable person to have on my team. She was right;

270

no one that knew me knew that I was that cool with her. They all thought that I had a regular parent, principal relationship with her. I sat there thinking about what Jewel said about not wanting to be separated from me anymore. That touched my heart, but I also knew that they needed to be in school, because of their responsibilities. "I'll tell you what. We can ask them; how's that sound? I mean I would love to have them, you know that. And you know where I stay. You know I don't have a boyfriend or husband or anyone for that matter." She laughed and continued, "So I think it would be perfect. Those two girls are so special; it would be my pleasure to have them as house guests." She said smiling. I thought about it some more and decided that we should ask the girls like she said. I didn't want to make a decision like this without them. They were old enough to help me decide, and besides, it was their life.

I was just there to make sure they did right. "I like the idea, but I'm not sure how the girls will take it. I don't want them to think I'm trying to get rid of them. You know I promised not to leave them anymore. I told them that whatever happened, we would be together. And I'm not sure how they would take it, them leaving and Eric and Diamond staying." I said. "Well, let's get them in here and explain. I'm sure they won't mind. They seem to

271

like me." She said with a smile.

She pushed the buzzer and told the secretary to call the kids down. I was taking them home after, so it made sense to call them all. I sat there waiting on my kids and I didn't know if I could part with them again. I didn't want them to think that every time something bad happened I was abandoning them. "Don't worry. They won't think you're abandoning them." Caprice said with a smile. She had read my mind without me saying a word. "I know that's what you are thinking and don't. I will let the girls know that it was my idea; so don't worry. Once I explain, they will understand. You'll see; the girls are very mature and understanding. That's why Jewel is the team captain of all her teams and that's why Sapphire is running the student body. You have raised them well, you should be proud. Don't worry, watch." She said giving me a little pep talk before the kids arrived. I thought about what she had said, and figured she was right. I was proud of the young women they had become and were becoming. I hoped she was right, but even if they didn't want to go then I would be fine with that. I really didn't want them to go anyway.

The secretary buzzed us to let us know that they had all arrived. Caprice wanted to know if I wanted

272

the little ones to stay in the front office, but I said no. This was a family decision, and I wanted us all to be here. Caprice told the secretary to send them in. Each of my children walked in the office and I was filled with pride. These were my fruits of labor, and it felt damn good. I had some of the most beautiful and exotic children anyone had ever laid eyes on and it made me burst with pride. "Hey mommie!" Diamond said, and ran over and gave me a big hug. "Hey baby; how was school today?" I asked hugging her back. "It was good; I made a 100 on my test today in math." She said. "Wow, that's great sweetie. Come here Eric and tell me about your day." I said reaching out to him. He came over and gave me a hug and a kiss. "It was cool; you know the usual." He said nonchalantly. "Oh it was cool huh?" I said pinching him on the cheek. "Hey ma; what's up?" Jewel said and gave me a hug. "Nothing much; just had some stuff to talk to yall about." I looked at the kids to see the expression on their faces. They each looked at the other and went to sit down on the imported Italian leather sofa that was in the office.

"Shoot, and just so you know; you better tell us everything. You always leave stuff out. Not this time ma; keep it real; we can take it." This coming from Sapphire. I looked at each of my kids and suddenly I was pissed. I'm sick and tired of living

273

T.E Cooper

like this and putting my kids through this shit. This bitch was gonna get handled and handled soon. "Well guys, remember what happened 'tween me and your Auntie Ky?" I asked. They all nodded and I continued, "Well, mommy has reason to believe that it's not over and your Auntie Ky got some other stuff in mind." When I said this, I looked directly at Lil E. I could tell he knew that some of the other stuff meant him, but he didn't say anything. "So I gotta make yall safe. First, Ms. Byrd will help me find a teacher to work at the house with yall; someone that can teach on all levels. That way no one would have to miss any of their studies. We are also moving. Not out of Charlotte, but out of our house for a while, until I get things handled. We are going to stay at our other house. Now Jewel and Sapphire, I know that both of you have responsibilities here at school and I wasn't sure how you would take this. Do you want to come to the house with us or would you like to stay somewhere safe, where each of you could finish out the school year here. I am making this decision yours because I don't want you to think I am running your lives or trying to get rid of you. If you decide that you want to continue school, I have a possible solution. But no matter what I want you to know I love you and I am not trying to get rid of either of you." I said then stopped and looked at each of them, I wanted to see their reactions.

274

Welcome to My Hood

"It's okay with me mommy." Diamond said. "Me too." Said Eric. Okay I had the approval of my two youngest, now I wanted to know what my oldest had to say. "Well, it would be kind of messed up if I leave now. I mean we're in the conference, and I need this for my scholarship. But I don't want to leave you ma, or E and Diamond; I mean where would we stay?" she asked. I could tell she was wrestling with the idea of going with us or staying at school. "Well, I still have the prom to organize and a few other school events; I couldn't leave now. But like Jewel I don't want to leave you all." She said also looking a little confused. "Well... you guys know that me and Caprice; Ms. Byrd go way back." I said, and looked at the girls to see if I had their attention, I did so I continued. "Well, she offered to let the two of you stay with her until I get this all sorted out." I said. "Yes girls, as a matter-of-fact, I was the one to suggest it; I want you to know that. I would love to have the two of you as my house guests. I never have company and I would love to have you, I would be fun. I have 5 bedrooms, all with their own separate baths with Jacuzzi tubs. I also have a swimming pool and a tennis court. Please stay with me, your mom won't say yes unless you agree. She loves you very much and doesn't want to part with you." Caprice said with a smile to the kids.

275

"Wow; are you for real?" Sapphire said amazed. My kids thought I worked miracles all the time, so no doubt she thought this was my work. "Now really girls, Caprice offered, I didn't ask. I want you to understand that. So what do you think?" I asked them both. "Well, I love the idea. I mean, we can still see you guys, right? And plus we get to still come to school. I mean, why not? Do you think it's gonna take a long time to straighten out this mess?" Sapphire was saying. As of yet, Jewel had not made a comment. I was curious about what she was thinking. "Baby, you haven't said a word, what are you thinking? You know you don't have to agree to this. It's only if you want to." I said hoping that she understood. "I know ma. And I think it's cool that Ms. Byrd said we could stay with her. It's just that I would be worried about yall. I mean; you did say we would never split again, right?" she said. I could tell she wanted to come with me and I was cool with that, I just wanted to be sure that she understood that if she came with me, she wouldn't be in school, but taking private lessons at home. "Baby it's okay if you want to stay with me, as a matter-of-fact, that's what I want. I just wanted to give you and your sister a chance to make a decision, based on what you had going on here at school. I'm cool with you being home 24/7." I said giving a hint without saying a word.

276

"Girl, you trippin, ma ain't dumping us. This way she knows we're safe and we get to come to school. Come on, now you know ma gonna have us with security and all; this is gonna be cool!" Sapphire said with excitement. I hoped she knew this was serious and not some kind of joke or popularity contest. I knew some of these kids had bodyguards just for show. "Now, you can't tell anyone what is going on in the family, Sapphire. We don't want anyone to know what's going on. So please don't tell." I said giving her a look that said I wasn't playing. She nodded in agreement and said nothing else. I looked at Jewel to see her reaction. "Well, I guess so. It looks like I'ma havta keep Saf out of trouble. You know how she is." Jewel said with a smile, letting me know that everything was okay. "Well, now that's settled, when shall I be expecting you?" Caprice said with a grin.

I could tell she was loving this; she had no kids of her own and I could tell she couldn't wait to get my girls to herself so she could spoil them. "Well Jewel has practice, and Sapphire has a student body meeting; so why don't you come by and pick them up then we can go to your house to get some of their belongings. How does that sound?" Caprice said, rushing to answer her own question. "Sounds good to me. What about you guys?" I asked the

277

girls. "Sounds good to me; I get to stay for practice. Thanks mom; we'll see you later." Jewel said with a genuine smile. She got up and walked over then gave me a hug. "I'll see you guys later; love you." She said and with a wave she was gone. "I sure hope she understands." I said a little worried. "Oh don't worry mom, she gonna be alright. She's just a momma's girl." Sapphire said with a laugh. "Well, I hope you are too. I hope all of you are." I said giving Sapphire a hug. "I'll see you later mom. Oh and thanks Ms. Byrd." She said and left.

"Well, that was a lot easier than I thought; now how 'bout that teacher." Caprice said, and pushed the button to tell her secretary to ring up a teacher by the name of Ms. Hoke. I had heard of Ms. Hoke; all the kids loved her from what I gathered. "Are you sure you can spare her? Isn't she one of your best teachers?" I asked. "Girl, all of our teachers are amazing. We can spare her, trust me. And plus, I happen to know she is in love with Diamond. She has yet to meet Eric, but I'm sure she will love him as well. When she gets here, I will explain that you need her services for an undetermined amount of time. At which time I think we should discuss money, well I'll let the two of you talk money. Hopefully we can settle things today. I'll let her know that it would be a personnel favor for the board." Caprice said with a smile. Being her friend

278

was turning out to be a good look. Just then Ms. Hoke walked in the office. She was about my height and had a nice shape. She had long jet black hair, so long that it touched her very round bottom. She had an Asian look about her, but you could tell she was black. When she smiled she had one dimple in her cheek on the left side. She was dressed comfortable, but classy. I liked that. Any woman who can pull off teaching at school with a bunch of rowdy kids and still dress nice was fine in my book.

Caprice did the introductions and got down to the purpose of the meeting. I let Eric and Diamond sit in on the meeting so they would know what was going on and so they could look over Ms. Hoke themselves. They seemed pleased, and that was all I asked for. After everything was settled and money was discussed we parted. I felt good because I had that handled and the kids were set. Now all we had to do was go home and pack for the move.

When we reached the car I apologized to Clara for staying so long. "It's cool; I knew you had some stuff to handle. I took the time to make a couple of phone calls. Where's Jewel and Sapphire?" she asked, as I pulled the car out of the parking lot. "Oh they both had some stuff to do. You know; Jewel

279

T.E Cooper

had practice and Sapphire had a student body meeting. I'm going to pick them up later. Who did you call?" I asked as we pulled onto the main street. "Oh, we'll talk about it later. What's up yall? Yall can't say 'hi'." Clara said talking to the kids. I kinda figured that she had been working on our little problem, so I didn't press her for any info. We traveled the distance to our house talking about stuff that wasn't really important. I don't know about Clara but my gut was telling me that something was about to jump off. As we entered our subdivision, I looked back at my two youngest and couldn't help but feel fucked up. I mean, kids ain't supposed to go through this type of bullshit. I made a promise to myself right there that this would truly be the last time they had to go through this shit. It's a good thing that I don't have to send them off. At least they know this house and I'll be there. We pulled up to our house and entered the garage.

"Now, when we get in here, I want yall to go to your rooms and start packing up the stuff you wanna take to the other house. We leaving tonight and I'm not sure when we'll be back. Don't worry about your homework; you'll have time for that later." I said as we exited the jeep. When we got inside the kids asked if they could get a snack before they started getting their stuff together. I took them into the kitchen and fixed them some sandwiches. I told them to eat and get to their rooms. "Okay, girl. Now I have to find someone to be at the house with the kids when I can't be there. You know that you gonna have to stay with us until all this is over don't you?" I said to Clara.

"Girl, that's fine with me. I figured we would need to be together anyway. Now let me tell you who I was talking to while you were in the school." She started towards the fridge and got herself an orange before she started. "Darryl." She said and got quiet and looked at me. I thought about it and I didn't know who she was talking about. I tried digging in my brain, but I came up with nothing. "Okay, I give. Tell me, who is Darryl?" I said exasperated. "DARRYL! You don't remember Darryl. The guy that Kyra used to go on and on about; I think he rented yall a Porsche jeep once." She said. "Oh; that Darryl; what about him? What does he have to do with any of this?" I asked. After figuring out who she was talking about; I wanted to know how he fit in the equation. "Well, first of all she never lost contact with him and in case you didn't know, she's known him longer than you." She said with a satisfied smile on her face. I thought about that for a minute, and well I still didn't see what he had to do with this mess.

281

T.E Cooper

"Okay, still, what does he have to do with this shit that's going on now?" I said, getting a little tired of all the guessing games. "Okay, miss impatient. This nigga knows everything; I mean everything. He can tell you whatever you want to know about Kyra; and he's willing to help us."   I thought about what she had just told me and I had to admit, Clara sure knew how to get what we needed. I had already starting thinking of ways to pick his brain for info. "Oh, you don't have to interrogate him, he's a willing participant. As a matter-of-fact, he's willing to meet with us today. He's just as anxious to get her as we are. He knows some good shit too. Trust. You know I got you." I just sit and smile. "I think we just got our smoking gun. Are the two of them still on good terms?" I asked, getting excited. This could be just what we need to end this thing quickly. "Of course, but for some reason he seems scared of her; like she got something on him too. I just wanted to give you a heads up about that vibe. Come on, we got about 30 to get downtown and to the restaurant." She said pulling me up off the sofa and towards the door. I call for the kids to come with us; can't leave them alone. Gonna have to get another nanny. We grabbed our purses; walked out then locked up. Neither of us said anything as we walk through the garage and towards my CLS. I guess it's just natural that we drift towards that car when things seem to go wrong.

282

I picked up the phone before we drove off to see if Lil' E and Diamond could go over to one of their friends house. Once that was confirmed and we dropped them off; we were on our way. Once we were on our way we talked; I mean really talked. "Man, did you ever think things would come to this?" Clara said. "Never; I don't even know what to expect. I mean, that was my girl, you know? What is she thinking? Don't get me wrong; the girl got peeps, it's just the violation of everything. I mean, damn." It hurt to think that someone I loved like my own blood would do this to me. And the fucked up thing was I didn't even know what type of shit was going through her head. I mean, Kyra had a very cruel imagination, if I wasn't mistaken and now she wants my son. Oh hell no! "Girl; what you thinking 'bout?! You got this puppy hittin' 150!" Clara said. Except when I looked at her she wasn't scared, she was smiling like she was having fun.

"My bad; I was just thinking about how good I know this bitch, and the shit I know ain't good. Ya feel me? I mean this chick has one helluva' imagination. And when she wants something, she can be lethal. You see my life, don't you?" I said, getting off the exit. "What spot?" I asked as I came up on Davidson St. "Rock Bottom, on North Tryon.

T.E Cooper

He supposed to be sitting at an outside table. So we should see him. I'm quite sure they have valet." She said.

I maneuvered my CLS down Davidson cautiously, 'cause Charlotte has some of the most fucked up streets in the world. I took Davidson straight out and bussed a right. I took that all the way to N. Tryon. We looked over from the light at the corner of N. Tryon, and there he was; sitting at an outside table like he said. When the light changed I pulled up across the street and put some change in the meter. "No valet today." I told Clara smiling. We walked over and told the Maitre D' that our party was waiting. He led us over to Darryl. "Hello ladies. How are you today?" Darryl greeted. "Fine; thank you." We said in unison. "Well; why don't you have a seat. Would you like anything to drink? I would suggest it." He said with a knowing look. Oh shit. This can't be good. I ordered an Apple Martini and Clara ordered Vodka on the rocks. Damn! Not good at all.

When the waiter left, we got down to business. "Okay, ladies what is it you want to know first?" Darryl offered. I was still a little suspicious of him so I said, "Why are you here?" Now of course I wanted to know, but more importantly I wanted to see his reaction to my question. Would he look me

284

straight in the face and the eye, or would he avoid eye contact? Would he start fumbling with his utensils and clothing? Or would he get right down to it, no sweat, no lies, and the simple truth. "Because she has to be stopped." He said simply while looking me in my face and making eye contact.

He had a straight face and he didn't avoid the question, but he also didn't go into details. Interesting. "What do you mean, she has to be stopped? I mean, I thought the two of you were pretty tight, so I really don't understand what you are doing here." I kept it short and to the point. At this time the waiter arrived with our drinks and asked us if we had decided on what to order. We all told him not at the moment, but we would let him know shortly.

"Okay check it Memorie. First of all, I have seen the destruction she can do. Your husband is a perfect example. But the thing is; she's been doing shit like this. And did she tell you she has killed before? I mean, not some damn dog, either. I mean her step-dad. They all thought that he died from complications with cancer. Nope. Sure the old man had cancer, but that ain't what killed him. And now, she wants you real bad. She wants her son, and she wants to see you suffer and fail. She hates

285

you, and always has. You might have been a friend to her, but she hated your guts. She would come to my house sometimes and just go on and on about you. How you had everything and how you didn't even deserve it. I am sorry Memorie, but she really hated your guts. I can't even repeat some of the things she said about you. And Clara, sorry, but, you too are on her shit list. And only because you are loyal to Memorie." He said then took a long swig from his drink.

I sat there for a moment and thought about what he said. Did I believe him? Why not, I mean, Kyra damn sure has left a wake of destruction in her path. But how can I be sure he's not trying to set us up. I mean get info from us and tell her. I don't know. "Let's hear some of the stuff she said about me; Clara too but mostly me; 'cause she's known me the longest. But before you do, tell me why you want to help us?" I asked. I really didn't trust this guy. There was something more to this than he was saying. "Well, what gives?" Clara asked noticing the pause. "Well, there are a lot of reasons I want her to go down. I mean, all she ever did was use me, just like she used you. She is a horrible, sick person; can't that be enough?" he said looking at us with a pleading look. Okay, something has to give. "What the fuck is up? I mean, you expect us to believe that you want to help us 'cause she's a sick

286

person? I mean, what's the deal? What she got on you? 'Cause it's more to this than you trying to tell us and we can't trust you with secrets. I mean if you were us what would you do?" Clara asked. "Okay, okay, listen. No she didn't put me up to this; she found something in my past that I don't want to be exposed. If it got out; it could destroy me, my business, everything I worked so hard for. Why do you think I gave her anything she wanted?" he said with a stricken look on his face.

"Shit, I thought you was just a sucka' for the bitch, to be honest." I answered. "Hell no, I ain't never even fucked that bitch! This bitch has a way of knowing shit. I mean....Damn! She got film of me, that can't get out; okay. Some from when I was a boy and my fucking sick ass stepfather and others when I got older." He said on the verge of tears. Damn! How the fuck could she blackmail him with some shit like that?! That's fucked up. "Listen, you don't have to go into detail. We'll just take it at that." I said, patting his hand. His story was fucked up, but still I didn't trust him like that. We sat and talked some more. Mostly, Darryl, telling us of all the stuff that Kyra had planned. He told us some pretty disturbing shit, I will admit but still there was something missing. "Well Darryl, thanks for coming to see us, we appreciate it. We'll call you once we start getting shit together." I told him

287

rising from my seat. Clara stood as well and told him goodbye. We both left the restaurant with nothing to say, until we got in the car. "I'm not going back to the house." I stated. The whole scene just clicked.

I was flying downtown headed towards the highway. "Shit!" I say then punch it on the ramp. "Meme, what the fuck is going on?" Clara said concern all on her face this time. "That muthafucka was a decoy; I gotta get to the school. Clara, call and speak to the principle and tell her to get my kids out of there ASAP! That bitch is going for my kids! Damn! Why didn't I see this coming?! I knew I should have just let Diamond and Lil E ride with us, instead of going to the school with their friends. At least then I would just have had to worry about getting Saf and Jewel. "Tell them to put security in place and get my kids OUTTA SIGHT!!!!" I yell, at Clara. She's already ahead of me; she told Caprice that they needed to all stay in her office with security at the door and on the grounds.

"Damn, why didn't I think of that? This nigga was too sincere with the pictures and shit! OOH; wait 'til I see that muthafucka' again." She said, punching the console. "As long as I get to my kids before she does. Listen, call Jewel and tell her what is goin' on. Never mind, dial the number and give

Welcome to My Hood

me the phone." "Oh, hell no! Speaker phone!" we both said at the same time. "Hey ma', what's up? How come Ms. Byrd got us all in her office? Is something going on?" that's my girl. She always knows. "Yes baby and I need you to listen real good; you hear?" I say and ask. "Yes ma'am." She says. "Your Aunt Kyra is coming for you. I don't know if she's gonna try to take you all or if she's just coming for E, but baby whatever you do; don't tell the little ones, not even E. I want you to listen to Ms. Byrd and I'll be there in 'bout 10; I swear. Yall stay right there and momma's coming for you okay? Now, put Ms. Byrd on the phone; and baby I love you more than life itself, you hear me?" "Yes ma and I love you too. Ms. Byrd, my mom wants to talk to you.

T.E Cooper

25. She's Coming.

"Talk to me." Caprice said. "She's coming. I don't know how or even if she's coming or sending someone else, but I know she is coming. She might come for all or maybe just E. Pre, please don't let her get my kids. I'm on 485 now and I will be there, don't let her get them." I say sounding desperate. "I got you; don't come to the school; just listen. The school has a tunnel, it goes about 20 miles towards Matthews, I know you have the locator on all the kids phones, activate it as soon as you get off the phone with me. Follow that beep girl, and I promise I will hand you your kid's safe as a button; that's on my life." She said and hung up. "Clara, turn that damn locator on. Dear God please." I say I'm 'bout frantic now, and then Clara yells, "Hey, there they go. I can see each of them or at least their phones and this says we should be headed towards Matthews; just like she said." Clara said with a smile. Yeah I can trust her; I had to be able to believe I could trust her. Well we were about to see. We followed the navigated directions and after about 20 minutes pulled up at the Hyatt. At that moment we got a text that said come up to the penthouse 15 floor.

I parked my car so fast and was out of that sucka' in a flash with Clara on my heels. We got to the front door then slowed down, we didn't want to look anxious but I knew I looked crazy. The walk to the elevator and up to the 15th floor was the longest minutes of my life. When we reached the 15th floor and rung the only bell on the whole floor, my stomach did flips. Please God, let my kids be here and safe. After a minute or two; Caprice answered the door. "Come on in, the kids are in the den." She said with a smile. I almost broke my neck getting to the den to make sure that what she said was true. And it was! There they were, all four of them watching TV like nothing was going on. "What's up, ma?" E asked, not taking his eyes off of the T.V. "Nothing much. How you guys doing?" I said back like everything was okay. "Oh we fine, we're watching, Sponge Bob." Diamond said. To say I was grateful would be an understatement. I looked over at Caprice and told her thanks, without any words. "Well, let's go into the living room and let the kids watch T.V." Caprice said leading me and Clara out of the den.

This shit was happening too fast and I didn't know if I could do what I had to do, to finish this

291

thing. Damn! Why the fuck did Ky have to turn out so fuckin foul! She got my kids on the run as well as me. I said I was through with this madness, yet here we go again. I swear after this is over, me and the kids are moving out of Charlotte. As we were headed towards the living room I got a text from Leo. Boy, what timing. "Damn!" I say out loud. "What?" Clara asked. "Leo, just texted me and told me he was in Charlotte. Damn! This is fucked up." I said. "What do you think I should say?" "I don't know, but I know we ain't got time for no romance right now. Not trying to bust your bubble or anything, you know." Clara said. "Girl, don't I know it. I'm just gonna tell him I'll hit him later." I said starting to text back as we entered the living room. "Well ladies, what's the plan? I called the school a little while ago to see if we had any visitors. And like you said, we did. They said a young black, light skinned woman with a big butt came to the office with some guy that looked like his nose had been broken before." "Darryl." Me and Clara said at the same time. "Who is Darryl?" Pricee asked. "He's this guy that tried to play us but I caught on before it was too late. We had lunch with him today, before I called you. She must have sent him to get info from us." I said.

Just then I got another text from Leo. "Damn, don't that nigga know when to chill? We ain't got

292

time for him right now Meme." Clara said. "I know. Hold up, listen to this. 'Meme, I talked to your cousin Bam. I'm here to help. Call me.', Well, what you guys think?" I said. "Well, let me call Bam first. That way, we won't have any more surprises. Ya feel me?" Clara said already dialing. "Yo Bam, this Clara, I wanted to know if you talk to that nigga Leo?" she said right to the point. "Oh, you did? Cool, but how can Leo help?" she asked. While Clara was engrossed in the conversation she was having with my cousin, I called Leo. "Yo, what up? Where yall at?" Leo answered. "Wait, you don't even know what's going on? And besides, how I know I can trust you?" I said being as cautious as possible. "He's cool, I talked to Bam, tell the nigga where we at." Clara whispered in my ear. "Come on shawty, you know me better than that. Besides I wanna see my little man, E. where he at anyway?" Leo was saying. "He's in the den. I haven't told the little kids what was going on, just Jewel and Saf. I mean I don't know what to tell them. This all happened so fast and unexpected. I never thought my girl would go crazy like this." I was saying to Leo. At the same time, both Clara and Caprice were on the phone trying to figure shit out. We needed all the help we could get right now. "Well, I'm going to scoop Bam and we're coming over; yall hold tight." Leo said hanging up.

293

T.E Cooper

"Well, Leo is going to pick up Bam then they'll be on their way. Now what did you guys figure out?" I said. "Well, first things first, we gotta find somewhere to hide these kids. I mean we don't know what Kyra wants right now, so we should hide them all." Caprice said. "Well, from what happened today, I don't think we can hide them in Charlotte. We gotta find somewhere she doesn't know about. And even though you said she hasn't been to the other house, I wouldn't take any chances." Clara said. We all got to brainstorming, thinking of where we could hide the kids. We sat in that living room and went over every place we thought we could shelter the kids. Just as we thought we would have to keep the kids here, my phone rang. "What up?" Leo said. "Where yall at; me and Bam are on the way." I told him where we were and to watch his back, 'cause someone might be following Bam, then I hung up. "Well ladies, reinforcements are on the way." I said as I hung up. "Good, we're gonna need them.

Listen, when you told me about what was going on, I took it upon myself to find out a little more about your girl, Kyra. And ladies, this shit ain't good. First of all, did you know that her dad died when she was 10 and she was the main suspect in the murder? And... she spent time in a mental institution for killing animals?" Caprice said. I was

294

stunned; she never mentioned anything about any of this. "Well what else did you find out?" I asked, wanting as much info as possible. "Well, the bitch is loony. Not like you didn't already know but this is way more serious than we thought. Her name ain't even Kyra, it's, Crystal Blakeny and her mom isn't her mom. She was adopted when she was 2 and the woman you know as her mom, was her adopted mom. And from what I found out, she was crazy too. She always treated her real son better than Crystal. I mean she would beat on Crystal for anything and believed her son over Crystal all the time. Her adopted dad was a sick bastard, he used to molest her. I guess that's why she killed him. Plus, her adopted mom used to threaten her about sending her back to foster care." Caprice informed us. Damn! Was all I could think of; what the fuck is going on? "Okay, where did you get this info and can you trust it?" Clara said, still not believing what we just heard. "Hey, I got it from County records. You know all that shit is public information and the stuff about Crystal's mom came from a neighbor that used to live beside them. She had a daughter that was good friends with Crystal. Some girl named, Tiffany. I'm still trying to find her." Caprice said. "Well at least we know what we're dealing with. All I can say is, how in the hell did SHE become your best friend." Clara said trying to make light of the situation.

295

T.E Cooper

We all just sat there for a moment then the bell rang. "Well I hope that's Bam and Leo, 'cause I can't handle any more surprises right now." I said, going to the door. "Girl, wait a minute. How we know that's them? It could be that crazy bitch. You better take this gun and don't look through the peephole. People get shot in the face like that." Caprice said giving me a 9 milli. I looked at her thinking 'Where did she get a gun?' but took it gladly. "Thanks; take the kids into the back room near the fire escape. That way if shit goes crazy, yall can get the kids out." I said. Caprice and Clara went to take the kids in the back room as I made my way to the door. Lord please let this be Leo and Bam. "Who is it?" I asked from beside the door. "Yo cuz, it's us. Open the door." I heard Bam say. Still cautious, I opened the door so it swung in front of me and had the pistol ready. When the door opened, my heart started pounding. "Yo cuz what up?" Bam said with a smile. "Don't shoot me, I'm here to help." He said pulling me into a bear hug. "Boy am I glad to see you! Its Bam girls, it's okay!" I yelled towards the back room. "This has been a crazy day; I can't believe this shit is happening. I sure wish I would have listened to you cuz; you were dead on the head with that one. Leo it's good to see you and thank you for coming. I really appreciate it." I said giving him a hug.

"No problem, shawty. I told you I got you. Now where is my little man?" he said referring to Lil E. "They're in the back in the den. You can go back there." I said showing him to the den. When we got there all the kids jumped up, including Jewel and Sapphire. "Hey Leo!" they all shouted at once. "Sup yall." He responded. They all crowded around him asking questions galore. I just let them have their time and went into the living room with Bam, Clara and Pricee. I wanted to know what the game plan was and if there was any new information. I came in on the end part of what seemed like a very interesting conversation. "What yall talking 'bout and what's this I hear; you got somebody that wants to help us? What's up cuz, tell me what's going on." I said sitting down on the sofa. "Well first off, your girls crazy for real. I mean some of the shit I found out 'bout this chick is scary. Not only was she a suspect in the murder of her father, but also her baby sister, baby brother, and little cousin. And I'm thinking we need a DNA test, 'cause I ain't really sure, E is her son. I went to get the real info from Lala and found out, she was dead." Bam looked at me with a solemn look on his face. Just then Leo walked in.

"Okay yall it's time to get this mess figured out. I don't know what kinda psycho people you down

297

wit', but we gonna stop this bitch. Check it, I think I got in touch wit' ha' real fam'. And yo' this bitch is loaded! I'm not talking about a little bit of money; I'm talking, like generations." Leo dropped this bomb and sat down next to me. So that would explain a lot. She had me thinking she was out pimpin' niggas, when she had doe all along. I mean I can't hate on her for being born rich but what the fuck she want my life so bad for? If she had so much then why did she want my so little? "Okay, all this is making me dizzy. Let's start from the beginning, if there is one. Can anyone tell me what the fuck is really going on?" I said feeling frustrated and at the end of my rope. I was getting tired of this ride called Kyra, or Crystal or whatever the fuck her name was. "I thought she was an abused foster child. Where are you guys getting this info? It just doesn't sound right. First she was abused by her foster mom and dad and now she's a multi-millionaire. This is all too much." I said looking from Pricee to Leo. They had both just told me some very different stories, not to mention the murders. This was all very strange to me and suddenly I didn't trust anyone. "Kids! Come in here a minute." I yelled. I was trying to figure out a way to get them in there with me and out of this damn hotel room. Something suddenly sounded and felt real funny.

298

"What up Meme? Why you calling the kids in here, this is grown folk talking." Leo said, looking a little suspicious himself. "No reason." I said looking in the doorway. I looked right in Jewels eyes and she knew what that meant. We were going to try and make a run for it. "You guys hungry?" I asked getting up and walking towards them. Clara had been with me long enough to know what the deal was and so did Bam, but he couldn't get up right then. "Yes." All of my beautiful and smart kids said at the same time. "Oh we can order room service." Pricee and Leo said at the same time. I knew it! They were working together and they wanted us to stay here until that bitch could make it. No thanks. "Aw, that's alright Pre, these kids always want stuff from different places and it would be too much hassle for the kitchen. Me and Clara can just run down the way and pick up something from by the mall. That's right around the corner right? Yall want anything? 'Cause I know this hotel food ain't the best." I said trying to play it off and get my kids out of there. "Yeah," said Clara, yawning. "These kids can never make up their mind. Yo, the three of yall can go over notes and by the time we get back, yall will have come up with something. I mean, with the resources yall got combined, we should be able to do something 'bout this crazy bitch." Clara finished grabbing her coat and handing me my purse. That's my girl.

T.E Cooper

"Yeah, yall go ahead. Bring me back something from Steak-n-Shake." Bam said, sensing he needed to help us get out. I love you cuz. I said with my eyes. "Anybody else?" I asked, while heading towards the door. "Leo what 'bout you; did you want something?" I asked, for good measure. "Naw, shawty, yall ain't got a JR Cricket's; so I'll pass this time. You got some doe? Yall ain't stopping at the mall are you, do any of you have any clothes?" he said, looking from one face to the other. When he got to mine, I could see this was his out for us. He was in this shit knee deep, but still I could tell he was trying to help. Damn, what a waste of a good nigga.

"As a matter-of-fact, no we don't. Why, you gonna sponsor a little shopping trip?" I said with a smile. He didn't even respond, he just reached in both his pockets and gave me a few g's; just like that. "Wow, that's a lot of money." Pricee said, and she didn't look happy at all. "Well she got the kids; so you know, money ain't a thang. No worries, I got a feeling it's gonna be worth it." He said brushing it off. "Yeah, cuz let me give you the money for my food." Bam said coming to the door. I knew he wanted to talk in private. "Cuz, I don't know what is going on with these two but I'ma find out. And don't worry; I'll get out just fine." He said, stuffing

300

another stack in my hands. "Just in case." He said giving me a hug. "Alright, be back in a minute." I yelled, from the door.

Once the door was closed, we booked it to the parking deck. No one said a word until we got in the car. Even though we were kinda packed, not one of the kids complained as I sped out the hotel parking deck, damn near at full speed. "I don't know what was going on back there, but it wasn't cool. What the fuck was that Clara?" I said looking to her, like she had some answers. "Girl I wish I knew. But it sure seemed like Leo and Pricee knew each other, was I trippin' or was they...." Clara said then fell asleep; right in the middle of her sentence. What the fuck? I looked in the back seat and all the kids were sleep too! What the fuck was going on? Oh my god, the bitch had poisoned them! How? When? I had to get them to a hospital quick, I didn't know what she had given them but it had to be in that snack she gave the kids and the drink she gave Clara. I'm sure glad as hell I didn't take anything from her. Who the hell is this bitch, and she better hope she hadn't done anything serious to my family, 'cause if she did that bitch was gonna die. I don't even remember getting to the hospital. All I remember was yelling at the nurses on duty that my kids and sister had been poisoned, and they needed to hurry.

301

T.E Cooper

By this time I was out of my mind, I didn't know what to think, I just prayed that they were okay. While the doctors worked to see what type of poison was used and to make sure none of them was gonna die, I spoke to the police. I told them who I was and what I thought was going on. I told the hospital staff to put my family under assumed names and asked for police protection outside of their room. One room, so we could all stay together; I wasn't playing this time around. All the staff that originally helped my family, I paid double to make sure no one new came on staff. I was out of my mind with worry. The doctors assured me that they each had only been given a small dose of sleeping meds and they would each wake up as soon as the drug wore off. They told me I was very lucky not to have drink or eaten anything, seeing that I was the one driving.

Yeah, plus I'm sure if I would have drunk anything I wouldn't have woken up; this shit was crazy. How the fuck did that bitch get to the fuckin Dean of the school my kids went to. I asked the officers not to leave the door and told them I would be right back. I had to get a bigger whip and some more clothes, cause we was leaving the hospital today, no matter what the doc had to say. Clara had woken up a little while ago and I told her where I

302

was going, and to continue to play sleep so they wouldn't try to take her out of the room with the kids. I told the cops not to let anybody in the room until I came back, not even the doctors or nurses. They had no reason to return so soon, seeing as to how they had just left. I left the hospital confident that they were safe for the time being.

I had to get some fresh air, 'cause this was some crazy shit. I mean, Pricee and Leo? How did they know each other; I needed some answers and I needed them quick. I hopped into my CLS then took the road. I made a couple of calls and found a spot where I could rent an Excursion for the low with straight cash. That's just what I needed. This car was too small for my family and I couldn't risk going to any of my spots to get a bigger car. This was perfect. I thought about who I could get to drive my Benz and thought about my cousin Bam. I hadn't heard from him since the other night and frankly I was kind of worried. Ring, ring, ring. Answering machine; Damn! Ring, ring, ring. "Hello." Bam said, into the phone. "Oh god, thank god you're okay. What the fuck happened; I need you to drive my Benz for me. I needed a bigger car so I went to the side street rental. Oh god where are you? I can come pick you up." I said rushing, I was so glad nothing happened to him I didn't know what to do. "Yeah, I'm good cuz and wait 'til I tell

303

you the shit that went down after yall left. Come out to the south side. You know the spot; I'll see you when you get here." Bam said, and hung up the phone. Boy was I glad I still had him, if I couldn't count on anybody, I could count on him. Thank god he was alright.

I made my way to the south side of Charlotte with the quickness. When I pulled up at the condos, Bam referred to as the spot, I checked out my surroundings to make sure everything was straight. Never could be too careful. I drove around the complex a little and figured everything was okay then found a park. I parked in the back of the complex then walked to the front; something E had taught me a long time ago. After I took a walk around the complex; I headed towards the condo that Bam was held up in. I say that 'cause that's the only time he uses this particular spot. When shit is hot and he doesn't want to be found. I walked up to the door and was getting ready to ring the bell when the door opened wide and I was yanked in. At first I was startled but then I saw my cousin and his girl. I ran and gave him and Christie a hug. Christie was my home girl. "Hey, girl; I hear shit been kinda crazy for you; you alright?" Christie asked sounding concerned. "Well, right now all I'm focused on is getting my kids out of the fuckin' hospital and out of Charlotte, 'til I set this crazy

304

bitch straight. So what was up with Leo and Pricee? You know that bitch poisoned my kids and Clara." I said talking to Bam. "Yo, those muthafucka's is gone cuz; I had to handle that shit. They was in the room talking to Kyra on the phone and talking 'bout what they was gonna do to you and the girls. All she want is E and she's willing to do anything to get him. Shit, that shit had me hot. I mean this nigga Leo; know how I get down, so he should have known." Bam said, slamming his fist on the coffee table almost breaking it.

"That's what I thought. But why did he give me all that damn money, if he was down with Kyra?" I said bewildered. "First off that nigga knew what time it was and he knows what I was capable of so I guess that was his way of saying sorry. Shit I don't know cuz, but spend that shit; he don't need it. And that bitch Caprice, she was down with Kyra the whole time. She knew Kyra before she was Dean at the school. They go way back from what I figure and she owed Kyra, big time. She had killed her boyfriend cause he was beatin' that ass. Well guess who helped her, Kyra. She buried the body and Pricee doesn't even know where she buried him. Kyra just told her not to worry and when this shit popped off it was the perfect time for Kyra to pull rank with Pricee and the rest is history. I still don't know how or why Leo was involved but you

305

know I don't show no mercy for nobody." Bam was saying. I was amazed; I mean this is the bitch I thought was my sister for real. I didn't know what to believe anymore. "Come on cuz, I need to get back to the hospital before somebody wakes up or some other shit goes down." I said, walking towards the door. "A'ight, here I come." Bam said. I waited at the door for him to tell his girl bye and get a kiss. "Good luck. Let me know if I can help." Christie said. "Thanks." I said and gave her a hug then me and Bam was on the way.

"A'ight cuz, tell me what the fuck to believe right now, cause I'm totally freaked out. Is she a killer, is she rich, was she adopted? I mean what the fuck. I can't take this, I gotta know what's going on." I said as I whipped the CLS in and out of traffic. "A'ight, this I got. Yes, the bitch was rich, no, she wasn't adopted, the lady was her nanny, and yes she is a killer. Her family tried to have her committed but the nanny took her and ran. For some reason the nanny didn't want her to go to no crazy house. Her family has been looking for her ever since and that was over 10 years ago! And yo cuz, that nanny was just as fucked up as she was, so you know that didn't help matters. When she met you she wasn't pregnant, either; that was just to set things in motion. She can't even have kids; can you believe that shit!" Bam said, mad all over

306

again. "Well, that means that E ain't her son. So what is all this about? Why would she be after him if he wasn't hers? Now I'm really confused." I said, not understanding anything that was going on.

"Well, he might be. She wasn't supposed to be able to have kids is what I meant to say. She did get pregnant but I don't think it was by E, cause she really didn't know him like that. I don't know who the daddy was but it wasn't E. I guess that's why I found Lala dead; she knew too much. Now I want to find that damn nanny. She could shed a whole lot of light on the situation." Bam said as I pulled into the rental car spot. "Listen, I'ma follow you over to the hospital then we going over to Christie's. Something ain't right about this situation so I'm a stay close to you." Bam said.

"K." I said and got out of the car. As I walked to the door of the rental car place all I could do was thank the lord I had my cousin. I got the rental in no time flat. They just wanted their money and a copy of my license. I gave it to them and bounced. I waited out front 'til they brought me my rental and I was off, with Bam following close behind. That made me feel better that's for sure. Now all we had to do was figure out if E really was Kyra's son. This shit is too crazy; I don't know what to think or feel right now. I do know that I want to get back to that

307

hospital and get my babies.

I pulled into the parking garage on a mission. As I pulled into a parking space I noticed Bam doing the same thing. That put a smile on my face. My cousin was always there for me. I'ma have to do something special for him after all this drama ends. Together we walked to the elevators and waited. "Yo, I hope you know I'ma be here from now on. For some odd reason cuz you attract danger; It's like you're a magnet for that shit or something. So me and Christie talked it over and decided that we should all just get a big ass crib and move in together. You need help with those kids and somebody to look after your ass. Ha,ha,ha." Bam said as we entered the elevators. "Well cuz I can say that, for the past couple of years drama has followed me. I don't know if it's bad karma or what but I sure will be glad when it's over. Shit! If I wanna keep it real, we do need a body guard, cuz. And that shit's fucked up. But if you and Christie wanna watch out for a sista, I'll at least pay you and buy the house. Sounds like a plan to me, and I know the kids and Clara will feel better knowing you got our back." I said as the doors opened to our floor.

"Well you don't have to pay for the house, cuz I got that all taken care of. I just want you to stay

308

away from any kind of drama, danger or anything else after we get this done and over wit'." Bam said as we walked down the hall and to the room. The police were there just like I asked and when we entered the room everything seemed okay. Bam searched the room and found nothing out of order so we proceeded to see if I could wake the kids. Clara had gotten up when we walked in and she helped us get the kids up one by one. We got them dressed in silence and walked out the hospital. That's the very reason I had to get my fam out of there. No protection at all. If it wasn't for the police that I had to pay DOUBLE their normal salaries, ain't no telling what would have happened. We got in our cars and pulled off. Without one ounce of hospital staff even noticing. After we left the hospital I followed Bam to the crib on the south side. The kids were still kind of groggy, so they didn't say much, and I think Clara was still in shock that she had been duped but then again, so was I. Who would have thought that Pricee was down with that bitch and even more who would have thought she would have drugged anyone. Well she got hers that's for sure.

As we pulled up to the condos, Bam and me split up then circled the complex just to make sure everything looked cool. After deciding that it was, we each parked and got out. Just like before we took the scenic route to the condo, looking around every crack and crevice; didn't want to get surprised. When we reached the condo, Christie was there waiting. One good thing about her, she was a Registered Nurse. So I felt the kids and Clara were in good hands. Bam said we would chill here for a few days before making any moves. Which was smart; considering he had two bodies at one of the most exclusive hotels in Charlotte. At least no one knew where Christie stayed. Thank God for that one. That was one thing Bam was good at and that was keeping everything and everyone away from Christie. I mean, her peeps knew where she was but they had never actually met Bam. So they didn't know him like that. All they knew was he kept Christie laced and treated her good. So that was enough for them. So this was like a safe house of sorts, which was just what the doctor ordered.

After Christie had Clara and the kids settled, we sat down to talk. "First off Bam; what about what happened at the hotel? Did you take care of it? I mean really take care of it?" I asked concerned that he might have left some type of small piece of evidence that could lead straight back to us. You know the police and their forensics. "Oh you know I did my thing. Ain't nothing in there but two dead bodies. A homicide, suicide; the way I heard it; oh girls boyfriend went crazy on her and shot her then

310

turned the gun on himself; sad story." Bam said with a smile. That's my muthafuckin' cousin. "Okay, with that taken care of, would you like to fill me in on the real story, the whole story behind this bitch that wants my life." I said referring to Kyra.

"Okay this is the deal. Well a lot of that shit was true 'bout 'cha girl. She was a suspect in her stepfather's death but they couldn't pin anything on her; ruled it as "Accidental". So she got off on that and from what I hear 'bout that nanny, she helped her. As far as the deaths of her cousin, sister and brother, I'm afraid all that shit is true too. This bitch has been psycho since she was a little kid. From the stories, she had to have all the attention and whenever anyone got any type of attention she would be crazy jealous. Her parents didn't want to think something was wrong up top with the girl until after all the deaths. I mean, come on, she was killing everybody and each time it was ruled some freak accident. Her mom's and real dad got tired of it then tried to put her in an insane asylum but the nanny took off with her and they haven't seen or heard from her since and that was a little over 10yrs ago. So that's where we are right now with a crazy bitch and her nanny after us." Bam said; taking a swig out of the beer Christie had brought him.

T.E Cooper

"Well, that's a lot but that still doesn't explain why she wants my life so bad! I mean come on cuz, there's got to be more to it than that." I said. Okay she was psycho but what did that have to do with me? "Cuz for real what does all that have to do with me?" I asked; the stress showing in my voice. "Well you met her a long time ago, apparently you used to mess with a guy she either dealt with or was related to. Some guy at a pizza parlor?" I thought back and then I remembered, "Oh shit, you mean, Ashton! I thought she knew him through me. What the fuck?" I said bewildered.

"Well he must have been someone close to her and she swears you dogged him or something." Bam said. "Well I met Ashton, after I met Ky, so that still doesn't make any sense." I said still confused." Naw cuz you knew that nigga from school or something and he was all into you but you dissed him or something then embarrassed him real bad. That's how I got it and that was from someone that went to school with you; not Ky." I thought for a moment to see if I could remember what it was he was talking about. I don't remember dating or dissing anyone in school. Let me think, damn let me think. Oh shit, oh shit, I fucking remember. " Damn cuz, I remember. Man this was in like the 10th grade or something. I mean Ashton did go to West Charlotte with me and we were in ROTC

312

together. I mean when he said he wanted to be my boyfriend, I wasn't' feeling him but I said okay anyway. Oh my God, when he used to call me in the halls; I used to hide from him. But then when I saw him again working at the Pizza Parlor on the Ford he was all grown up and it didn't seem to me that he was holding any grudges from school. Shit we had a good time together and we ended on good terms, so I would have never thought he knew Ky." I said.

"Well, there it goes; the bitch crazy and she just wants some kind of revenge on you for hurting her peeps feelings in high school. I mean, a boys feelings are crucial during those times." Bam said and laughed. "So what do we do now; how we gonna stop her?" I said, my mind spinning from all the stuff that had been going on. I couldn't believe I really had some psycho bitch stalking me trying to take my son. I agreed that I needed some rest then went into the guest bedroom. I wasn't sure if I would be able to get some sleep with all the stuff going on. I was in the guest room that was attached to a bathroom and on the other side of the bathroom was the bedroom my kids were in. Clara was in the twin bed across the room knocked out. She was still kinda out of it from the shit Pricee had slipped in her drink but she had enough in her to help me get my kids out of that hospital; I will be

313

forever grateful to her. I don't know where we're gonna go from here, but it can't be nowhere but up, 'cause it can't get much worse than this.

At least I got my kids with me this time, and no matter what I will protect them, with my life. I laid down in the bed thinking I would be up all night tossing and turning, but to my surprise, I fell right to sleep. I must have been exhausted 'cause I don't even remember going to sleep. I must have felt safe, 'cause this is the first time in a long time that I just slept. No dreams, no nightmares, just sleep. The rest was what I needed and what my body must have been craving, because when I woke up the next day I felt refreshed. I hadn't felt this good in a long time. I hope it was a sign of what ly ahead; I was ready for some good news. I lay in bed for a minute just thinking of the events that had just went down. For some reason I didn't feel antsy or strained, I felt at peace and relaxed. Yeah, this is where me and my kids belong; with family. I hadn't felt like this in a long time. I felt, safe and I hadn't felt like this since before E was taken away from me.

I looked over to the twin bed across the room to see if Clara was woke and she was, she was doing the same as me, just lying there. "You know what; I haven't felt this safe in a long time." Clara said. I

Welcome to My Hood

just smiled, because I was feeling the same way. "Yeah, me too; I hope this feeling sticks." She said, with a smile. "Well, for starters look what we have on the bottom of the bed." I said with an even wider grin. "Man, that cousin of yours is alright with me." Clara said with excitement. On each of our beds was a set of new clothes. And not some bullshit either, my cousin knew I liked to be fly no matter what the situation, and he damn sure delivered. I had the matching Gucci pants, shirt, belt, panties, bra and shoes and Clara had the same in Vera Wang. That's my cuz; I didn't have to go look at what the kids had 'cause I knew they would be just as fly. Me and Clara took turns in the bathroom, 'cause apparently the kids were already awake.

After we had gotten dressed we went out to the terrace where everyone was eating breakfast. " Good morning." Everyone said to me and Clara. " What do we have here; did you cook all this Christie?" I said, looking around in amazement. There was fresh fruit, omelets, sausage links, eggs, waffles, pancakes, muffins, and all sorts of stuff. "Chile no! Ha-ha, ha-ha, I can't boil water. We have a personal chef that comes in the morning." Christie said still giggling. Well I'll be damned; my cousin was alright in my book. Me and Clara sat down then ate what had to be a breakfast for the

315

history books. This was definitely what the doctor ordered. The rest and the food were definitely what I needed to get my focus back. After we ate, we went back into the living room so we could get things together. We still had a lot of work to do before we could actually relax. And how much work we had to put in, nobody knew just yet.

"First things first; we gotta get a tutor for the kids. That's only until we get things settled, so they don't fall behind. Then after shit cool off they can go back to school. Next we need to find a house, something comfortable that we can all agree on and with enough room that we won't get on each other's nerves. After seeing how trouble follows you cuz, I would feel better if you were with me so I could keep an eye on you and the kids. I spoke to a realtor and she wants to meet with all of you at 1 o'clock. She said she had some properties that we would like. I told her, yall would meet at her office in University then follow her to the locations. And since the kids are playing hooky today, they can ride too. That way I can go get some things together. How's that sound?" Bam said after a while. Damn, cuz wasn't playin, he meant it when he said he had my back. "All that sounds fine but cuz, what is it you want us to do?" I asked; "'Cause from the sound of things, you want us to sit in the background while you handle shit. You

316

know I ain't gonna feel right, with you doing everything." I said, not wanting my cousin to feel responsible for handling my problems. "Listen, right now the most important thing is to get those kids settled; I can handle the rest. Just chill, I got yall. Quite frankly, I'm tired of you going through a bunch of bullshit anyway. I got this and if I need yall, I'll tell you. Right now, yall need to be heading out to meet with the realtor." He said giving me a hug and his girl a kiss. Wow, that's why I love family.

26. A long time coming.

"Well ladies and gentleman are yall ready?" I asked. "Yeah!" they screamed back. Yeah, I loved my kids, because no matter what they always were ready to take on a new adventure with me, and not complain, or whine. I loved my kids they took a lickin' and kept on tickin'. It is time to lead a normal life, if not for myself and my own sanity, then for theirs. They deserve it and I'm about to do my best to make it happen. We all got together and headed out the door. I wasn't sure what had to be done, but one thing was for sure, this bitch gots ta' go.

As we were headed down the highway towards University, I turned and asked Clara what she thought' bout the whole situation. "Well to tell the truth, I'm glad Bam said he was gonna handle things. I'm kind of tired of doing all the dirt. It's time to sit back and relax. Shit we deserve it, with all we done been through in the past few year and so do the kids. I know that look and let me tell you, sometimes it's better if someone else handles things for you so just chill. Look there's the office, what

Welcome to My Hood

did Bam say the realtor's name was?" "I don't know, call him right quick, while I find a parking space." I said whipping into Century 21. I drove around the parking lot while Clara got the realtor's name. "Okay, her name is Jessica Williams and he said she was looking out for us; so come on." Clara said getting out of the car. We all got out and walked into the office.

"Yes, we're here to see Jessica Williams." I said to the receptionist. "Name please." the receptionist asked. "Memorie Watts." I responded. "Oh, Ms..." "Mrs." I said correcting her; for some reason I still wanted to be addressed as a married woman. I would never get over E completely. "Oh, I'm sorry, Mrs. Watts, Ms. Williams is expecting you. Please right this way." The receptionist said, getting up and showing us down a corridor towards a corner office. She knocked on the door and opened it then informed Ms. Williams that we were there and walked away. "Oh hello, Mrs. Watts; how are you today?" An Asian woman said, walking towards me with her hand out. "Oh, I'm fine, and you?" I responded. "Oh, I'm good. Please have a seat, I'm sure there's room are these your children?" she said, looking at each of the kids. "Yes ma'am they are. This is Jewel, my oldest, Sapphire, Diamond and Eric Jr." I said introducing the kids to Ms. Williams. "My, you do have a beautiful bunch and

319

T.E Cooper

their names, after precious gems. I like that and you young man must be named after your father." She said smiling at Eric. "Yes ma'am." E replied. "Well, I know he sure is proud of the lot of you." She said unknowingly. "My husband passed a few years ago." I informed her politely. "Oh, I'm sorry to hear that; I thought the gentleman I spoke with earlier was your husband. Excuse my rudeness." She said apologetically. "Oh that's okay, you didn't know and that was my cousin. For some reason he thinks that we need to be taken care of." I said with a smile.

"Oh well, thank God for cousin's and guess what he told me, money was no object and to find something that was huge and nice." She said, with a smile. "Thank God for cousins. Now what do you have in mind?" I said, with a smile. I liked this lady, she had swag. "Well here are a few pictures of different homes that I thought of. You know when someone tells me money is no object, I truly test that theory." She said, laughing and handing me the pictures of the homes she had chosen. She wasn't playing either. These were some of the baddest homes I had ever seen in my life. I mean she really meant what she was saying. These would test the saying, 'money is no object.' Well we would see if Bam meant what he said. "Well girl lets go. I can't wait to see the inside of these. You have

320

superb taste to say the least. Are you riding with us or driving your car?" I asked. I really liked this, Jessica Williams she was my kind of girl. "Well company policy states that I should drive, for insurance purposes but to please a client, I guess I could bend the rules a little. Just let me get my stuff and we can go." She said gathering her things.

The first house was located on Lake Norman and to say it was gorgeous was an understatement. Jessica told us it was located on 100 acres, had a gate with a guard, and the house, well let's just say I was speechless. "I know, it made me speechless when I first saw it too. Well, let me tell you all about the place. First off it has an Olympic sized pool inside and out, there's a tennis court, a dirt bike track, a track, a basketball court, a bowling alley, a movie theater, 3 Jacuzzi's, 4 guest houses, 2 pool houses, 4 living rooms, 5 dens, 4 playrooms, a laundry room on each level, 15 bedrooms, 16 full bathrooms, 6 fireplaces, 2 main kitchens, 1 half kitchen, 3 entertaining dining rooms, 3 family dining rooms, a dock with 3 boats of various sizes, a stable with at least a dozen horses and trails all over the place. You have to be careful with the kids, they could get lost. Good thing that gate goes around the whole property and security does rounds all day to make sure no one gets on the property." Jessica said, in what seemed like one breathe. "Wow, this is the

321

T.E Cooper

life!" I heard Diamond reply. "Ha-ha, Ha-ha, well you got that right. Now tell me how in the world are you gonna top this house?" I said laughing. "Well, you would be surprised what Charlotte and the surrounding area has to offer. We have property that would make a dead person jump out their graves. Come on, let's walk around inside so I can show you some of the amenities that come with the place. I think you're gonna like it." Jessica said taking us inside the massive building that could be called, home.

We walked up the stairs and it reminded me of something instantly. My house with E; it didn't have all the stuff that this one had, more like an upgraded version but I knew right then and there I wanted this one. "We don't have to look at the other houses, I want this one." I said with finality. Everyone turned and looked at me at the same time. I guess they thought I was crazy, since I hadn't even looked around first but this was it for me. "Excuse me?" Jessica asked stunned. "I know it's a nice house and I'm not supposed to oppose if you say you want it, but are you sure? You haven't even seen the other houses, not to mention this entire house. How do you know this is the one you want?" Jessica asked. "Yeah Meme, if this house looks like this, imagine what the other houses must look like. Don't get me wrong, I love this one too

322

but maybe we should look at the rest of them, or at least this whole house first; it's a big decision." Clara said. I appreciated what she was saying, I would explain to her later how I knew this was the one.

"Trust me yall. I'm not trippin', I just got a feeling of home when I came in the door; you know. Like when you've been away too long and you come home; it's just where you wanna be." I said with a faraway look in my eyes. This feeling, this is what I was waiting on. To feel like everything was over and I was safe. Safe in E's arms once again, with no problems, and no worries. Yes, this was home. This was home. "Uh, Meme? You okay?" Clara said with a concerned look on her face. "Yeah, for the first time in a long time, I truly am okay." I say with a smile and a tear sliding down my cheek. "Mommy, why are you crying?" Diamond asked. I looked at my kids and they all had a worried expression on their faces. My babies always worried about me. Damn I love my kids. Why did my man have to be gone?

"Hey, kids, why don't you walk the grounds with Ms. Jessica while I talk to your mom, okay? She's okay, we just need a minute." Clara said looking at Jessica. As if on cue she said, "Hey, why don't we go visit the stables? You can pick your horses that

323

T.E Cooper

way." she was telling them as she ushered them out the door. "Okay girl; what's up? And don't tell me nothing, 'cause I know you girl. What happened just now?" Clara asked, taking my arm and leading me around one of the countless rooms. "Well, I don't really know but I am okay. It's just that, when I walked up those front steps to the house, E was all in my head. I mean I've never had this feeling before, not since he's been gone. It was like peace all of a sudden, and safety, and love. It was like he led us here. Look around, does it look familiar at all to you?" I said to Clara, who by that time was already looking around. "Oh my God, you're right! It's a little bigger with some extra stuff but this damn sure is the house. Oh my God!" was all Clara could say. It was like he brought us here. I had the same feeling I had when he took me to what was his house. The same feelings, all of them came rushing back. It was overwhelming and I wasn't the only one who felt it.

"Wow, it's like he brought us here. You're right we don't need to look anymore." She said then fell silent. The two of us took our time and went through each room and bathroom and by the end of the tour we were sure our angel E had sent us here. Everything from the old house was in this one, just upgraded; I couldn't believe it. "Well maybe Bam told her some specifics that he knew

324

you would like. I mean he knows how you feel 'bout E, so maybe this is his way of, I don't know, giving some good memories. No pun intended." She said, laughing and looking all around the room. Maybe she was right, I mean, we damn sure need some good times and that is what we had at home with E. "Okay, find ya' girl, tell her we're not looking anymore. This is us." I said smiling, walking off. I walked around the whole house in amazement; this is what E had planned for me and my kids. This is what we had talked about on those nights we just chilled. You know, no work, no friends, just us. I miss those times so much, I miss E so much. Without even knowing it I was crying and walking, crying and walking.

Clara and Jessica found me standing in the breakfast area looking out the window, tears still streaming down my face. "Hey, sis; you okay?" Clara said, walking up to me patting me on the back. I turned around and both her and Jessica were standing there with concerned looks on their faces. "Oh I'm fine; I was just thinking, you know about everything. If we stay here, how long will it last before that bitch fucks it up? Can Bam really handle this girl without getting hurt? And my kids, they've been through so much already…" I trailed off. I don't know what made me say all that, maybe I was just tired. You know tired of everything that

325

was going on. We had been through a lot, and I was so ready for it to be over with, to live a normal life. "We got this girl; we've done been through everything and this ain't shit. We got this and the kids are straight; you know that. As long as they got you, they don't care. Now stop worrying and let's get the paperwork done so we can start living." Clara said giving me her version of a pep talk; it worked for now.

I wouldn't be satisfied until I knew for sure that Kyra, Crystal was out of our lives for good. We all piled back in the car and went back to the realtor's office. I called Bam on the way and told him about the house. "Thanks so much cuz. The house is gorgeous. Are you sure we can afford it? Don't get me wrong, I got some money stashed and it should last for a while even if we buy the house but I don't want you to be strapped trying to help pay the bills." I said, the sensible side taking over. "Naw, we straight cuz; trust me on that. Yall just go and get the paperwork done and call me when yall get through. I got some news for you." He said. "Okay talk to you later." I said, not wanting to think of what the news could be. I sure hoped he was gonna tell me that he had done away with that bitch. We pulled up at the office and Clara told me to go ahead and do the paperwork while her and the kids went across the street to Chic- Fila.

326

Jessica showed me to her office and proceeded to get the paperwork together. "Well, that was one of the fastest sales I have ever made; are you sure about this? I mean, it is a pretty big commitment. That house is selling for 5.2 million." Jessica said with emphasis on the 5.2 mill. "Trust me girl; it's what we want and the money is really no object. I didn't know the price was that low, for that property I would have expected more. What about the furniture? Did it belong to the previous owners? It's beautiful." I asked hoping the furniture was put in place for effect. "Oh no, the company furnished the home for showing purposes. Why; do you want it to stay?" she asked already knowing the answer. "Oh yes please. I love it. It's all so beautiful; who picked it out?" I replied getting more excited by the minute. "An interior designer from the NoDa district; she's very good at what she does and you don't have to worry about the furniture. If you want it, it's yours, nothing extra." She said with a smile.

"Now here are the papers; would you be purchasing through a loan or direct?" Jessica said; all business. "Direct; not messing with any loans; I think we are gonna put up half today and the rest in about six months. How does that sound?" I said, taking out my check book. "Sounds good to me; my

327

T.E Cooper

boss is not gonna believe this. I am so glad you walked into my office." She said smiling like a chasseur cat. "Well the feeling is mutual. Now where do I sign and who do I make this check out to?" After we finished all the necessary paperwork, Jessica walked me back to the reception area. "Hey mom." Diamond said smiling with a kid's meal on her lap. "Hey baby; guess what, the house is ours!" I said yelling, all the kids jumped up and gave me a hug. "Hey that's what I'm talking about; I can't wait to move in." Clara said standing and gathering the kid's things. "Well, I'll contact you when the rest of the paperwork is finished; for now if you want the keys, you're welcome to them." Jessica said walking towards the receptionist desk.

She said something to the young lady and walked back over to us. "Now, I want to be invited to the house warming. Our receptionist will be right back with the keys and the instructions to the security systems, the codes for the gates and so forth. You can change them of course and I would recommend that you do as soon as you get a chance. Other than that, it was a pleasure doing business with you. Tell your cousin I said thank you. He just got me one helluva' commission." She said, laughing. I gave Jessica a hug and promised to call and invite her over sometime. I mean, she seemed cool and she damn sure helped me to get the best house on the

328

block.   The receptionist returned with the keys and the codes. It seemed like everything was coming together. "Oh yeah, Jessica, I meant to ask you about the security guys and the other help that's on the grounds. Do I need to find others or can I just contract them?"   I asked thinking of the grounds and horses that would need caring for. "Oh don't worry about them. Each of their companies will be contacting you with their fees and all in about a month. They've already been taken care of for the month so you don't have to worry about that now. Just go and enjoy your new home." She said with a smile and a wave.

Wow was all I could think to myself. "Well guys, are you ready to go home?" I asked the kids. "You bet." Lil E said with a smile. "Ma guess what? I already picked out my horse! It's all black with a white star in the middle of his head. His name is 'Midnight' and he likes me too. When I get home that's the first place I'm going." He was saying, while almost running to the car. "Me too mommy; I picked out a pony; she's only 9 weeks old. So I really can't ride her yet, but I can go see her and play with her and everything! She's so pretty! The man that takes care of the horses says she's one of a kind 'cause she's all white with blue eyes! You gotta' come see her and guess what else? I got to name her myself; nobody else named her for me

329

and her name is 'Honey'." Diamond was telling me, just as excited as her brother. It felt good seeing my kids this excited over something. It felt real good.

"Okay yall we need clothes. I know we got stuff at the other houses but we can't go to any of them to get anything so I think we need to hit the mall." Clara said buckling her seat belt with a smile. "I think you're right. What do you guys say to a shopping spree?" I asked the kids as I pulled out of the parking lot. "Yeah!" they all yelled. Everybody loves shopping. As we pulled onto the highway I called Bam. "What up cuz?" I said cheerfully. "Well you sure sound happy; I'm glad. I ain't heard that many smiles from you in a long time; what the deal? Where yall at?" Bam said. "Well we just left the real estate office and we're headed to Northlake to do some damage. I still got all that cash and we need some stuff to take to the new house. Want me to pick you or Christie up anything?" I said maneuvering through the traffic. "Naw, we straight; yall have some fun. Me and Christie got a surprise for yall when yall get to the house." Bam said, sounding happy with himself. "Oh you want us to come over to Christie's or do you need keys to the new house?" "I already got the new keys and stuff, so just meet me at the new house. I'll see you when you get here." Bam said and hung up.

330

"Well what's up?" Clara asked looking at me intently. "I don't know, but Bam was in a good mood, so that's a good sign. He said he had a surprise for all of us when we get to the house. So I guess we'll just have to wait and see." I said, smiling at Clara. "You know what, Meme. This is the first time I've seen you smile a real smile in a long time." "Bam, just told me the same thing. That's strange." I said, still smiling. "Well I for one, like it. My best friend is finally happy." She said and starting smiling too. I looked back in the back and all the kids were smiling too. I will take it as a good sign.

Well to say we did some damage to the money Leo gave us would be putting it mildly. I was right when I said he gave me bout 100 g's, but I was a little off, it was more like 500 g's! Yup, 500 stacks! I couldn't believe it either, but when me and Clara counted it before we went to the mall, that was the total; 500 stacks. And we did it justice too, we didn't miss a store. We had everything from Gucci to Jimmy Choo; we were not playing. That's how I like to shop. I miss shopping like that; don't get me wrong. For the past few years, me and the kids have been fly, and yes we spend at least 20 stacks every time we shop but this was different. It was

331

like shopping with my boo; just go in and go crazy. Ya' know.

   That was one of the things I missed most about my husband, not the shopping trips but the free spirit. Just live and it would all come together. "Girl, what are you so deep in thought about? Whatever it is, it sure got you smiling." Clara said teasing me. Girl, I was just thinking about E again. I mean, it's been what; 7 ½ years since he's been gone and I still think about him every day. Is that crazy?" I asked Clara while putting bags in the back of the jeep. "'Chile no; you ain't crying; so that has to be a good sign. 'Cause before; you would tear up at the sight of anything E related. It's good to see you smile when you talk and think of him. From what I can see, he was the love of your life and that type of love never dies." She said shutting the door, as I walked around to the drivers' side I thought about what she just said. The love of my life; I hadn't even lived that long and yet she was right. E was the love of my life and I don't think that anyone could ever measure up. Oh well, that's their problem. Right now, my life is good, and I'm happy to accept it as that. We whipped out of the mall and hit 77 northbound headed home.

As we came up on the Lake Norman exit the song that I told E would be our song forever came on the

332

radio. "Is that Beyonce's 'Dangerously In Love'?" I asked Clara. "Yup, girl that's my song! That girl got skills. Why you ask?" she said humming and nodding her head to the beat. "That's me and E's song. I haven't heard that song in so long and now with all that's going on it comes on the radio. I wonder if it's a sign." I said, turning the corner that lead to our subdivision. "Well if it is, it's a good one. Look at all the good luck we've had the past couple of days. No drama, no one following us and no one shooting at us or trying to poison us. If it's a sign, I take it as more good things to come. Watch when we get to the house and Bam come over; he ain't got nothing but good news." She said, smiling. Well I think I agree with her; so far we've managed to elude this Kyra or whatever her name is. I mean, with my cousin on the case, we may never hear from her again; I hope. Well, I guess it does seem like things have finally come together for us. As we pulled up to the gates of our new home, I got a funny feeling, and couldn't shake it. It was like going to school on the first day, you know the butterflies that you get in your stomach. Like that, except maybe a thousand times worse.

As I pulled the car up to the front door I noticed that Bam was standing out front with someone. As I took a closer look I decided that I didn't know the guy and he must be one of Bam's close friends or

333

T.E Cooper

else he wouldn't be here. We parked the car at the front door and proceeded to get out. As we walked towards Bam I told the kids to go on in the house. "What up cuz? Who this you got with you?" I said smiling and giving him a hug. "You don't know who this is?" he said grinning like a chasseur cat. "No, why should......" I stopped in mid-sentence; no this wasn't happening; this was crazy. What the fuck was going on?

"WHAT THE FUCK!!!!!!!!!!!!!!!!!!!!!!!!!!!!!!!";was all I could get out, before I passed out. When I woke up I was in the house on the couch with everybody looking at me with concerned expressions on their faces. I looked around to see if I was hallucinating. As I looked into each face that was staring down at me and came on the one I thought was a hallucination.

No, it just couldn't be. "What up princess? You okay?" the mouth on the face of the hallucination said to me. And it was funny; it had the same voice and the same eyes. I got hysterical and just started laughing and crying at the same time. It just couldn't be. "Daddy, is mommy okay?" I heard Diamond say, to the hallucination. "Baby, that's not daddy, that's just a figment of my imagination. Now come to mommy, so it can disappear." I said holding out my hands to my daughter. If this thing

334

was gonna disappear it wasn't gonna be with my daughter. "Baby, I'm no hallucination. It's me, for real, it's me." I looked around at everyone and it seemed like I was the only person in the whole room that was in a state of shock. Did everyone know except me? Now, I was pissed. What the fuck was going on? "Okay, now I'm mad as hell. Somebody better get to talking and that shit better be good or there's gonna be trouble in this muthafucka!" I yelled, rising up from the couch like a soldier ready for battle. I couldn't believe what I was seeing, this nigga was alive! After all the bull shit I put up with, and he's alive!

"Somebody better start explaining right the fuck now! You're alive! You're alive! After all the bullshit I went through, and your ass is alive!" I started towards his ass and Bam had to grab me. "Calm down cuz! Damn man, yall kids go outside or in one of the dens until your mom calms down." Bam was instructing the kids, while I twisted and screamed and punched and kicked. I know my cousin wanted to kick my ass for what I was putting him through but shit, he wouldn't let me get hold to the person I wanted to really get, so he had to. The kids all got up and walked out the room looking at me like I was really crazy. I must have looked like a mad woman for real, 'cause that's how I felt. "Meme, come on baby. Do you

335

really wanna hurt me?" Eric asked; giving me that look that Diamond had used on me many a time to get what she wanted.

"Let me go." I said as calmly as possible. I still had fire in my eyes and I knew they were changing colors, but if I acted like I wasn't going to kill him, then maybe Bam would let me go, and then.... "Ain't nothing; I know you better than that. First, let my man here explain then we'll see if I can let you go. Oh and Clara, close your mouth, or a fly is gonna fly in it." Bam said and sat down on the couch with me on his lap and Christie by his side. Clara was still standing with her mouth wide open.

And Eric, my dead husband, father of my children, the man that was sitting here in front of me looking just as he did before he left for jail. How many times had I dreamed that he wasn't dead, and oh how I have missed this nigga. "Okay, listen to me baby. I'm sorry, but I had to do it. I don't even know where to start. First off, let me start by saying that I had no idea that Kyra would cause so much trouble but I took care of that myself, so you don't have to worry about her no more, and now let me see...." I cut him off. "What do you mean, I don't have to worry about Kyra? Is she really gone? Bam?" I questioned, and you had to be deaf not to hear the pain and anguish in my voice as I asked

336

those questions. I looked from one to the other settling on Eric. The look he gave me showed so much pain, I almost cried. "Well? Is she really gone?" I asked again, afraid that somebody was playing a sick joke. "Yeah cuz, she's gone. I don't even know where to start." Bam said.

"Let me tell her; I owe her that much." E said. I just looked at him. I still couldn't believe he was standing in front of me and not dead. "Well go ahead and talk, cause you have a lot of explaining to do but tell me about Kyra first. I want to hear that first." I said, finally calming down enough to sound sane. "Well first of all E ain't her son. I really was fucking with Lala, sorry and that's who E's real mom is for real. I'ma keep it real; I really didn't know that they was cousin's and shit. Listen, baby, I have so much to say and I have some major daddy duty that needs to be taken care of. All you need to worry about is the fact that Kyra is gone and I'm back. Can't that be enough for now?" E said to me. I thought real hard on what he said. I mean, could I really ask for more? Did I really need the answers to the questions I asked? Yeah, I did deserve the answers but did I need them? I thought back on these past few years without E and thought, 'Do I want to live without him?' No; I wanted my husband, the father of my children and the only man I ever really loved. Yes, I wanted him

337

back in my life, my children's' lives but does he deserve to get us back so easily. After all the shit I had to go through without him! Oh Hell no! This nigga has got a LOT of making up to do, before I get back in a relationship with him. I want him, yes, but I went through too much hell while he was gone.

"Uh Meme; what's the deal beautiful?" I heard somebody say. I looked around out of my thoughts, trying to focus on everyone. Then I settled back on E. "You sure are quiet; you were fighting mad a minute ago and now you ain't saying anything. Do yall think she's in shock?" this coming from my cousin's girlfriend; Christie. I looked at her and gave her a half smile. "I'm okay; at least I think I'm okay." I smiled at her then turned my attention to my cousin. "Nigga you got some explaining to do but that can wait 'til I got you to myself." I said with a sinister look. All he could do was look away. He knows, oh he knows. "Now let me ask my best friend something." I said and turned to Clara. "Did you know anything about this?" I asked her with a serious look. "I mean, 'fess up; everybody else is." I said and waited. As I looked at her I knew she didn't know a damn thing. She was the one looking like she might be in shock. "Clara, girl, are you okay?" I said with concern. This has been my dog from the beginning of all this craziness and I

338

couldn't lose her to something like shock. "Clara!" I yelled and got up and smacked the shit out of her. That got a reaction. "Girl! What the fuck! Is that E?!!" she said, not even referring to the helluva smack she just received. Well, I guess that answered my question. She was clueless just like me; well at least I wasn't the only one.

"E! What the fuck! Do you know all the hell we have been through while you were on your fuckin' vacation! What the fuck is wrong with you, making her and these damn kids think you were dead! I should fuck you up myself but I gotta talk to my girl to see what she wanna do. All she gotta do is say the word and I'ma fuck you up!!!!" Clara went off! You hear me! I mean she tore that nigga a new asshole and I had no doubts that she would fuck him up if I said, let's do it. That's my girl. "No, Clara; we ain't gonna fuck him up, just yet. You see he has a story to tell..."

I don't know what happened to E during our time apart but I know that if it was anything like what I had been through these past couple of years then it should make for an interesting story.

339

T.E Cooper

T.E. COOPER

First and foremost I would like to thank God for giving me the ability to get this project done. I'm not sure exactly where it will go but hopefully straight to the top. I would next like to dedicate this book to my children. They are the reason I even gave this a try. I never thought I could actually get my thoughts written down but here they are. I hope they are finding an audience that will stay with me through the years. This book was special, it started out as an auto-biography but after the first few lines; I decided against it. Yall ain't ready for that. LOL!!! Anyway, this book has a lot of depictions of people that I have come across in my lifetime. I don't mean to offend anyone, which is why names have been changed and likeness and

Welcome to My Hood

personality's switched. So no one gets confused.

The events in this book are totally fictitious. The places are actual places but the people are not. I did grow up in Charlotte, as a matter-of-fact I grew up in the hood. So here's to the hood and all the talent it spits out. This is for those of us who were never heard and for those of us who are trying to be heard. Keep trying; it's never too late. No matter how long it takes you to see your dream through, see it through. Keep dreaming and keep pushing. Everyone gets a time to shine. Keep trying and look out because your time is coming!

T.E Cooper

Thanks for reading; Welcome to my Hood by T.E. Cooper. We hope you enjoyed her first release. Be sure to leave a review and visit our website for more titles from PRINTHOUSE BOOKS Authors.

PRINTHOUSE BOOKS.

Read it, Enjoy it, Tell a friend.

VIP INK Publishing Group, Incorporated.

Atlanta, GA.

Welcome to My Hood

www.ingramcontent.com/pod-product-compliance
Lightning Source LLC
Chambersburg PA
CBHW060418030726

47495CB00003B/640